a novel

OLLIE, OLLIE, OXEN FREE

MICHAEL WILKINSON

Contents

Preface

Men don't make a point of shopping with friends. They rarely set lunch dates. They typically don't belong to book clubs. They will golf or work out at a gym or serve on a committee or enjoy a poker night. My friend and I were interested in none of the above. We simply enjoyed meeting and talking about our lives. And we wanted to meet with a regularity that would be safeguarded, not just haphazard. And so, from the imaginations of two "creative minds", we decided to proclaim that we would meet weekly for coffee so as to make plans for writing a musical.

Don't ask.

Neither of us had any experience with this kind of venture. At all. I had written two plays. Neither featured singable tunes, choreography or overtures. David had sung and played an instrument all his life, but neither of us knew what we were doing. This meant, after one month of packing last week's notes to a coffee shop, we abandoned our "Millard Filmore" Broadway mega hit, and we settled for venti mochas and saying what was on our minds, no matter the tune it struck.

In the course of these meetings and finding a need for resources when our discussions cooled, we adopted the reading Emily Wilson's vivid and moving translation of *The Odyssey*. Sparked by Homer's lively tale and Wilson's wonderful retelling of it, I returned to thinking about the epic story which I had shelved since my teaching days. Why had this classic been taught to so many in their high school years, then again in their college studies, and why had it remained as part of how we thought and even spoke ongoing? What was it about this story that made it "classic"?

I returned to considering Odysseus and his effort to return home. I examined the trials he underwent and how they had anything to do with a more modern life. Out of this set of considerations came *Ollie, Ollie, Oxen Free*. A telling of anyone's effort to get where they want and need to be: home.

And suddenly the story began to write itself. We all have those questions about directions, charting, recharting, obstacles and ultimate challenges. So, I sat down to sketch and reflect and revise and populate the pilgrimage anyone faces: to man the ships for the adventure of returning home.

From this odd circumstance was *Ollie* born. And reared by a multitude of parents and aunts and uncles to whom thanks comes later in this volume. Much thanks to the village.

As you travel with the characters of the story, may you enjoy the telling.

And give thanks there are no show tunes.

May 1, 1956.

(The Prelude)

The school was on one corner. The old parish church was at the other, behind the school.

The children had to play alongside the old collapsed church.

The parish had opted to skip painting it for the last few years since it was obvious that the derelict building could not be saved. So, when the crews came in and took out all the glass and all the doors and whatever might have been still inside, all they really needed to do was give it a metaphorical shove, and the old grey wooden wall nearest the playground crumbled as a final piece in the passing of the ancient sacred structure.

Like a blinded beast, the carcass lay collapsed on the asphalt, its sharply broken wooden claws threatening what should have been the playground for the kids in recess.

Not too long after, as children will, they fearlessly found their way behind the temporary cyclone fencing and rescued balls of all kinds that let them play at their games. Holding this or that ball aloft, they would run from behind the fencing. Once they grew accustomed to the fence and the places to enter, some even played hide and seek among the wreckage, and with uncanny accuracy, called "Ollie, Ollie, Oxen Free", pulling hiders from their niches and notches mere seconds before the school bell ended all games entirely.

Although they had played with muted intensity, they had been discovered and taken to the school principal. They were made examples.

There was no reverence for the old building. It lay there until one Monday when it was gone. Only the foundation and a few waist high, raggedly stacked piles of weathered lumber remained. The fencing had been moved closer to the fractured cement walls, and the games resumed in their proper allotment of space.

The children had reclaimed the playground.

Across the street, the new church was already begun but not finished. Until it was completed, the parish would continue to use the school auditorium filled by special metal chairs with kneelers on the back. Catholics needed kneelers.

Whatever the broad parish plans might be, the children would surge, twice a day, for a break from studies. They were rowdy at morning recess. A meager 15 minute break after the endless drone of Social Studies and Math and Religion classes.

Recess was the exercise in socialization that school provided. One could make the case that these kid games foretold futures. Tag suited those who might become business people. Red Rover attracted those who might aspire to be athletes in contact sports. Kick the Can polished the swift, the coordinated, the would-be politicians, unafraid to elbow others out of the way. Hide and Seek was perfect for every individual ever. In fifteen minutes of Hide and Seek, one could learn to blend into the surroundings just before the seeker opened his eyes, and narrowing beyond belief, all but disappear. One learned to race once flushed out into the open, to duck, even to touch base in unorthodox ways. Safe!

Screaming worked as a measure of excitement in every single one of the games.

It did make you wonder about the boys who sat on one or other of the benches near the brick walls. They sat, nearly always alone. And mum.

Perhaps working their mouths, cracking open elusive sunflower seeds. Perhaps watching the other children, but with an odd, distant interest.

The scattering of shells the only clue as to how they spent their time.

Recess was a time to run and yell if you were a boy. If you were a girl, a time to stand with your friends, long school sweaters pulled tight against the Seattle breeze, arms folded, glances bouncing in and out of conversation.

◆

Matt was always in trouble. With nuns in the classroom, with the parent monitors on the playground, with Father McMilton even, whenever he wandered across from the rectory upon hearing the screams of recess beginning. Matt was one singled out. Fr. M was always curling his finger at him, making him come over. "Matthew Thomas." Then he would muss up Matt's hair and grab the back of his neck and ask him questions with the other boys watching askance.

"Have you been good this week, Matthew?"

"Yes, Father."

"No more taking lunches or saying things you shouldn't, eh?"

"No, Father."

"Have you done something good for anybody this week, Matthew?"

"Yes, Father." He had to think fast now.

"And what was that, Matthew?"

"I tried to do a nice deed to Weiner." Weiner. Joey Weiner. The smallest kid in their class. He had just been called "weiner" forever.

"What did you do?"

"I passed by him and didn't pants him even though I thought about it." Joey Weiner wasn't fun to pants anyway. His belt was so tight over his hips and around his skinny white belly that it left a big red scuff mark on his stomach that didn't even go away when he put on his swimming suit in the summer.

"You're starting to grow up, Matthew. That's good. Especially since you'll be off to high school at the last of next year. We don't want you going with the bad marks on you."

"Yes, Father."

'Bad marks?' Whatthe . . . Matt lowered his head.

They better not send word home again. His backside remembered the last time . . . Bad marks!

The priest was silent. Matt looked up and saw him watching some of the children sneak from their hiding places behind the fence and race to the safety of home base. "Who's the best at Hide and Seek?"

Matt, unsure of why the priest asked the question and not wanting to betray any of his classmates, watched alongside the priest.

"Well?" The priest was going to demand an answer it seemed. But priests were always tricky. What they seemed to be saying often turned out to be something else.

"God." Matt blurted the answer as it came to him.

Father McMilton looked. And then he laughed. And then he scrubbed at the top of Matt's head as he repeated Matt's answer, "God!"

And Fr. M was off. Without even saying anything else. Just walked off like he owned the place and grabbed another kid to talk to. Matt had to stand there and try to fix his hair and shift his sweater around. He curled his lip and made an ugly face as the priest walked away. The other boys laughed.

He had what he needed. Matt turned and finished straightening his sweater.

He hated being grabbed by the priest. What the hell?

What was the deal with priests anyway?

When they got close you could smell them. Not like his dad smelled after work. It was a used smell worse than socks; you didn't want to have it on you.

And Fr. Richards had had a red face a lot of the time. When he talked you could see the wet at the corner of his mouth.

And they stayed in the house. He had never seen one at the beach or at the store when he was sweeping up. And he never had seen one walking the neighborhood.

But then something happened.

That evening, Matt had served at the novena and was the last server to leave. He was doing up his jacket while he cut through the buffed hallway outside the auditorium church. A youngster, maybe third grade or fourth, was looking through pamphlets on the table while his aunt was talking with the new young priest assigned to the parish.

Matt was taken by what he saw.

The boy was all blotchy. Blush red, like meat for a barbeque. The raw scars ran down the side of his face and onto his neck. As Matt fiddled with his coat, he could see the youngster's hands were also blemished. The boy picked up a pamphlet and, waiting, turned to see if the adults were about done. Matt saw then that the raw stuff was not just on his cheek but had patched one eye to be almost shut and heavy looking. He tried not to see the monstrosity of it all. A rough red mache-like mask of hesitance and fear applied over the nearly hidden smooth skin of innocence. The near blinding of one eye.

Matt stood still as he watched the youngster.

Matt was mesmerized. While he had never seen wounds that he could almost feel, and while he didn't know the boy, there was something oddly familiar. Something Matt seemed to know very well.

Matt searched for feelings . . . He knew the image . . . Bright red welts across his white behind. The struggle to walk, to sit. The effort needed to carry on, no matter. The effort to seem intact though every step reminded you that you were broken.

To appear. To appear despite . . . He knew that feeling.

The boy looked at him. The one eye was hard to read. Matt could not tell whether the boy was alarmed or glad to see him or something in between. The two stood, totally still for a moment, as if each was looking into a mirror. Seeing Matt's curious stare, the boy blanched and turned away.

Matt wanted to say something, but he didn't. He thought he should go, but he couldn't. He was caught, immobilized by the youngster's scars. If he had those marks, those bad marks, he could never be seen in public. He would have stayed home. He would have gone into hiding.

"His burns are much better, Father," said the woman approaching the boy. She finished tying her headscarf and put out her hands to summon the boy. Her eyebrows jumped as she spoke. She was smiling. "My sister is so grateful the church has been praying for Lucas even though her family no longer goes here." She gathered the boy to her hip like she was going to tuck him under her coat. He looked Matt's direction, uncertain.

"It's what we do," the priest smiled at her. "And we're glad to do it."

Matt watched as the boy squirmed almost free while the aunt and the new priest walked toward the big door to the outside. The boy looked at Matt as if Matt might do something for him . . . Or was it something else?

As he stood watching, Matt wanted the boy not to have those sores over his face and hands. He wanted his eye not to fall down the way it did. He wanted the boy not to be afraid. He wanted the woman to leave him alone.

Matt would have wanted to play ball with him maybe. Something normal. They didn't even have to talk. Matt had an extra mitt. They could use a tennis ball. Anything. To let them connect.

But there was nothing to do except watch the boy follow his aunt and the priest into the night.

Lucas.

◆

All the way home, Matt heard "It's what we do." Wrapped in his thoughts, in his jacket, inside the night and the cool spring air. To the pounding of his good shoes on the hard cement he heard it, and he thought of playing toss with the kid with the burns. He could almost hear the leathery slap of the glove with his footfalls. . . Every kid, no matter, deserved someone to play catch with. No matter what bad marks he had.

And he thought of the new priest who never mussed up the kid's hair or grabbed his neck. Not once.

May 9, 1974.

The Day Before His Ordination

As if in a glider plane stalling out at a great height, Matt felt himself slip into an ominous silence. A hiatus. An interbreath.

He knew only the memory of movement, and now the suspension, the lift up his spine to get over the ridge.

He felt his workings rise as a glider might, over a crest, before committing itself down, down and over the highest of tree tops into the falling blue gray expanse of the next wide depression.

Silence seeped up in him— only the wind of his imagination sounding.

Then, ignoring how ruthlessly he scattered his papers over his desk, he pushed himself to a stand.

He needed to get out.

Lacing up his tennis shoes with thoughtless efficiency and grabbing a light jacket, he exited.

Would there ever be enough exercise to settle his anxiety?

Meese had his radio on loud. Some rock and roll this time. Matt walked away with the beat of the music fading. But the sound had made it into his memory. Whoo, whoo, whoo. Matt saw no one in the hallway, and no one was on the stairs. He passed successfully out of the empty lobby of the residence and into a late afternoon light.

His ordination.

Tomorrow.

He pushed his hands to the bottom of the jacket pockets and aimed for the street corner. He would have to be directive with himself at first.

The calendar had been ruthlessly steady. He had felt a different twinge daily. Perhaps on a morning he would be pierced with the thought. Perhaps nothing all day, until he saw it, creeping at the edge of his awareness. Perhaps it would choke off his breath as it rose up his gullet – it, the word he was meant to say.

Or not.

He was not afraid. He was nervous. Everyone had said that. He was nervous. You work through nerves. Bridegrooms do; ordinands do.

Work through it.

He crossed to walk along the busy arterial toward the hill.

Whoo, whoo, whoo.

A year ago at this time, he had asked his Superiors for another year. He had not been ready to commit. And they had given him that year and placed him here, in Spokane, at the university. It made him seem nearly normal.

He didn't feel nearly normal. He felt unsettled still. The other three ordinands seemed at peace and even joyful about the day of becoming a priest. He, however, felt like a street performer barely balancing on a board on a ball upon a hot sidewalk in the sun — surrounded by a crowd, waiting. How had he got on? How would he get off?

He waited for the light to change.

He had fought these fears hand to hand for more than ten years now. Why was he so beset when no one else seemed to be?

Whoo, whoo, whoo, whoo.

The light changed.

He didn't know exactly why he felt this. He had done well in all his classes. His teachers had told him that he had a good pastoral sense: he generally listened well and considered the person in front of him when giving advice.

It was as if his latest dream was right: over the top of the ridge he had glided, letting the sun and the air stream lift him. He had hung almost. Suspended. For the longest time the dark mountain valleys opened below. The width of it all. Beneath. Beyond. He could not take it in, all the beauty before him. The horizon beyond.

But as he drew closer, the expanse had grown treacherous. It seemed steep and hard in its disappearance off into the valley. The coldness of the knuckled cliff and the deep fall off into the punishing trees below.

And how would he climb back up to save himself? Could he?

He should not have gone over the ridge. This was no place for a glider. What was he doing, thinking he could fly? He should have stayed on the smooth predictable side. Over the plotted fields and along the road that led him back. He should have followed the poles and their wires home.

He felt the regret, the confoundedness becoming sheer confusion.

They would never find him.

His plane had shown its belly to the cliffs and fallen. The trees had pointed him out as an intruder.

He did not belong here.

And the plane dropped and sped silently to where it was going. And he had no control.

None.

Ch 1

May 10, 1974; The Day

His headache had moved into his eye.

The cathedral was full for the four of them. They had stood in the sacristy and been vested. His priest friend Larry had tightened the cincture. "From now on, do your own." He patted Matt on the butt. "Go, get 'em."

And then—the sudden immensity of the organ eliminating all other sound—their entry and the beginning. It worked just like rehearsal: The promises, the lying prostrate, the laying on of hands, the bishop's prayer of ordination and step by step by step.

The *Suscipe, Domine* hymn in Latin had floated with great clarity over the ceremony. Those casual worshippers did not know, but all clergy understood the meaning: "Take, Lord, receive my liberty, my mind, my will, my memory." The prayer of St. Ignatius. Sung only at special moments of dedication or renewal. "Give me only your love and grace; that is enough for me." The small choir of seminarians all but sanctified the air with their voices.

And now as he faced out, it was real. His years of preparation were over. He had been accepted; he had been ordained. It was over. Finally.

He looked out. KT was near the front. She didn't quite understand but was enthusiastically there. Proud of little brother who had been away for such a long time. It was down to just the two of them. He caught her eye. She waved her small, private wave.

The Tritons. Doc, Elizabeth, and Marianne. Matt smiled at them and nodded. Beautiful, vulpine Marianne. Her deep laugh. He and she had gone up to the train tracks by the beach to watch the bonfire and the train. Her wild, red blonde hair was tamed and coifed around her face. She was a woman now.

All the different bodies out there. All the different souls. All the different faces watching with joy and remembrance and earnestness. The McKinnons from the block had made it. The Russells. The guy who had worked with his father. Dressed to the nines. He had been at the mother's funeral as well. Matt should learn the name. The man stood with a broad smile on his face as if he and Matt were fast friends.

Then Matt noticed the man's straw hat tucked beneath his arm as he applauded. Matt felt something change inside of him. He could not catch his breath.

◆

The chesty organ startled him out of his thoughts in the hot, still air. The recessional. Thank God. The last slow parade before fresh air. He was hoping he could make it. He was feeling a chill in the warm air. He could feel the sodden neck of the robe. There was a . . . wavering. As if something holding him up had been yanked away.

Then, in the slowest of motions, he darkened like Jesus himself and fell.

Ch 2

Carol was seated toward the back of the church. She had made a careful assessment of where she might sit and still be hidden. Behind her were enough tall people that she would be shielded. She could be comfortable.

She had taken to thinking like this over the last months. As if she were on the run. As if, beyond all likelihood, he was still intent on finding where she had gone.

Surely, he had let her go, had forgotten her.

She had not forgotten him, however. She had still experienced alarms. In the market, at the mall, once in a movie theater her body had twitched into an alert response.

No matter. She needed to get beyond that.

Here she could do what she intended: report on this year's ordination of new priests. She had a life to live. Fuck Gene, anyway.

She laughed at herself. "Such language in a church," she scolded, smiling.

◆

Something had happened in the front of the church. Being in the back, Carol could not see yet, but a few men had rushed out of their pews and hurried to the altar rail. The organ continued, covering this confusion in a screeching discordance.

Something had changed.

The new priests behind the rail moved beyond where she could see. Those faithful around her and down through the church were standing, singing, in their suits and colorful dresses. In the front however, something unexpected was happening.

One of the men from the pews had opened the altar rail and moved rapidly out of her view. The bishop stood on the top step looking down toward where the man had gone. Then another man, carrying someone draped in vestments, crossed quickly toward the sacristy. The bishop raised his hand, and a broken applause began. All was well.

See? Things happen. The unexpected. The unplanned. And then often true drama replaces ritual. Rarely is it just a service. That's what drew her to moments like these. She liked to observe them, to scribble cryptic notes in her small notepad, and to wonder. This was why she had dressed and found her way to the cathedral. The off chance.

Once she discerned what had happened and played it up right, she would be able to sell a human interest piece to the *Spokesman Review* or a freelance piece to the *Catholic Northwest Progress*. With the best of luck, both would accept her work.

Had she been a photographer, Carol would have dashed up the side aisle and captured images in several snaps of light. As it was, it would take longer. Words take longer.

She sat, hurriedly finishing her notes and then stood in time to see the procession pass: the adolescent servers in cassocks and surplices but with tennis shoes beneath, looking like what they were – boys from the court beside the church who had been called in to dress up and help out. Three of the new priests were next, shining with pride and humility, thanks and exhaustion. Waving like Super Bowl champions in a victory parade. (Maybe she could throw in some confetti somewhere. That note left a smile.). Then came the older priests who looked oddly impatient and discomfited. Their secret mantra seemed oddly contrary: "Smile . . . Such a long service." The bishop, in his tall hat with the tails, passed next. Waving or blessing or both. Nearly like a beauty queen, she thought , though she couldn't write that.

The pews emptied, one hushed, excited knot at a time. Up every aisle they came. Men already fishing for car keys; women remembering; children agape or quietly tagging behind.

The organ music ran like a marauding, newly loosed monster over the tops of it all until, with a breathless echoing stop, it had exhausted itself and collapsed. The line of abrupt silence made stragglers of those still wandering on toward the open exit.

She imagined a single, small, spectacled female musician in the wide loft slapping the large book closed and tucking it away for the next unleashing.

The church was nearly empty. The servers had circled back and in some secret game searched the pews for lost and found, returning hymnals to their places. On silent signal they swished away.

The sacristy door opened. The man in the blue suit came first – the man she judged to be a doctor. Then the fallen man who had his robes taken off, likely to help him catch his breath. Next came the man who carried the fallen one. They came down the stairs and out the open rail. The carrier shut the rail and genuflected before catching up with the others.

Still looking faint and a bit ashen, the new one stopped to drink from his glass of water. He looked haggard, worn. Beneath his deep brown eyes, dark rings brushed the tops of his cheeks. She could see his struggle for balance. His full head of blonde hair had spilled onto his forehead, and he brushed it back. He was still recovering. He pushed at his glasses. Then he stretched to his full height, easily over six feet, as he sought to catch his breath. She watched him settle.

She smiled encouragingly. He started to laugh in return and then lapsed into taking two more big breaths. In some way he was still searching for stability.

He smiled, almost as a mask it seemed.

The carrier caught up with the doctor and clapped him on the shoulder. The new one left his empty glass in a pew. Passing, the two leaders laughed. The new one—still aware of her, politely, perhaps embarrassedly, but genuinely— smiled and half waved.

"Congratulations, Father," she offered.

He pivoted and walked away backwards, not knowing who she was.

And they were gone.

But she had what she came for, perhaps. There may well be something unusual here. She would see.

Grown men rarely faint on the most important day of their lives.

Ch 3

Larry had thought ahead. At the reception he had leaned in and urged Matt to take an hour before they met at the tavern.

Matt hung up his clerical shirt over the curtain rod. They needed airing, he had perspired so. And he lay down for whatever part of a nap might happen, leaving his lamp on to keep his sleep light.

Today had not been what he had thought it would be. All the anxiety. All the years of wonder: "Was it the thing to do?"

And then the morning knock at the door. "I'm up." And "getting pretty," as he loved to say. Catching the ride. Grabbing the alb from the car. Crossing over to the back entry of the sacristy.

Larry had strapped him in, tying the rope cincture over the alb. Matt remembered feeling like a rodeo rider in the chute. Cinched. Or maybe the horse, cinched. It was quiet now, he remembered thinking, but the rope was for when all hell broke loose.

Odd that he didn't know which he was . . . Understandably tired.

◆

So, he was different now. Ordained. His role was set. A relief. No more the conditions and the wonderings and the subtle misgivings that had soaked his clerical clothing with unspoken anxiety.

He had needed a year more than the others. To think, to pray over things, to wait for an answer. Thirteen years it had taken. But that was past. He had been fine with the year of college teaching. He had got what he needed.

1974 from 1961. Arriving with a comb and a cotton shirt, black jeans (per the list), a pair of black oxfords, and a trunk for everything else. A big black box. In storage till the next move.

◆

As he lay on his bed, he finally let himself relax and breathe in a memory or two from his training years. Such a simple life, the training. Spartan. Spiritual.

And here he was now: a professor and priest.

◆

Living at the University was different. The only brother he had was Meese. And Meese rarely left his room.

Matt would have to make his way without the same close brotherhood he had known.

He could do that.

He felt himself relax . . .

◆

It seemed he had only taken a few deep breaths.

"Matt, Larry just called." His door shut again, firmly.

"Thanks." He was never good at the alert voice when startled awake. He took a second to calm his breath.

Larry had led him through the ropes from the early days. Showed him how to climb stairs in a cassock, how to tie the black cincture at the waist. What went. What didn't. Larry knew.

That autumn seminary evening in the red wash of sunset, Larry had kept his gaze on the soup while Matt had been kneeling while the whole community filed in for evening meal. Matt had had to kiss the floor and apologize aloud to all for his "culpa" or error. He had been singing songs from musicals on the Rosary path. Someone had heard him and turned him in. Turned him in! Had helped him realize this error. For that he was grateful, fathers and brothers. Reverend Fathers and Dear Brothers in Christ.

Made him laugh now. The innocence of it all.

He had sung "What Kind of Fool Am I?" in his strongest and best tenor assured that the cows, looking up, loved it.

The memory made him laugh as he searched for his shoe.

He found his glasses on the nightstand, then laced up his shoes tightly.

Time for the tavern. And up.

Ch 4

The walk felt good. Half a mile was good for blood flow. Especially after keeling over this morning. Right in the middle of things. Let it be. One of those things no one would forget. Least of all him.

Nice of Larry to arrange something informal, a time to tell war stories, after all the smile time this afternoon. Matt didn't care for formal things. Saying Mass would be fine since he had some distance. Other than that though . . .

KT was going to be hyper. Marianne would probably be quiet. He hadn't spoken to her, but he had heard that divorces often leave people off balance, out of character. Doc would not say much at all, and Larry would MC.

Matt was up for beer with friends and his big sister, KT. She had stepped in as mom after their mother had passed. She was good for him. Always had been. A pal as well as a sister. One you choose, and the other you inherit. Maybe someday he would end up in Portland, and they could connect even more. Portland would be fun with KT and Larry both there. But that would play out as it would.

Time with the Tritons would be easy. Doc (Matt couldn't call him Robert, let alone, Bob) was easy enough, even though he would clam up in a crowd. "Let my sax do the talking." Listening to Doc play the sax was like listening to him grinding for a crown. You were never going to be the same.

Despite that, Doc and Elizabeth had been there for both the kids. The Tritons maintained what he had overheard Elizabeth call "the safe zone", the twenty feet of fenceless space between houses. But more, not just a nearby house to run to.

Doc and Elizabeth had helped the night Matt's old man had threatened the family for the last time. Getting off the couch, he had hurled the empty bottle. It had smashed against the painted radiator, splintering into angry glass flying everywhere. Grabbing his coat from the chair, he had cursed at them all. Then punching open the flimsy wooden screen door, he had slammed the heavy front door on his way away. Then the revving of the raw V8 and a grating impact sound that must have been the violent uprooting of the newly planted Hawthorne tree, as speeding off, he left deep tire tracks on the front parking strip.

They had both helped KT with the arrangements after the mother's death. Good people. Elizabeth could be high maintenance. Probably why she wasn't there this evening. But nice people.

Why did he leave Marianne to last? She was actually . . . what was she? She was nearly a sister. But not. Something else. Same age as KT, and they had all grown up together. Matt and KT ate as many times at the Tritons as they did at home. The Turners didn't even have a barbeque.

Marianne was always confident and physical, a tomboy sometimes. She had no hesitancy about trying things. He often was in awe of her abilities.

Marianne was around when KT was around. So, Marianne watched him grow up. When he started getting tall, she could cut him down and keep him in his place. She knew how to punch. . . she had hugged him tightly with her body that first time and totally confused him. He remembered that.

And they had done a school play together. He had a second lead, and she had taken her bow alongside his, and they had run into the wings, and he had lifted her into a twirl, and the whole cast had erupted into a cheer Mr. Pitonzo called unprofessional.

Mr. Pitonzo probably never did a play as demanding as *Our Town* where they had to make their entire lives believable even though nothing at all existed on the stage.

They had every right to cheer.

And he remembered the night at the train tracks. Mostly because he didn't know where to put it.

◆

The tavern was loud. They were in a booth along the side wall.

Larry saw him first. "Here he is. The man of the hour." All lifted a glass.

KT rose to give him a passing hug. "Lazarus, back from the dead. Are you ok?"

"I'm fine. Wasn't it really hot in there?"

"Not really." Marianne finished her sip of beer. "Nerves probably." She flashed a brief, mischievous smile.

"Nerves for sure," Larry raised his beer as testimony. "I can't even tell you how mine played out."

"Please!" KT defended herself with both hands raised. "Don't go there! I can only imagine . . . Thank you for sparing us . . . " She turned to Matt, "So, you've already performed your first miracle? Become a father without anyone being born! Badumpbump."

Larry was quick to admonish her. "You didn't wait long to get that in."

"Thought of it in the car on the way up . . . I don't tell you everything, you know."

Matt broke in, "You guys. You made today really special. You're my closest friends . . . (nodding to KT) and sister. Seriously though, without you all, I don't think today would have happened."

KT saw the opening: "'Seriously though.' Nice transition. I remember you always being in trouble."

"I was. But for stupid stuff. Making fart sounds when Sister would turn to the board or making my pen into a blow gun and launching spit wads at people. My favorite was making people laugh by turning my eyelids inside out and waiting for them to discover that. That always worked. I called it my "handsome Matt" face.

KT explained to the table: "when he was in trouble, you knew. Only then would our mother use his full first and middle names. She would call upstairs: 'Matthew Thomas!' And you just knew he was in for it again."

"Thanks, KT. Great interlude!" Matt rolled his eyes for comedic effect.

Folks laughed.

KT undeterred, "And so?"

"So." He looked at her with mock intensity, "I got tired of being the school fool and holding my gum on my nose for punishment, or standing in the hallway by myself during class, or staying in for half of recess. I got tired of being bad.

"And then what pushed me along was Sandy someone. . ." he paused, searching. "Anyway, she had never smiled at me when I was bad."

KT, on her own search for the name, "Sandy?"

Matt smiled, remembering. "Sandy Manning. Beautiful girl, but I had never had a glance from her. Anyway. During math, when Sister was writing on the board, Fat Ted Lally was showing off, playing mumblety-peg in the back of the class. He accidentally stabbed himself in the hand with his switch blade. He yelled and started writhing in his desk as if he was dying. I grabbed the knife and wrapped his hand in my handkerchief and kept pressure on it so he didn't bleed so much.

Sister was stunned I think. "Quick thinking, Matthew." And they took Ted to the office. But I mostly remember Sandy as I was going back to my desk. She was just smiling at me."

"What does that have to do with priest stuff?"

"I liked the feeling so much, I kept trying to do the good things. I started as an altar boy; I volunteered for the choir and promised to sing and not to poke or blow at anyone in front of me; I rejoined the crossing guards and was on probation for a month until I proved I would no longer point intimidatingly at cars and swing the flag over my head while I danced.

"For the altar boy stuff, I worked diligently on my Latin study card so I would be on the altar as soon as I could. *Ad Deum Qui Laetificat Juventutem Meam.* See? To God who brings joy to my youth.

"By that time even the nuns smiled at me."

Marianne, who had been quiet at the end of the table, looked up from her beer. "And to think all this came from one cute girl's smile."

"That and the young seminarians I had as teachers in high school. I had already decided to become a teacher, and they showed me the way."

KT spoke again. "I remember when you changed." She looked to Marianne. "We had just started high school. Mom thought something was up. She wasn't used to the good Matt."

"Who was?" Matt laughed into his beer.

"And here you are!" Larry toasted again, feeling the beer. "You made it, man!"

Matt demurred as his friends raised their glasses.

Larry spoke up, "You're too modest!" He looked at each of the others. "No matter how it all began: A toast to a new Jesuit priest, Father Matthew Thomas Turner. Bad boy made good."

Matt smiled with some embarrassment. "Just 'Matt' is still fine, especially to all of you . . . Doc, thanks for making the drive."

Doc, quiet all evening, nodded and raised a small lift of acknowledgement.

Marianne put her arm around her father's shoulder, "We were glad to get out of the office. Thank you for the excuse. Is there another something we can come to next month? Some kind of one-month anniversary or something? We could make this a progressive, year-long celebration, couldn't we?"

And with that began the evening of jokes and laughter that the beer heightened and that his rawness absorbed and cherished. Larry went on about the awkward days of the hilltop seminary with students violating rules, such as always to speak in Latin during times of silence. This begot wonderfully cobbled and contorted phrasings as were never heard in any era of Rome.

Then there was "modesty of the eyes", which drove some to watch their toes so diligently that they bumped into walls and people. It was comedic to see those bad actors skewing down dark hallways, brushing off walls or people, and shambling on. If you saw one of these literalists angling down the hall toward you, you shifted to the other side and immodestly watched them make their next collision.

"So, what was the point?" asked Marianne.

Matt said he never knew for sure, but when he had gone off the hill and into town, he had seen some attractive young women his age, and they had visited his thoughts in the next days. Thank god he lived on the hill.

"I think it's about protecting us from ourselves," Matt began.

"But here's my theory: instead of separating us from our lower tendencies it activates them. So in the seminary, requisite modesty fosters immodest thoughts; just as requisite silence fosters belting show tunes; and requisite sacredness fosters giddiness and snorts of laughter. Requisite rules foster imagination. Not sure what I've missed. Anyway: Bent but not broken, the human spirit. Squeezed but resilient. My theory."

All toasted after his lead.

"I've noticed that your requisite poverty fosters a slowness to put money down for pitchers of beer," offered KT.

"And your requisite obedience fosters insisting on your own way," said Marianne. "Otherwise I'd be drinking wine."

"Not even going to speak about requisite chastity," Larry said to the laughter of all at the table.

Then there were the crazy stories of doing unbelievably stupid or excessive things, such as the boy who hit himself in the chest as a sign of repentance or humility but did it so many times that he was sent to the infirmary to be treated for the massive bruising.

◆

Then, with the ricochet logic that such conversations take, everyone threw some random neighborhood or childhood memory into the center of things, and whether the story was regrettable or fascinating, laughter ensued.

KT raised a toast to friends and reached across to place her hand on Doc's. Matt had looked up and seen Marianne watching with a distant yet maybe wistful smile. They connected in that glance. She had always been in his corner. He smiled back warmly.

Doc ended the evening with tapping his watch and reviewing aloud the driving plans for the next day. KT leaned into Matt and said, "I am so proud, little brother."

Matt shrugged. "Just my lot in life."

"Lucky you." She kissed him. "Lucky me. A priest in the fam."

Everyone emptied the booth, and Marianne took a moment as folks pulled on their coats. "Come see us; we miss you." She kissed Matt almost on the lips and stepped away.

"You'll never be rid of me," he heard himself say reflexively.

◆

Everyone said good byes at the door.

He should have checked. An unusual misty shower was drifting through the street lights. Spokane was not known for misty rain, but . . . he had made his choice. At least, he thought, he had a collar on his jacket.

He stepped into the rain.

◆

The "Pretty Girl Conversion" story always worked. If folks didn't know you well, they couldn't but be amazed that something as special as a vocation came from an incident as simple as that. If folks knew you well, it could function as a joke to carry you through the impossible explanation of where vocation comes from. That had worked again tonight. People really would rather drink their beer and laugh along with you than dive into some deep and serious story.

Like faith probably. Vocation came from examples. The opposite of "I don't want to be like my mother." It also came from some kind of affirmation that this seemed to be a place where one belonged. A role that suited.

He could feel the rain through his clothing.

Vocation was not much different from finding one's inclinations and abilities and following them where they led. Dentist, Lawyer, priest. The calling was in part interest and aptitude, in part conviction, in part successful exercise each step of the way.

But where had it come from? Matt remembered always being around priests. His mother had taken him to Mass weekly since his birth. Priests spoke to their classes every year in parochial school to try to get to know them.

Fr. McMilton had wandered the playground as long as Matt was at St Brendan's.

Matt would never wander a playground. He would never be that kind of priest. But he had learned from the good young ones just how good the calling could be.

"It's what we do."

That's who he would be.

Ch 5

As Matt entered his hallway, he began to hear the radio. Meese's. Either ads or news but on much too loud. Meese's door must be open again.

Now that he could see a little better, his suspicions were confirmed. "Rev. Jerome Meese, S.J." had left his door open while he worked. "Meese" was how he was known. For all his oddities he was upheld as a legend. A seer. A scholar who presently was living among what seemed like a dozen boxes of files. Rumor had it he was studying priestly defections. He had already published his works on celibacy and sexual aberration.

Meese was an introvert. Rarely spoke with anyone. Aside from his radio, Meese was in his own complicated world. On occasion, if the door was open, Matt had leaned on Meese's door frame and made frivolous comment, just to be neighborly. The room seemed almost always carefully untidy. Beyond the desk with its stack of files was a scattering of boxes filled with books and other files. It was impossible for the outside eye to tell which box had been processed and which was yet to submit.

Beyond the scattering of boxes was Meese's bed and his drawn curtains which Matt had never seen open. The bed was never made. It was as if Meese was always prepared to retire or to get up. There was little difference.

In the corner was a saxophone perched on a narrow vertical table. Matt had never heard it played. A thin cord hung from the instrument and coiled onto the table. For carrying the thing along, he supposed. What a sight that would be.

An oddity to be sure. But then no more unusual than the man himself.

Matt had developed a story for Meese. Meese was faithful. He was at one altar or another every morning saying his Mass. He had his meals promptly each day. Never late.

Meese had found a rhythm for his life. Mass, meals, work.

In Matt's story Meese worked to compensate. He earned his keep not with people but with data. Meese poured his energy into research and developing statistical reports for national magazines. Meese was an outcast, a maverick, a man who might live in just such a room no matter whether he was in cloister or no.

A true introvert. A Montanan: strong and silent.

Unless you counted the radio.

To know him you needed to add his affection for loud music. Mostly in the evening hours, whatever that said about his work process. (Perhaps that he needed to work through the fatigue by listening. Perhaps it was just washing the data off. A rebaptism, this music.)

Meese, the story told, could not speak. He had had a trauma early in his life and was left without a voice. Matt knew that to be false. Meese could speak only in a raspy whisper, but he had often responded to Matt's remarks with gesture and a few whispered words which Matt had always had to supply for himself. And Meese was an eccentric they said. Stayed to himself. But Matt had found him almost always ready to lift his head from his work whenever Matt had stopped at the door.

Matt thought they had given him this corner room across from Meese because Matt's stay seemed likely to be temporary. If there were complaints, they would be short lived.

Maybe they had isolated Meese for that reason: the radio bothered people. The only other rooms with priests in them were five doors down the hall toward the central stairs and the telephone.

◆

31

Tonight Meese's door was wide open. Who, besides Meese, listened to Elton John at full volume? Nothing like "Yellow Brick Road" to induce sleep! Matt almost shook his head and laughed as he opened his own door.

He had promised himself never to have a radio. It was the beginning of the end of your prayer life as he had been told in no uncertain terms.

Meese could get away with the radio noise. But Matt would never be like Meese. Meese had his own set of rules. He was almost sixty, or maybe even older, so there was no arguing with that. When Matt had been assigned his room, he had thought it strange that Meese was the only one living at the end of the hall. (Rumor was that Meese's room had been there from the outset and the rest of the building was erected around it.)

He closed his door as Elton John's backup banshees moved into the chorus.

With a few more drinks, yes, he might even sing along. . . Of course, he'd have to learn the words.

He stood still in the middle of his room. The muddled lyric still in his head . . .

At 11:45, no.

He stood in the dark to let his eyes adjust.

Was he drunk? . . . It took him a moment . . . No.

Matt had left his room dark. He would leave it that way. He would feel his way into the room. That was easier than the light and all that that entailed

He was soaked and blind. He felt for his bed and sat to unlace his wet shoes and to begin to dry himself off. His towel, draped over the foot of the bedstead, was handy enough for him to dry his hair and face once he had rid himself of his drenched jacket. He was wetter than he thought. He began to strip himself of his wet clothing. Naked, he dried off vigorously to warm up.

The dry scrubbing waked him from the effects of the beer. He thought of himself there, naked. Like a warrior before battle. Ridding the self of any imperfection, any impurity. Leaving the self purely prepared to engage in the fight.

He smiled at the incongruency; he was certainly no warrior.

Stepping into dry underwear, he sat on the side of the bed and pulled a tee shirt over him. Then he stopped all preparations: he was ready.

He opened the blinds. His room was darker than the outside world. In the world outside, a single streetlamp, arcing from a light pole, illuminated the lot next to the residence. In the day the light was natural; at night, artificial. In the day he could see the gap in the trees where the river ran. In the night, all things became one in the darkness. There was no distance, no separation. He had always found it easier to pray in the darkness.

On the desk his vow crucifix stood vertical near the window end of the desk. He could see the cruciform in the relief of the light. He rocked back in his chair.

God

Thank you for today. Thank you for all those who believed in me and cheered me on. Thank you for the call you have given me in my vocation. Thank you for the chances this will give me not to just be an ordinary teacher but to touch others in a special way with my vocation. You have blessed me and given me more than you have given others, and I will make every effort to make the most of it and help as many as I can to come to you.

I'm tired God. Please let me sleep well and wake refreshed. I'll try to do your work and see you in every student I see tomorrow. Help me to do that. Bless me with the energy and clarity of purpose to be who I am supposed to be.

◆

His ritual complete, he stood and closed the blind and, turning on his light for reading, he laid himself out.

His body told him immediately that the light would be useless tonight. He was just too tired. He would look at things in the morning.

He needed to shift gears and get ready to start class with *The Odyssey*. He was ready.

He would begin with the summary in Chapter 9. That might let them find an obstacle adventure that spoke to them. They had to engage with the epic if it was going to have any effect.

He loved being in charge of a class. The looks of expectation from the students and their hurry to capture insights into their notes.

He drifted almost to sleep . . .

Meese's radio . . . ? No.

He knew the sound. A distant thud. He turned to hear if it would happen again. It did. The sound was a ball. He knew it well. Most youngsters did. A ball being bounced off a hard surface. Like when you have to play catch with yourself.

Lucas, the burned boy, was back again tonight.

During Matt's years of achievement the boy had mostly disappeared. But with the doubts, Lucas had returned. He had a signature, this boy. The game of catch that was their bond. The game of catch that had never really happened. The game without which Matt had watched the boy step into the darkness.

The boy appeared more now both in sound and memory.

And in feeling.

Matt had yet to figure out why.

He had felt secure all evening.

◆

He sat up. Of course, the room was empty. There was nothing to look at in the darkness. The sound was in his guilty imagination.

Matt switched on his light.

He wasn't sleepy any longer.

Ch 6

Sissy had not responded to her letter. So that was the last of that for a while. If Carol had to be alone, she would be alone. Not the end of the world. She had been with; she had been without.

She moved to put into order loose articles that would be lost on her tiny desk otherwise. Her work on the ordinations was still on the corner chair. She needed to save those, her first work for those two newspapers.

She pushed her desk chair in and turned out the overhead light. She took up her notepad and pen and propped her pillow. Cool sheets. She loved cool sheets. She pulled up the blankets enough to cover.

So, enough of her success. What was to come next?

One cannot rest in the past.

She loved writing scripts. She had discovered that late in her undergraduate days. She had a good ear for how people spoke; she had a good eye for how they behaved. The hardest part was shaping a story line that moved naturally. Her first comedy was by the book. She had used George Kaufmann and brought a bull into the china shop of a very meticulous household. It had given her a number of situations, though nothing as complex as George K. was able to milk. Her story had not been very satisfying. It was an exercise merely.

There was always poetry, but that was so difficult to get accepted for publication.

She wanted to develop something about betrayal, perhaps. Or missing the clues. Or trusting too much or . . . Something everyone tried to avoid. Something people struggled mightily to keep a distance from. Her time with Gene had renewed her thinking about that.

Even the thought of him changed her. Gene. The one she had felt safe with. The one who laughed with such an open face, head tilted, as if throwing his heart to the sky. Gene.

She shifted.

Recovery perhaps. How one chooses to regain balance and momentum. Or was that too personal? Too revealing?

Her pen had not written a word. She was nowhere nearer. She would have to work with something small and specific and see where it led.

That's the beginning of something, she thought. The specific and the question and the listening.

The familiar soft thumping of her housemate's headboard on her wall. Mickey was at it again. With the new one. The headboard, louder now, kept crashing into Carol's wall as if Mickey regretted sharing the house with her and was trying to push Carol's little box of a room off the top of the house. Carol would have to get up. This likely would go on for a while.

She supposed the thumping was karma for her late night Hamilton St. escapades. Her landlady had complained. Carol had shrugged it off. There was no way of stopping such noise. A person should enjoy her life.

It did make her laugh though when she recalled that her tiny room had been in the basement of the three-story house. And that the landlady slept on the upper floor. " How loud must that have been!" She laughed nearly aloud.

Carol scribbled in her notebook: "You cannot mute fun!" She propped herself up.

Some nights she didn't get up. Some nights she lay there, feeling their energy affect her breathing. The changes. Decisions. Some nights her hand would go down there. The headboard would become a metronome for her own wide pleasure. Some nights she would listen and hear the beast with two backs grunt and stagger in the middle of Mickey's room. Not knowing who it was always turned things into a vague but gritty Beauty and the Beast.

She could always look for a new place. But Mickey was nice, and the price was very right. She had been lucky to find a place after she broke up with Gene.

She laughed a bit. "Broke up." She had had to run for her goddamn life.

◆

She recalled being at the park and how he had, without introduction, slid into the shade of her bench. "What're you reading?"

She had chosen to respond. He was sleek; he was earnest; it was an innocent question.

"*Jane Eyre*."

"Is that the one with the weird woman in the attic?"

"It's the one where the girl needs to find her way for herself."

"So, not the attic one?"

"I'm not there yet."

"Sorry."

She put the book down, holding a finger in place.

He was bold but not aggressive seeming. She could give up some time.

He had been many days shirtless in the sun. His brows were bleached as were the lashes of his narrow set eyes. His blonde hair coiled languorously into natural ringlets. His tan skin was unflawed. His fingers long with handsome nails. He was shamelessly handsome. As far as she could tell, he knew that. He knew of her interest; he knew that she needed to guard herself.

What had she heard about narrow set eyes? Whatever, it escaped her now.

"Want to get some exercise?" He held a football that he spun as he spoke. He nodded toward the sunlit grassy area busy with the people sunning, and the frisbee chasing and the dogs.

"I'm fine. I came to read."

There was a pause. He watched the scene in front of him, estimating.

As if to prompt something, perhaps some conversation, she added, "I'm fine. Thanks anyway."

He said not a word but rose immediately and running across the path tossed his football toward the sky and chased it before it hit the ground, only to throw again as if launching a spear that would deflate the sun.

She looked away.

She smiled. She had been right about him.

◆

He had found her at The Spar Tavern some weeks later. As suddenly as before, he placed himself next to her at the table where she sat with friends.

And her friends had liked him, and she had seen him again, and they had spent the night and more nights, and then everyone knew that you could reach her at Gene's. And she had closed out her tiny room in the basement of the Hamilton St. house. And she had moved in.

She took a deep breath as she remembered it all.

And he had been sweet. He had brought gifts. He had watched her prepare the little food they actually cooked. Sometimes he would dance to the radio while she peeled or sliced or layered the evening meal.

◆

The first time it happened was when she was still watching the flames after a late night session of wine and cigarettes in front of the fireplace. Friends had just gone. All but Gary. Gene had finished in the kitchen and had gone to bed. The fire was nearly dead.

Carol had been watching the embers when she felt Gary's hand on her back, stroking slowly. She glanced. Gary was watching the fire but continued with his hand on her blouse.

"I better crash," she said. "I have the early shift."

Gary had heard her and touching her on the back of her hand, tapped twice. She had always liked him.

She had seen him to the door and then had come back to close the chain screen on the fireplace. She picked up their glasses from the hearth.

"How sweet."

Gene was standing in the shadow of the hallway watching.

She had shaken her head in disbelief at what he had said.

"If I had gone to sleep, dear old Gary would have been inside your blouse in no time and probably inside you soon enough after."

"You're drunk. Go to bed." She finished rinsing the glasses and put them in the washer.

Next thing she knew, he had grabbed her from behind and twisted her to face him. "You want him don't you." She could still see his close set eyes in the puffiness of his face. He grabbed her at her cheeks, squeezing. She pulled away, but he was strong, even when drunk.

She had closed her eyes and tried not to hear the ugliness in his voice.

She had waited for it to stop, and it had. And she had gone to brush at her teeth, avoiding looking at her face in the mirror.

She should have responded.

◆

The next morning, Gene had wakened her by leaning a hand up the bedroom door jamb and announcing, "Coffee's on! Eggs?"

He had been drunk, after all.

She was fine.

This was his apology.

He hadn't really meant to do that.

◆

The next time had been just as unexpected.

They were to go shopping, something she normally did alone, but this morning he decided he would go along if they could stop at the Hobby Shop on the way back. He wanted to pick up a Mustang to add to his collection of model cars. With that, he had incentive.

He had already grabbed his coat from the hallway when the phone rang. She took the call and turned to him while he stood in the archway. "Give me just a sec," she said. "I'll be quick. I promised Beth we'd talk. It'll just take a sec. I promise."

He picked up some part of the newspaper from the back of his lounge chair and moved to the window.

Sitting on the front of the couch cushion, she tried to keep up the energy of her "quick" phone conversation as Beth went on and on about her failed date that had ended with a milkshake spilled all down her front.

Gene's glance at the newspaper led him to the fireplace and then to stand by the coffee table and eventually to sit in his chair. She looked up as, shifting, he rattled and snapped the paper. He was no longer reading; she could feel that. She knew that he really only read the sports section and then only if a headline caught his eye. He was never deep into anything he had to read.

He was listening. The waggle of his foot confirmed what she sensed: he was nearly out of patience.

Carol laughed her way into a moment when she might glance at Gene. She tried to find a movement that seemed natural. She slid the ends of her hair to inspect them.

She could feel him, his body taut, almost suspended, but watching, looking off.

She was uneasy suddenly. On alert. She twisted to face the door. She could barely listen as Beth went on. It felt to Carol that he was then as he may have been before at the park: that perhaps, before he put on his sly and handsome face, he may have been watching darkly, as he was now. Had she looked up then from her reading, she may have seen him, a dark figure watching from some distance. Not looking. Watching.

Her breath grew suddenly shallow.

What if that had been true all this while? That the chance meeting in the park was hardly chance; it was where his dark watching had prompted him to go.

If that were true . . . she had experienced the feeling that flooded in. That look had been what she had seen with little girl eyes in her hallway in Texas. She needn't look at it again.

She laughed into the phone, the laugh finishing in a sigh. She knew herself well enough to offer a good facsimile of naturalness.

She looked over, knowing he was upset. She raised her index finger and flaring her eyes, made an exasperated face at him. *One minute more; what do you expect me to do?* Taking charge of the moment, she pushed back into the couch. She could wrap it up ASAP. Beth was rounding a last turn. Carol leaned forward suddenly, in hopes of ending things. She cut in, "Right. I say, 'screw them if they can't take a joke.'" She laughed at herself. "I mean, don't screw them if they can't take a . . . "

She laughed. It rang false.

His eyes narrowed. He was around the table and on her before she had finished her breath. He grabbed the phone and pulled the cord from the wall. The phone clattered, landing upside down on the hardwood floor.

And then he did a remarkable thing: he stopped and seemed suddenly out of breath as he turned to look at her. She had not moved.

"You don't get to tell me to wait . . . That's what she . . . " He turned away and then quickly back.

He shouted this time. "You don't tell me that!" He was out of breath. Spittle had fallen onto his chin.

She looked at him steadily.

"You don't tell me, wagging your goddamn finger in the air. She used to do that, and it pisses me off. Do you hear me? You don't make me sit around until you're goddamn good and ready.

You don't." It felt like he had become confused.

She watched.

"I've been waiting this whole time." He stepped away, uncertain whether he was done, whether to speak or find his composure. He turned his back to her. Then, back again, he pointed toward her face, pumping that fist as he pointed, as if to say "That's for that!"

He actually said nothing, but she could see the confusion in his eyes. He didn't know what he wanted to be doing. He just knew she had upset him.

She simply looked at him. Then through him. Then away. Past him.

Had she not been so startled, she would have begun right then to argue. Instead she watched obliquely for a moment as he shook his head and, turning, moved to the fireplace.

This was her chance.

◆

She ran into the hallway and slamming the bedroom door never entered. Instead she flattened herself into the alcove and when he crossed the hallway and opened the bedroom door, she moved to slide her coat and purse out of the entry closet, and as he went into the bedroom and called her name, she blindly grabbed two shoes from the pile and slid silently, fast as she possibly could, out the front door.

She had run along the pavement still clutching the shoes in her panic. She ducked in along the driveway of the Callahan's house and pulled herself tight to the wet siding. She felt that her ears could almost see; she was so intent.

She was safe. Hidden. For the moment anyway.

He would never search. Not on foot. Not in the rain.

Still in her stocking feet, she ran to the back gate and into the alleyway. Searching for her keys, she lost hold of the sandals. One fell into a brown puddle. She scooped up the other and brandished it like a weapon. At the car she put the sandal on the roof and yanked her purse as wide as she could in her search for keys. Finding them quickly, she grabbed the car's slick chrome door handle and slid in. For once the Plymouth started immediately. And as she pushed at the accelerator with her stocking foot, she saw him open the small gate between the two garages.

She did not watch his face as she pushed the accelerator flat.

She did watch in the mirror, only glancing through the windshield.

She would remember that face.

She made the turn at the head of the alley.

He had not yet moved.

He would.

She knew he would.

◆

Watching the Plymouth leave the ally, he bent over to pick up the sandal that had fallen from the car's roof. He didn't know what he would do with that yet, but it was worth keeping. Who knew what could happen?

◆

What a mistake that was. Moving out had cost her most of her clothing. Beth had used Carol's key to get in and grab what she could carry the next day. Carol had yet to tally the loss.

But she had outwitted him, and she had escaped.

She had made a point to "stay low" and be where she could watch for his car on the street. She recalled the first time she saw it, his blue Chevy with the prime gray hood. She had hidden, camouflaged in a neighbor's rhodies like a deer hiding in the fullness of the forest.

She had no idea how he had found her new street. She didn't think he had found the house. She had run up the back steps. He was not searching the backs of houses yet. That would be later.

The Plymouth was hidden away in the garage.

◆

From the second floor window she had watched the Chevy on the side street. The slow passage was made even slower by her anxiety as she assumed the blue car possessed preternatural abilities to see and hear. It was no longer his thing. It was him.

Until he pulled over and stopped, she would feel safe. He would be watching the front doors. He was not clever enough to think of looking at upstairs back windows.

She loved the sliding doors. She had always felt safe looking out these back sliders.

But seeing his car had triggered a new phase in her behavior. Now she never stood in front of the sliders. Always now, she looked out from behind the adjoining wall.

It felt to some degree like he had vanished. And yet to some degree like he was watching from the darkness of her hallway.

She had to let go of that specter.

Of course, there had been the cot in the restaurant storage room if things had really come to worst. She could be around those who might help.

Gene was so explosive, so devious.

At least the places of his punishment had enlarged from the bedroom to the living room and now to the north portion of the city. You always need a fallback, she thought. She was her own best resource. She had discovered this early on, and it never had changed.

◆

The banging from the next room stopped.

The outside upstairs entry, she loved. And the view out the sliders. In the daytime she could sit on her bed writing and look out toward the river, over the maples that turned so brilliant in fall. And in the depth of winter the houses wore white caps while they smoked, and the bare trees showed the promise of where she could look in the spring.

It was like sitting in the bell tower of a church, her view.

She was not naturally thrifty. She had learned this when she lived with Gran. Gran had lived her whole life frugally. And from the time Carol arrived, she was aware that money was an infrequent visitor to be welcomed and treasured. Gran had taught her without saying a word. Carol might have learned that at home in Texas as well as with Gran in Iowa, but her mother had surrendered her "parenting credentials".

Her mother had . . . Was she going to think about her mother again tonight? A tongue to a bad tooth. Carol had rebuilt herself, and that was where the story was. Ongoing. Not back there.

The banging began again.

She got up.

Habit took her to the mirror that leaned atop the dresser. She combed at her dark hair with a hand and pushed out her chin. She hoped it wouldn't become a problem. But this was really her only complaint. Beyond the fact that she was really two faces fused together. Some days that was all she could see. Two faces. The right side had the arched eyebrow. It just never rested as low as the left. That eye sat just slightly higher, which gave it an alert, surveying, sometimes imperious look. It was the younger, more adventuresome eye. Her nose, she had been told, was aquiline. So, she joked, straight on was her best side. The left eye was less adventuresome, maybe more reliable, steady, older, more mature. Her dominant eye, apparently.

She peered into the mirror for a new assessment. Looks are looks. We make of them what we will.

She had struggled not to be two things, divided. Not Texas and then Iowa. Not Mom and then Gran. Not before Gene and after. Not even then and now. She was trying to believe that it all fit together in the now. She was still in Texas, and Texas was in her; she was still in Iowa and Iowa in her. She was still in some way with Gene. Even though a narration needed to have a before and after, all things that came into your life fit together. It was all one constantly unfolding story. Never done.

One day she would be brave enough to write it.

A play was hiding in her life experiences . . . Holding onto yourself when things get taken from you? Trusting instincts? Discovering truth beneath false appearances?

Life as a solo trek onto an outcropping and then a search for a way around the expanse that falls away on every side?

She jotted. An image, a metaphor: that's all she needed for a base.

So, was Gene a start or an impediment? She had no idea at the moment.

She tossed the notebook on the bed. How many of those books had she kept? She was always on the edge of starting a new one. In the three years since graduation she had two boxes full.

◆

She lifted her chin toward the mirror for the photo on the back of the dust jacket.

She looked one more time. She liked her face. She wouldn't borrow trouble. She looked fine.

Ch 7

The postman had a handful of mail for the office. He had to use a wide rubber band to keep it all together.

Rand had accepted the mail at his desk since he was closest to the door. The mailman didn't have to come in; he could have used the mail slot, but he had grown accustomed to leaving it where it would be dry since it often was so bulky.

It was unusual for Marianne to be on hand for the mail. She was usually out on errands regarding Doc's real estate. She moved to Rand's desk. He handed the bulk roll up to her. Marianne looked over the top of the mail. Rand might be someone to her someday. She sat on the edge of his desk.

She took the band away as she watched "Harps," the default office manager, scold the receptionist in front of two patients. Marianne was going to have to do something about that one day soon. She may even need to hire someone altogether new and start their training from scratch. Enough was enough.

As she undid the bundle and on her return to her office began her usual disposal of ads and surveys and sales requests, a personal letter fell to the floor. She picked it up.

Gonzaga University,

Spokane. Washington.

She kept her reserve as she opened the small envelope.

June 14, 1974

Marianne:

Thank you for coming to my ordination. When I looked out from the altar rail, I saw KT and you. It lifted me into realizing that I am loved and supported. Thank you so much.

As you know, this has been a bit of an ordeal, but those who know me best and love me most have seen me through.

Please extend my thanks to Doc and Elizabeth for all that they have given me.

Always, my best.

Matt.

She folded the card and balanced it and his envelope above her desk calendar.

It prompted her to sit, and soon she had lost herself in thought and remembrance. She remembered most the rangy, shy brother of her friend, the boy who had the secret devil smile as she had thought of it. The boy full of mischief. The boy with whom, a thousand years before, she had shared the stage, whose hand had taken hers during the curtain call and for whom she had waited while in the dressing room he had slathered cold cream across his laughing, shouting face.

The memory drew a smile even after the years.

Matt the priest.

Ch 8

September 10, 1974

Larry,

Almost six months since the big day. I have been trying to assess where I am . . .

Here goes. Please understand, this isn't easy. I am trying to push through, but basically, I see myself failing. I see myself as weakening, diminishing with each passing month.

On the surface things are fine. My work here is fine; and I like living in Spokane and in this community. It's just that I am not "right" as they say in athletics about someone still hobbled or affected by injury.

We've talked about some of this lots of times, but it's becoming more severe. I'm dealing with the public aspect of my priesthood like I would with an actor's role. (I don't mean that in a shallow or phony way). I've spent a lot of time learning the lines from the red Mass missal; the movements at Mass (blocking, if you will) are almost second nature. I've overcome any residual stage fright. All that is under some control.

Extending the metaphor, I have still a certain feeling of security and "rightness" when I slip into the "costumes" backstage, tightening my cincture and draping my stole for instance. (I never look in the sacristy mirror; that would bring all this crashing to the floor, I think.)

All that is passable . . . I look the part.

But you see, I know that what I'm doing during the Mass is not authentic, not what it should be, is false. And that, my friend, is death to any actor.

Am I wrong? Is it part of faith that we push through times like this and come out the other side, wherever that is? That's what I've been trying to do: to push through. And believe.

Larry, presently I'm saying the Mass only as a service for other people. The few elderly women who come to the 6:10 AM deserve to have someone put them in the presence of their faith. I can't pray the Cannon out of the conviction of my own heart, but I can do it as a service for them. I have nearly accepted that. And so, as any good actor, I find a way. When I am at the main altar, I can do that. For them. After all, I started all this to be of service.

It's even more complicated however. If I'm at the main altar, I have to preach; and that is problematic. If I am at one of the back altars, with no one there but me, I have trouble knowing why I am saying Mass at all, except as a remnant of what I used to dream. I have been reluctant to face this repeatedly, and so I have reduced my Masses to those on the main altar, three a week.

I'll have to explain this someday soon I expect. As soon as it's noticed.

Here's the crux. I have so many things that don't ring true any longer. The story I'm telling with my public Mass is a story about a hero who I've seen as being only human. And the story I'm supposed to tell is about him being something else.

Here's something: I sat in the pews the other day and tried to see what was around me. Tried with new eyes to observe where I was.

I was in a beautiful building. A stunning place, really. But then what I saw was an edifice built to separate us from the world. The massive shaped and fluted pillars reaching up to the vaulted ceiling on either side were lovely. But we don't look out onto creation; we look at stained glass.

As we proceed from window to window, we find ourselves at the suspended cross and the image of Jesus nailed there. And down to the altar table where sacrifice has always been executed, and to the expanse that draws the eye to focus on only one thing: Jesus' divine redemption story. The story that makes him different from the rest of us.

The one story that escapes me.

More and more I think the walls and windows and pillars and altar and crucifix and holy water font and pews – no, we should leave a pew, I guess—should all go away. The people should be invited to . . .no, I should invite myself to . . . sit in that space within the world and open my eyes. And go from there.

Maybe these— the world and I or anyone— are the elements of transformation. Each of us attentive to the world. The world present to each of us. The women of my 6:10 Mass time: people. On their search. Telling the beads of their rosaries. Sometimes blinded. Often baffled. In need. Struggling to find. Some out of hope, pressed down. Noble in their reverence. Nurturers in need of nurture. But resilient, strong, ready to listen. Present. Images of constancy.

And then there the young folks here on campus. People. Lovely in their innocence and in the wonder of new and earnest questions. Not easily confounded or content with tired answers. People on the search for models and pursuits to reverence, respect, or love. People who may become: capable of creating the spoken, the written, the played, sung, drawn, built visions and dreams.

And I am not even mentioning the awe and stunning revelation of intricate purpose in the primitive, eternal presence of mothering nature. The expanse of, the delicacy of, the constancy of it all.

But when we bring the walls and ceiling and pillars and all back in, the play changes. The pillars are like theology: stones stacked on stones to support something that doesn't need to be, at least to my mind. The unnatural edifice.

"Miraculous." "Supernatural." Confined to the stories of church. I don't think so. I balk.

Try this: I just see bread and wine. Before and after . . . They see more.

I will just read about an excellent man named Jesus . . . They will hear something more with the ears of faith. The way I used to.

Anyway. To some extent an actor's dilemma. How to believe in the flawed hero enough to play him honestly.

That's the script in my life these days. And I am always aware of playing a role I am not well suited for. Always on the edge of being discovered as a charlatan.

Anyway. I know you can translate all my theater jargon. Best way I had to describe where I am. Thank you for listening.

Pray for me. Whatever that really means.

I have fewer and fewer moments of belonging.

Enough! Gotta run. Have Odyssey class in ten. Just wanted to chat.

Take care, my friend. And thank you for your ear.

Matt.

◆

Larry heard the postman come to the door and push the mail through the slot. Three letters fell with a slap onto the laminate flooring.

A bill. A bill. Matt.

Larry tore the envelope open and moved over to the window, so he could sip his coffee and read the note. Finishing the note, he slid off the arm of the couch and onto its cushion, the letter still in his lap.

It might take a while before he knew what to say.

Ch 9

A young woman was waiting outside his classroom, notebook pressed to her chest.

"Father T?"

He began to unlock the door.

"My name is Carol Gordon. And I'd like to sit in on your class today, so I can start a faculty portrait for the Alumni News. Would that be possible?"

"Of course. You're welcome to sit in. We're doing *The Odyssey*, as you probably know."

"I do know. I also understand that you are auditioning actors for *Hamlet*. May I accompany you a bit on that venture?"

"I suppose. Too much of a good thing, as they say . . . " They both laughed. He opened the door, and she entered as he switched on the lights in the cold room. He put his books on the desk and adjusted the heat. While he opened the blinds, he saw that she had followed.

"I think it'll help the alumni to see the depth and breadth of talent on the university faculty. Win, win."

"And win," he said, pointing at her. "Is this the kind of work you do, this portraiture?"

"I'm a writer. So, I do whatever I can to keep feeding that dream of getting published. I hostess at Black Angus. I proctor professional exams.

I drum up article ideas that others don't yet know they would like. And in the time left over, I write as much as I can."

"Good for you. You're welcome to the class. And if you decide you can take more of me, come by for some doses of *Hamlet*, Carol."

"Thank you . . . " She hesitated.

He put out his hand. "Matt . . . Welcome, Carol. Feel free to ask any questions like any class member. Join in the fun."

"Thank you, Matt."

She proceeded up the stepped platforms to a student desk in the corner. As he unpacked his materials, he found himself trying to place how he knew her.

◆

Five minutes past the hour. The trouble with these early classes.

Might as well begin.

"Let's start with a bit of a review: We started with Book 9. Odysseus reviews the whole adventure to date. The one eyed monster who ate his men, the whirlpools trying to suck them down and the monster picking off his men while they sailed through the narrows, the sirens who tempted the men to put ashore only to have them crash on the rocks, the boulder throwing monsters who sank ships, the trickster Circe who turned some of his men into swine and would have done the same to Odysseus had he not had the help of the gods, the lethargic lotus eaters who tempted them to stay put, and finally beautiful Calypso who has delayed the Greek warrior in her cave. She wanted to marry him and offered to share the gift of her immortality. Remember that? . . .

Faces were blank.

He fussed with his notes on the desk, and, as he did, muttered to himself, "Of course not."

He selected a single page typed note to himself. Something he had written as a keynote to the lecture. He had forgotten to begin with it. He had actually forgotten exactly how it fit. He probably should have started with reading it. Better now than never.

"Having climbed to the crest of the hill overlooking our present harbor, we look out in the morning to see our mooring and remember that we are meant to be sailing today."

He put the page back into his notes.

"We are always to be on our way, ladies and gentlemen."

"OK, then. Chapter 9. All these were obstacles to his making a successful journey. And he doesn't know it yet, but there are even more roadblocks close to home."

"You likely have all that in your notes." He ignored the obvious.

"So. Polyphemus. Who is that?" A girl in the first row raised her hand.

"Polyphemus is also known as Cyclops." He wrote the names on the board.

"Correct", he said. "And what does that tell us?" Two hands up this time. "Yes?"

"He was the one-eyed monster who tried to eat Odysseus and his men." Two of the boys in the middle row smirked.

"Yes. Exactly. He was the one, as we remember from our reading (looking directly at the boys), who trapped Odysseus and his men by rolling a large boulder across the cave entrance and imprisoned them there, so he could devour them one by one." Several of the students were watching lethargically.

"I know this is an early class, but you may want to put that into your notes."

"*Polyphemus.*" He returned to where he had written it on the board. "*Many voiced*" or "*Much spoken of.*" May also be "*of many forms.*" Look at the name to tell us what the Greeks saw in this monster. Hidden in plain sight, boys and girls. *Hidden in plain sight.*" He underlined it.

"That means, ladies and gentlemen, that you can find him if you look."

◆

He looked, but there was no appreciable change in the energy of the room. A boy in a center desk put his head down.

"OK, then. On we go."

"This is the first of numerous strange creatures who will block or threaten Odysseus on his way home. Our warrior has been away from his loved ones for over ten years fighting the war in Troy, and for nearly as many years he has been struggling with all kinds of obstacles keeping him from home. Other Greek warriors we know got home easily or rather more quickly. Odysseus has not managed that.

"Remember." His voice changed, cuing the sleepers to shift and take up a pencil. "This story is about getting somewhere." He went to the board: "DESTINATION! That is where the frustration is for these men. They are overdue to be home. They are due to be alongside a fire with their abandoned families. Twenty years they have been away! Longer than you have lived, most of you. Twenty years they have been aliens *making their way home.*

Everywhere they have landed has only delayed their true destination: home. There are always false respites on our journey. You have to know where you are headed.

That's the whole tension of the story. It's not just an adventure story. Remember that. If the story is correct, it will be the same for you. You will be in some kind of tension until you are where you belong. Home."

He glanced up to see Carol writing diligently into her book.

The inspiration had passed. He began the hard work of excavating the chapter.

◆

At the conclusion of his questioning and seeing that there was still little engagement, he approached the board.

Some students picked up pens.

"OK then. So now we have the bones of the story. On their journey home, they land on an island. All seems well. Lovely setting. They find a cave or a haven. A place to gather their strength and rebound on the journey. However, they discover they have become trapped by a monster among monsters, who has only one eye. By trickery the Greeks escape.

"What the hell is this all about? Remember epics are not literal. They often employ one story line wanting us to think about another. What might the one-eyed monster represent? The room was silent, students intent on checking their notes or paging through the text.

He tried again.

"Do we have any monsters or monstrosities that only see with one eye? Or was this a phenomenon of the ancient world only?"

A boy two rows back offered, "I don't know if this is what you want, but anyone who refuses to see that there are multiple points of view." The girl in the front laughed a brief scornful laugh.

"OK." He wrote quickly on the board.

A call out: "Anyone who has only a company viewpoint." He wrote it.

"OK," said Matt. "Anyone with blinders on," Matt offered. "May I say that?" And, proud of himself as he moved to the board, "Yes, I may!"

Matt tapped the chalk as he finished the last word.

"Good. Now, why is that an obstacle to getting somewhere?" Silence had settled. "Anyone?"

Carol leaned forward over her desk. "It doesn't put all options and viewpoints on the table so the best choices can be made."

"Excellent."

"So, metaphorically Cyclops can be seen as any force that is selfish and/or narrow minded.

"Another time the Cyclops may be one who only sees one possibility and will not relent. Or again, a Cyclops may be someone stuck with just one way of searching for or explaining things.

"The monstrosity that blocks us is the narrowness of seen possibilities." Two students wrote the sentence down. Inspired, Matt continued, "Or put another way, the lack of imagination, of divergent thinking."

"So, what is keeping Odysseus from home at the moment? How powerful is this enemy? How does he overcome it?" He didn't answer his questions. "Just such an enemy threatens Odysseus and has killed and devoured a number of his beloved men.

"Remember, 'Polyphemus'. 'Of many forms'. "

There was no response.

◆

"Here is our work then. Write the bones; then write the non-literal meaning that might be made, and tell me why you think that is worth considering as the message. Remember as we said last time: the whole thing is about getting home, back to what should be.

"Do this analysis for Polyphemus —most of that is done if you were taking notes— for Circe and for Calypso. Don't leave it till late; it's going to take a while. And". . . dusting the chalk off his hands, "see you Thursday."

◆

Carol hung back until the room cleared, and then she approached. She smiled and sat on the edge of the table that served as a desk.

He began packing his books away. He glanced her direction. "You were intent; it seemed like you saw some things."

"I did, but I've also studied it a number of times: in high school, in college and afterwards, tracking things. Actually, I like him better as Ulysses, with his life unfinished, the way Tennyson paints him. Never really done."

Matt was silent.

"I've thought a lot about this, and I was interested in your take."

"On?"

"How this story is our story."

"Right." He wanted to turn away for something.

"We don't have a Trojan War, but we've all been called to fight. Our natural alliance supposes we'll defend our fellow humans as we hope they would us."

Matt looked at her. She was leaving him without a response. She puzzled him.

She shifted, as if giving him time to find his footing. "It makes him contemporary, to my mind."

Matt narrowed his eyes, trying to listen. He felt a need to say something. "Perhaps . . . I'm not sure Homer saw that."

She didn't speak. She looked directly into his eyes. Then, unexpectedly and nearly singing, she hinted at the melody, "You say Odysseus: I say Ulysses."

She was pleased with herself.

He admired her courage if that's what it was. It was disarming.

"As a female, the hero's journey always interests me. I love watching people have to transpose. It's not just singing up an octave. We have our own trials to overcome. Our own abysses to stare into."

He had no further response ready for her. He managed a smile. He would try to dismiss the rest. He turned to check the desk for anything . "And so?"

She would not be managed so easily.

"So, then we each have our own Odyssey," she said warmly.

"Right." He had packed and now clutched his materials to his chest as he turned back to her.

She seemed to find new energy. "Anyway, read Tennyson and tell me what you think. I think you'll like him. -I think that ending is more true to life. More inspirational actually. 'Always roaming with a hungry heart.'"

"So, are you a graduate student?"

"Coulda, shoulda, woulda. I graduated three years ago and have been scrabbling rather than spending dollars on more school. I figure, if they taught me well, I can teach myself. After all, I won't be in class the rest of my life, and I hope to continue learning always. Why write otherwise?"

"So, did you see what you wanted? Or what comes next?"

"Do you have a half hour for coffee? I see well, and I trust what I see. But there are some blurry spots I'd like to clear up." She waved a folded piece of paper.

"Such as?"

She spent a moment just looking at him. "Don't feed the monster." She winked and threw her head, amused, perhaps at her own private meaning.

He was uncertain what she meant beyond some intended classical cleverness. He would have to be careful with her.

Returned from her amusing birdwalk, she jumped in, "Do you have a half hour for coffee?"

"I can have."

She shifted and suddenly glanced at her watch as if in a hurry or perhaps even in distress. "This afternoon at 2?"

"2 it is."

He wrote it in his book as she hurried to the door.

◆

He had sat in the drafty Student Center for forty-five minutes. The music was so loud he wondered whether he would be able to converse if she did show up. He knew some of the most popular tunes. How could he not? That music invaded your blood stream as well as your ears.

The second cup of coffee had turned bitter and then cold. He no longer felt comfortable sitting alone paging with apparent industry through his textbook.

He had left the Center as though intent on a meeting for which he was regrettably late. Once out on the quad, he moved briskly to his room.

◆

She had returned for Thursday's class, coming in with the bell and returning to her seat in the back. At the conclusion of the class, she had approached the desk with a folded note. Holding her throat she had waved her hand as he read the note. *Sorry. I got sick. Laryngitis now. Monday, coffee. 9AM?*

He nodded.

She smiled, but he could see she was not well. Her eyes betrayed her.

◆

He wrote it out.

Perhaps for Larry; perhaps for himself:

> . . . *To begin with, I wasn't sure I should keep the appointment. And then thinking that I was simply being petty and exacting my revenge, I kept the appointment. I had her on the clock however. Should she be late, I would be gone.*
>
> . . . *I have to tell you I have been paging through that conversation all PM. And now I'll confide in you that she was exactly right. She sees well, and she does trust what she sees. We talked teaching, and she confided that she only sees a need for a teacher for what*

can't be done alone. She says a class should lift the heart and sharpen the ability to see. And that my class had done some of that. She said that she had loved my keynote remark for the lecture. Reminded her of Tennyson, she said. I had forgotten exactly what the keynote remark was and so I had started by asking her what else she thought, and she hesitated. Not a good sign. She stirred at her coffee.

She began with brevity. Listening to her voice, I was unsure whether she was still sick. "You did well."

"Damned with faint praise."

"OK, then. You were appropriately smart for undergrads. You laid the material out clearly." She rested her voice. "You were certainly in charge."

"I've always been taught to be in charge."

"Right. But I felt this had a different aftertaste. Kind of acidic. In a few years, you could become the bitter or closed up prof we all have had. The sarcastic one, the one who loves his own cleverness and will use it to safeguard his turf. The one who never really connects with the students. That one."

"Really?"

"Could be . . . What a waste that would be." She played with her stir stick and then looked up . . . "I just think there's a different you inside. He's the one who can lift hearts as well as sharpen eyes." And then she slid the box of artificial sugars to the middle of the table. "What if you relaxed and didn't need to be so protective? For instance, what if 'home' is a condition instead of a destination? Too easy to take the metaphor literally. Too difficult to move beyond the metaphor.. Don't you think?" She looked up after the question.

It dawned on me that this might be an altogether new tactic for teacher review. My turn to stare.

"I just mean, what if you let things come to you instead of needing to run everything?" *She bit at the corner of her mouth.*

"I'm not sure I understand what's happening. Are you mentoring me?"

"Not intentionally. I'm just observing . . . For instance, what were you hunting for with your question about Polyphemus? . . . I just ask because there was an obvious example right in front of them, and you didn't offer it."

I smiled, not knowing what she was referring to, exactly.

And then she went silent and looked at me. It wasn't long I don't think, but maybe it took a long while, I don't know. All the edge melted. She had a slow smile after. She winked and began to laugh.

"Think Socrates."

"I asked a lot of questions. Didn't I?"

Then, quick as a twitch, she was up and hoisting the strap of her purse to her shoulder. "Finish your coffee. I'll see you again later."

Ch 10

Carol looked over the paper. She loved how perfect things seemed when coming off a printer. Until you read them of course. Then all the warts would create bumps for your fingers, as it were. The prince turning toad.

Several evenings ago I was privileged to witness a master at work, Fr. Matt Turner, SJ. Many of you may have seen live auditions before. I had not. I sat in on his auditions for "Hamlet", which he is directing in the Smithson Theater in March. In these auditions I was impressed with the care and personal attention he gave to all.

Some actors were in way over their heads, and he would not be using them, but they had been brave enough to thrash to the surface of the readings and were rewarded. Some were readers without a spark really, but he spoke to them as if they had shone a light. Some showed good promise, and he found for each an angle of encouragement. Others were obviously in the running given their ability to understand and communicate Shakespeare. To each and all, Fr. Matt Turner was kind and present and encouraging. There was never a flip of the paper and the legendary, "Thank you! Next!"

Then last evening I saw a rehearsal. For three hours Fr. Matt was never seated. He worked back and forth in front of the Smithson stage, following each actor intently. If one watched carefully, they might have seen him faintly mouthing the words with the actor. And pushing and pulling and directing with his body language, nodding approval at moments, walking away from an actor choice that needed attention but not now. In the course of three hours, I observed Fr Matt leap onto the stage repeatedly to encourage and shape. What became obvious to this observer is that he could be playing any major role in this play with astounding depth and insight.

"Ladies and gentlemen, know who you are! As Shakespeare himself tells us:' The past is prologue.' What has happened has changed your character's path. Know who you are."

At one point he drew the actress playing Ophelia aside: "You are surrounded by walls in this fortress, boundaries to your freedom. Your father restricts the movement of your heart towards love; your brother abandons you, leaves you apparently to face the truth of how powerless you are; your king suspects you are angling for advancement through marriage to the Prince. You are hemmed in on every side. Only Hamlet allows you your power and now he seems overtaken by the death of his father. Everywhere you look is restriction. How does that make you feel and how will you act because of it?" What a good base of understanding to empower this young actress.

At the conclusion of the rehearsal this observer approached the director and asked him how it had gone. "We are exactly where we should be. This is an excellent cast, and they'll continue to grow even beyond all of our perceptions of them. Very pleased." And having attended just the one rehearsal, this reporter fully intends to follow this cast into production to see the magic this modest Merlin, Fr. Turner, is able to work.

He has already begun to spin dreams.

◆

She put the article in a file folder and into her bag. She would add it to all the incidental writing she had done. So far, the *Alumni News* seemed pleased. She would continue her work with this show. A big article at opening. A final report perhaps.

◆

Mickey was away, and the wall was silent for once. Carol luxuriated in the silence. Silence and her breath. Her two best mentors. She propped up a pillow and stretched out on her bed. How was it she was often alone? She had been alone really, from the time her mother had sent her to Gran's, then through high school and through college. Her time with Gene was never going to work. She had intuited that from the start, but moving was a pain if she didn't have to. And then she had to.

Who knew what the next bend would bring? She needed to get serious about her writing and either get something marketable or at least substantive. Maybe she needed just to sit and write the play she had been considering. She needed to make some decisions. She liked Spokane, but . . . options were limited. Prospects were few.

Matt was thorough. He knew how to get what he wanted. He must have acted at some point in his life. She wondered when. He had such an open face. And he was softening. She would have to ask. She had not lied in the article. She was astounded at his ability to take on each character with a different look and energy to the line. He even helped the Gertrude actress find the frustration underlying her character's life.

Carol liked how she had been included. How he had given her a nickname just as he had everyone else. She had become C. She liked being C.

And then the yawn happened, and she turned off the light. The sliders disappeared as she crawled into bed. The darkness and the silence were indeed a comfort. But someday she would enjoy company. Then she would show Mickey a thing or two about headboards. And she needed to get travel reservations for seeing Sissy. Why was she putting that off?

Enough. Good night, C. Sleep tight.

Ch 11

At the closet of the sacristy the boys had been fussing with the black cassocks, trying to find which they would wear. Matt had become caught up in watching them sort and reject and sort again.

"Just put one on! You probably smell worse than it does."

He pulled his rope cincture tighter in irritation.

His situation wasn't that big a deal. He shouldn't take it out on the kids.

He continued to vest in the chilly sacristy.

He usually dismissed as comical the servers sniffing down the cassocks, trying to find the least offensive ones. But we go through phases. He must be in the midst of one of them. Usually, he would be fine. Today he had found himself to be edgy. He needed to see it and then get over it.

Likely something every priest had experienced at some point. People go through phases like this. He remembered a time when he saw people as animals. The porcine waiter where his family had taken him to dinner just before he entered seminary. He had seen KT as a gerbil once. Her small hands and dark brown eyes. He was so glad when he had grown out of it. Grew out as blamelessly as he had grown into it. Phase.

He would have to ask Larry. Matt thought he might be getting tired with the rehearsing. Crankiness was a sure sign that resources were thin. This had all the marks of incipient crankiness. "Incipient crankiness." He would have to remember that. Larry liked good lines, and that could be one that he would like. On with the stole like a scarf around the neck against the cold. On with the stiff and noisy chasuble.

He moved toward the sacristy door and snapped his fingers for the servers to line up in front of him. As an effort to apologize for his outburst, he mussed the hair of the blonde boy in front of him. The youngster twisted, resisting the gesture.

That was fine. No matter.

Herd the mavericks toward the door, a deep breath, and . . . enter.

◆

Carol watched him from the rear of the congregation. On such a weekday, only a handful attended. She watched the teacher, the director, the priest, the actor even perhaps. She must remember to ask.

He wasn't like the others. They spoke in monotones, and you couldn't read their eyes, even if you were in front. They seemed past something. Past care? Past seeing for the first time. Past surprise. They seemed slightly bored. "And here's the story you've already heard."

Matt never seemed past some discovery. And he warmed the echoing church with his pleasant voice. He seemed actually to mean the prayers as he flipped his way through the fat red missal. When it came time to preach, he stayed out of the pulpit and ambled down toward the altar rail. Toward the people. Personable. Warm. And there was a hint of something humorous there. It sometimes seemed as if he paused and listened for what to say and in that pause, became amused at what he seemed to hear. She found herself sitting up even though she could hear and see perfectly well. He was connected to each person there. To those in front of her, to the balding woman off to the side. To the woman in the felt hat across the aisle.

Carol smiled. He smiled as well. To her?

For Matt, having walked back up to the altar, the rest was his service for the women attending. For them he lifted the bread and wine at Offertory.

For them he genuflected deeply as the server rang the consecration bell. For them he brought the wafers to the communion rail.

His slow thoughtful exit was honestly him.

◆

She waited on the walk in front of the church. For him. And he walked down the few cement stairs directly to her. He took her hand. He was warm.

"I saw you in the back. It came to me this morning . . . Where I had first seen you. You were at the cathedral for my ordination last May. So you probably saw me at my worst. By the way, back flipping onto terrazzo is not recommended."

She laughed. He winked and touched her arm briefly. "Nice to have you here. Thanks for the great article on *Hamlet*. I got a promo of it."

"You may see more of me. I may come by this week, if that's OK."

He started away. "You better come by. Just over three weeks and we open. It's down to the push." His breathing changed, and he was away for a moment, looking at the others.

"For sure, this week," he said in parting. He turned to shake hands with the others who were waiting, but he looked directly at her. "I look forward to seeing you."

Ch 12

The Office tavern provided unexpected drama.

Maybe Will's Laertes was still intent on killing Chris's Hamlet. Who knew how it started? Matt didn't.

Will and Chris had seemed fine. Will, Chris, C and himself. The four of them had found a way to depressurize post rehearsal these last, almost four, weeks. This night everyone seemed in agreement: one beer and home. Of course, and he should have been able to predict it, one beer had turned to a couple pitchers, and then when he had looked at the clock, he shuddered. He had an early class tomorrow. Shit, today.

"Gotta go, folks." Just as he turned to see if C needed a ride, it erupted. Will jammed both fists into Chris's chest, sending him tumbling backwards with his chair and a half full pitcher. Chris got up with his chair lifted, and Matt hurried around the table to grab it.

"Enough! Get out of here." The boys stood, silent. "I don't care who goes first, but the other one will clean up the mess. Whoever goes first will get the hell out of here. I want to talk to both of you first thing at rehearsal tomorrow."

Chris bent to get the pitcher.

"Hold it! Before anything, an apology."

The two young actors mumbled and shook hands embarrassedly. Will looked ready to help when Matt signaled him to just go. He went. Matt came back to his chair. C put her hand lightly on his leg as he sat.

C confided, "They'll be fine. Don't you think?"

Still watching Chris, he briefly put his hand almost on hers. "They better be. Right, Chris?"

"Right, Matt. Sorry." Chris left to take the pitcher to the bar and asked for a rag.

C brushed by Matt's cheek once quickly with her lips as she took her hand to his shoulder and stood.

"Alright, I'd better head out," she said. "Thank you for the beer."

He reached for his jacket, "Do you need a ride?"

"I think I'll walk."

 His eyes narrowed.

"I'm OK. I'll see you tomorrow." She walked a few steps away. She turned and looked at him and let her head loll to one side slightly. She smiled. He had seen those eyes before somewhere.

Ch 13

It was good that at the tavern meetings she had told him about Gene and about how it had ended so badly. He had grown silent before expressing his concern for her. He had told her that he hoped she felt safe, and when she assured him that time had healed that, he watched her face for the truth.

From that point forward, if it was a night when she hadn't driven, he would offer her a ride.

She loved how solicitous he got.

On this night, she would be fine, she had told him.

◆

She turned the key in her front door lock but glanced back before entering.

Gene was already onto the high bank of the front lawn. He leapt onto her wooden stairs and stopped.

"You thought I'd never find you." His smile was boyish and wide – as from a game won.

It took her a moment, looking at the bright face before her. It was a strange accusation coming from the man who had hunted her through the hallways of his house and even out into the pelting rain. She remembered his face in the alley. It was not as it was now.

This was a mask.

She spoke, as if to herself, "I had hoped that."

"Yeah, well . . . "

It seemed he was done. As if he had only practiced the line he had given her . . . How had she ever fallen in with such an oaf?

"What is it you want, Gene?" A preternatural calm had settled in her.

"I got some of your stuff in the car, if you want it back."

"I don't. Whatever is there I don't need." She considered saying, 'like you', but she held her tongue.

"You should at least come and check . . . before I throw it." He had crossed down to below the stairs. Perhaps to make her feel less threatened.

When she didn't move, he sat, straddling the iron hand rail.

"Gene, I'm not going anywhere with you . . . Throw the stuff." She had moved down the stairs and walked off as if to coil the hose Mickey had left sprawled across the lawn.

He stayed sitting, turning as she moved. She thought how attentive he was to letting her feel some distance, some freedom.

She felt neither.

She began coiling the hose.

He seemed unsettled, needing to speak. "Some of it could be important. Some books." She glanced up, into the relighting of his smile.

His eyes were so close set, accented by the shadows over his face . . . An animal with wide set eyes . . . An animal with narrow set . . . Why could she not remember?

"I have what I need, Gene. And you need to leave me alone." She had put her hand on the shovel still lying where Mickey had dropped it.

"I'm sorry," he said. "I didn't want things to turn out like they did."

She had not looked up from her careful coiling.

"You mean with you threatening me and hunting me down like a bad dog you were going to whip?" He slumped at this and took some time.

"If you'd just come back . . . I've changed. I felt really bad. That's what I came to tell you."

"Is that why you brought the box of stuff?"

"What?"

"Gene," she had the shovel between them now, "get off this property. Get out of my life." She had lifted the shovel and held it now like a baseball bat. "If I see you here again or near me again, I'm calling the cops on you."

"For what?"

"You know what. For threatening me. Get out!" He slid off the rail.

"Leave me alone!"

He stood at the top of the cement stairs. His stare was uncertainly fixed between question and threat. His bicep showed strong against his chest. She remembered him naked, sleek, strong.

She raised the shovel. "Go!" The shovel seemed to her an awkward threat.

He stepped toward her. She swung, and he ducked behind his arm just before contact.

"Fuck!" He staggered as he said it.

She had clipped him somewhere, enough to make him turn away as the shovel clattered onto the sidewalk below. She grabbed at her face with the suddenness of it all.

"Why'd you do that?" He seemed not to understand. At the foot of the stairs he turned his face to her. The blood had already stained the one side of his face beneath his hand.

With that look, he turned to go. He pulled his hand away from his bloodied face, studied it and shouted into the night sky.

"Fuck!"

Pulling off his tee shirt to staunch the head wound, he bolted to his car.

The car stayed dark.

She presumed he was tending to his wound.

She watched the dark car and descended to retrieve the shovel. As she returned to the upper walk, the car headlights switched on and the car started.

She did not watch longer.

It was only when she closed and locked the door and then put the shovel in the corner, as if that was where it always belonged, that she began to shake.

And it came to her: what had been hidden away beyond words, what she had known but lost control of: wide set eyes; narrow set eyes. Wide set eyes meant prey, unlike narrow set eyes. She could not even dare to say it to herself.

She did not stop shaking until after her shower.

She lay curled naked in her bed.

Ch 14

He turned the key to enter. On the day of his ordination he remembered how the Jesuit residence had felt: open and warm and welcoming. A house of mystery and holy smells. He was part of the private cloister, and he belonged.

Tonight, entering, he saw the same house differently.

He was drunker than he thought. He felt chilled. He would need to be quiet.

The dark linoleum floored hallway was lined with door after door, with the lingering smells of smoke, aftershave and male odors. The hallway was ill lit, and at the end near his room, an ancient white gauze curtain, now grey yellow, which blocked the view in the day, seemed oddly like a dancer's mysterious veil, hanging.

Meese's door was ajar. The smell of cigarette smoke filled the corridor. It draped itself over Matt almost like the arm of a drunken buddy reeling a bit.

Matt turned the cool handle to open his door and to escape any chance of an encounter.

Nothing had changed since the morning. Except him.

He threw his jacket on the bed.

Actually, nothing had changed since last week when he had put the heavier blanket on the single bed. Actually, nothing had changed for the year he had listened to the window rattle and meditated on the spreading stain on the ceiling over his bed, from time to time remembering the obscene history he had given it and laughing at the memory. Actually, nothing had changed along the entire second floor: except for the new TV and the ice machine in the recreation room midway down the hall.

He lay on his bed and, looking at the stain, could not laugh. He could only think of himself as dirty clothing tossed on the bed. Discarded. Not where it belongs.

He closed his eyes. The room broke from its moorings and spun, like Dorothy's house, up into the sky. Spun and spun and spun. He felt liable to fall off.

He shook the room down and sat up. He was in a new place. He did not know this place. He felt lopsided: heavy and light. Empty and full. Still spinning in a slower turn. His breath was heavy in his chest.

And then as he hunched on his bedside, the grade school catechism reflexively rose:

> **Why Did God Make Us ?** *God made us to show forth His good-ness and share with us His everlasting happiness in heaven.*

He had always been good at knowing his catechism. From the time he was a kid. He laughed.

> **What must we do to gain the happiness of heaven?** *We must know, love, and serve God in this world.*

> **From whom do we learn to know, love, and serve God?** *We learn from Jesus Christ, the Son of God, who teaches us through the Catholic Church.*

Jesus Christ, the Son of God . . . The man who had sat on Matt's bed.

He found himself rocking.

He knew that the bed and prayer were not a good mix, and so he slid off the side of the bed and into a kneel at the desk.

Dear God, I guess I drank too much so this won't be a very good prayer. Pray-er. He stopped.

Dear God, help me know what to feel. I am loose. And I don't know what to hang onto. I just feel untied and drifting. There's nobody . . .

Her touch and her kiss and her look. What did that mean? And who would he become?

He stopped praying.

From the hall he heard the distant bounce of perhaps a tennis ball against a wall.

Meese?

His anxiety told him otherwise. Meese never made noise. Their empty hall was silent unless the radio was on.

No, it was Lucas. He was back again.

He heard it twice more, but he would ignore it. Were he to go open his door, there would be nothing there. It was his psyche, bringing Lucas around again. With that boy always came unsettling thoughts. He would ignore it.

He lay out on the floor.

◆

"Pull up your pants and get up to bed." His father stood next to him.

And the bathroom door swished behind the fury of the exit. But not slammed shut.

He could come back.

And the boy was left standing on the cold linoleum floor, still holding tight to the gathered top of his favorite cowboy pajamas, his pj pants still pooled on the floor.

He could still feel the grip pressing his face into the father's shirt, the thrumbing of the father's heart, the torso twist that meant delay and then the pain he could not endure until he had to.

He hadn't cried this time. Not in front of him. He wouldn't. Not anymore.

But it had hurt bad.

He reached for his mother's hand mirror and angled it behind. He wasn't just angry red; he could see the stripes. The long one ran across his butt and onto the soft back of his thigh. It already had a darkness coming. That was the one that had hurt all the way down the inside of his leg. He had thought he might pee it hurt so bad. He couldn't pee, he remembered thinking, he wouldn't.

He looked down at his tiny innocent penis. It was a point of pride that he had held the pee in during all of that. He felt numb all down there. But he had held on.

He put the mirror back.

He still hadn't moved his feet, and he bent to lift his bottoms. That was when he saw it. He was peeing. He was peeing onto his bottoms and as he stood up, onto the bathtub, and as he moved, out over the floor.

He couldn't stop it!

He squeezed down hard, and it finally stopped.

Panic rose immediately.

His father would know. And he could be back any second to shove him toward bed.

He opened the cupboard and grabbed a hand towel. Wiping up all he saw, he hurried into his bottoms and buried the damp towel deep in the hamper.

It hurt to walk, but he had other things to think of.

The tv was on, so he made it to the stairs and up to bed.

In the morning he had taken the damp towel from the hamper and tucked it under his jacket before he left for school. He had turned up the alley and shoved it deep into the first aluminum trash can he saw. They would never find it under all the garbage.

They would never know.

And he could forget about it.

◆

And this was what happened now when the boy with the burns came round.

Matt rocked once.

He was exhausted. And drunk.

This was not the night to chase phantoms.

He crawled over to sit alongside his bed and must have grown cold in the night since the next morning he woke in bed with little memory but only a dull, thick taste and some remnant anxiety from what had happened.

No matter.

He took the first breaths of the day.

He would be fine.

He knew how to deal with the daylight.

Ch 15

She had not come to class for days now. And he had found it increasingly hard to press on with any purpose. He knew what was required to cover the material, but, with her absence, the passion, the excitement of sharing the moment, the insights: all that had been tamped down. He was working by rote. He was there resentfully. He was punching a non-existent clock. He had become short with the students.

He had discovered himself changing his position in the room even. He noticed one day that he was playing with the cord for drawing the shade on the old tall window. He was facing the outside with his back to the class really, turning from time to time to keep up the momentum but then pivoting again to face outside and playing with the drawstring. Odd. Remarkably unusual for him.

He wished that she had been there during these last days to consider the full return of the hero to home: Odysseus to Ithaca. Seemed like something she would have had unique insight for. He missed her observations.

He missed her at rehearsal. Her attention to what was taking place. She never wandered off to do her own thing. He missed her glances, watching. How she would find a way to tap or touch him when no one would notice but him. He missed the excitement of watching for her entrance into the theater, knowing that she would be with him for the next hours.

He hoped, despite what she had said, he had not overstepped or offended by asking her to help him show his student playing Hamlet how to react to the death of the queen.

After repeated instruction, the actor still was not feeling the moment. Matt had pulled Carol aside and asked her to trust him and, whenever she chose after he said the word "Hamlet", to collapse and play as if she had been poisoned to death. Then setting the scene for the death of the queen from Hamlet's point of view, he said, "For the moment I will play Hamlet, but I want you to notice that he drops everything else [*Carol, briefly choking, had fallen dead*] to get to the queen. There is nothing [*as he knelt, he took her into his arms, but she gave no response at all*] that he understands except that the mother he had loved so much has been killed by someone who apparently had poisoned her. He cannot lift her back to life [*he tries*], he cannot embrace her back to life [*he rocks holding her and crying out*], he cannot kiss her cheek and wake her, he must hold her slack body to himself and feeling the loss, turn his eye to find the one to kill. It is not about any thought other than revenge, immediate and final. And then Laertes speaks. And we know . . . We all know . . . It was the king.

He let it hang in the air. He looked from one to the next to the next.

Carol had never seen such passion make a moment electric. His breath was everyone's breath. His intensity palpable.

She wanted to know where that had come from.

"Now run the scene again."

"Carol, thank you for helping us find our way."

She had saluted to all, stepped off the stage and sat in her usual place.

Upon review the scene worked.

At the end of rehearsal, he had thanked her again for helping. And as a group of them walked out, and he was locking the door, she and several others laughed about her fall and regal death scene. Matt had smiled to watch that.

But as he had held her, he had been moved in a way he did not plan or expect. He had started to become aroused at holding her body, and only his fervent instruction kept him on track. It had not been noticeable that he could tell. But he needed to pay attention.

He had feelings for her.

◆

Flush with the memory, he walked along the first row of students, pretending to monitor their essays. His fingers brushed against the card she had left him. The card he had inserted as an apparent bookmark in his text.

The poem he had almost memorized.

Untitled

I was in jeans and a cotton blouse.
There were no jewels for me to wear
No flourish of trumpets at my ascent,
No drapings of royal colors.

A tangle of feelings accompanied my ascendancy
Onto the naked stage.

I was no monarch true.

Until you,
Like the magic for Cinderella, transformed me.
Until you beckoned, called, summoned, smiled.

Then I became the queen.
And though I was to die
I lived every moment I was given.

That's what I recall.

The elegance of belief,
Of being believed in.
The excitement of creating,
Of being made.

I do not recall the tragedy.
There was no poisoned cup.

There was only possibility
Shining like the glass gem
On the back of the prop chalice,
Seen by me alone.

I have never smiled so truly.

Thank you, Matt. "Gertie"

◆

He made show of scanning the students at work before he placed the card into the book and folded them both into his arms. Still clutching the book, he sat on the front of the desk.

And he missed her promo work at *Hamlet* as well. She had done such a nice job publicizing the show for the students. And he had thought she intended to do another piece, for the closing.

And only now was he able to think of her without feeling the residual excitement of that evening. He remembered whatever the beer had not blurred. He found himself assigning writing in this class more and more so that he would have time to consider and wait.

He had written to Larry.

She would be back at some point. He simply needed to be faithful to that hope.

"I'm OK. I'll see you tomorrow." (And tomorrow and tomorrow and tomorrow creeps, my god.). He had heard her. He took her at her word still.

He had taken to calling her C. He was not really sure what it stood for, other than a shortened and affectionate diminutive form of her name. To some extent it amused him. "C" was the abbreviation he used for both Circe and Calypso in his lecture notes. "C". He liked the sound of it as well. It was actually very personalized. No one else in the cast had it.

Larry had not yet returned his note. He would. He was just letting it settle before he responded. That was Larry.

And then he told Larry about C and how she had become part of his class and his production work. About how she had become an important associate in his life. "She sees me," he had said.

He thought that telling Larry brought things more into the light. That seemed good. More honest.

◆

The bell roused him from his thoughts as he stood to the side and gave a space for the students to return their work.

Ch 16

At the party, he assessed.

He thought *Hamlet* had been successful. Audiences had invested in the performances and seemed to be taken when it ended the way it always does: the noble heart cracking and flights of angels singing him to his rest.

Hamlet, the character searching through the ill-fitting pieces of a murder mystery for who he is to be. Another cautionary tragedy. Not the way you hope a hero story ends, but . . . sometimes they do.

The last show had been good. Good enough to get the audience up on their feet, as had been true for most of the shows. Enough to remind him why he did theater. The lump in the throat, shortness of breath, water in the eye. Those things were death to the actor; they got in the way. But to a director, they were life itself. Like the throes forgotten with the nuzzle of the newborn, all the hours seemed fleeting with the rise of the audience. He thought that C should have seen the final show. She had such a strong hand in promoting it and supporting him. Besides, without her, he was the only old one and feeling out of place.

There was a philosophical frame that came with beer, tiredness, and not fitting in. A frame that led to slow sips and a temporary seat on the arm of one piece of furniture or another. And the occasional nod/smile to kids passing. These were the people he was meant to serve. The gathering had started in the front room, where he was, but there seemed to be a migration to some game laid out on the dining room table. And then there were the disappearing folks who hung out at the edges and at next glance would be exiting through the kitchen door to the basement.

Cast parties in college are fairly predictable. Pizza: in or out. Beer: either place. And maybe a random guilt salad. And all the onstage and backstage stories fit to tell. And not.

The party was "in." At Ophelia's. And her roommate's. They had helped with costumes and perhaps had something to do with hanging some of the soldiers' belts a bit lower than usual, loose and with a come-hither sway in front. He smiled. When asked, he explained it was a Danish fad. It gave the girls great pleasure to have had a hand in it.

His plan was to hang out for a while and then home to bed. He had had the early Mass today and was starting to feel it. He needed to ask for relief the next time he was in production. Too much. He finished his beer and needed to decide whether to start another or to offend Ophelia by an early departure. How Hamlet like. He was going to have to find a new reference set for his thoughts. He walked to the kitchen once his feet decided.

On his way back, a giant cheer arose from the dining table. Someone had won or lost a nation or a continent or a war or something momentous. He watched over shoulders for a second and deciding he didn't really care to fake caring, started toward the front room.

Someone was seated on the arm, where he had been. Two cast mates were standing by, chatting. There was no place for him. He didn't want to commit to sitting on the couch. He moved across the room from the couch to lean on the fireplace.

The couple at the arm of the couch moved away, and suddenly she appeared there before him. The dead was alive again! Was this real? Or had he breathed in too much of the Bard?

He laughed at the silliness of it all.

She saw his response. She patted a front space on the arm where he could sit.

He was certain anyone watching would have seen how his heart was working. He sat while she moved to lean over the back of the couch casually. She had that lolling angle to her head. The one he remembered from the tavern.

"I've missed you," he started, "I thought you were going to be onboard for the final weekend."

"I was. And then I heard from my sis in San Francisco and flew down. We hadn't seen one another for maybe three years." She reached for his beer and took a sip.

His breathing all but shallowed out. It was as if he had run to the party and was just now catching his breath. He leaned his shoulder into hers. "Well, you missed a good closing week. You could have written something that would have had John Simon salivating."

She shoved back and held. They fused. She reached for his beer again. "Can I get you one?" he asked.

"I'm fine with this one. If you don't mind, I mean."

He couldn't answer with words. He redirected the conversation. "How was the visit?"

"It was good. We don't talk enough, and she's the only family I have left. So, I decided it was time for us to connect. And she left me a message that said, "this is the only bloc of days I have for a while. It's now or wait a while." She sipped and handed him the beer.

"So, I flew out on Thursday." She took his elbow. "Sorry. I should have found a way to tell you."

"I just missed you. You were a part of what we were doing with that play. An integral part of it, really."

"That's nice to hear." She pushed against him for emphasis. "Now that it's closed, what can I become an integral part of I wonder?"

The question excited him. It really wasn't his to deal with; could very well have been a musing that escaped into the air. But he took it to himself. He thought it was that that excited him.

"We'll see. There must be something."

She stood up and stretched her back. Put the empty long neck bottle into the fold of the couch.

"In the meantime, I need to get home. I came here from the airport. That's my suitcase, in fact." The bag was next to the front door.

"I can give you a ride."

"I'd like that."

◆

Once he started the car, she gave directions to her house. It wasn't far. Street parking. For some reason he turned the engine off.

"Do you want to come up?" It became a strange moment of contemplating the house in the dark.

"Your housemate?"

"She's sleeping; otherwise, there'd be a light."

During the ride she had slid over on the bench seat. He liked having her next to him. He liked her touching and pressing on him.

Turning to him, she put her hand on his thigh.

She was beautiful with the dim cast from the street light giving her a dramatic glow as if she were in a stage light "special" that was set to shine just for that purpose. She paused to look deeply at him. He knew her eyes and gave her his. He kissed her on the side of her face. She swiped her hands along his cheeks and kissed his mouth.

He had never felt this in a kiss.

She removed his glasses.

Her tongue played at his lips, and, still holding at his temples, she laughed as his body responded. She put her hand on him. She kissed him deeply; he met her kiss with his own arching push. He was with her as he had never been with anyone in his life.

She embraced him and then took his hand to the smoothness of her belly beneath her shirt.

She moved to guide him.

◆

The nice thing about coming home at a late hour was that you didn't have to pretend you were sober or pretend that you were glad to see anyone or pretend anything at all. You were just who you were, climbing the stairs or walking the hall to your room. You were just who you were as you entered your room. You were just who you were.

He sat on the side of his bed, his clothing thrown across the foot of it. He would deal with that in the morning. He never reached to turn on his light to read. He was beat. He sat and breathed in the feel of her skin and her mouth and her energy as she had touched him.

With her was where he wanted to be. She was so soft and her body so warm. They had touched and struggled with one another to find more to touch. He had kissed her body and listened to her pleasure at his kisses, and he had burst with an excitement he never had felt before.

They had lain together in the darkness of the car. He had covered her with his jacket as he held her in his arms.

He might never sleep again. He lay out flat. Aroused.

"O My God."

He closed his eyes.

He could hear the old warnings, the seminary warnings . . . "Don't", "Mustn't", "Careful" . . . They faded into his breathing . . . new voices calling out. His *Odyssey* voices calling.

He taught the story every semester. He knew all these warnings. But now . . . Why were these voices in his ear?

He was lashed to the mast. Intent on the men rowing. Rowing. Rowing past. He could see, from the corner of his vision, the young women waving and raising their hands to shout. He knew he mustn't hear. Must not. The men had plugged his ears so he could not hear. They had told him, "Don't look!", "Don't listen!", "Keep to your course."

"Keep on!"

He did not even hope to listen, but he had twisted to search out a view of them. They were not hags as he had been told . . . Their vitality. Their vibrancy. The promise in their cheeks, and the hope in their movement. The directness of their glance.

They were young like he could never be again.

Even so, he wanted to laugh with them and toss his shirt into the air.

He felt the burn of the ropes that held him.

And was he like a cruciformed one: pinned and needing to ignore the limits of being human?

Or what was the myth he was in?

He had no idea.

He breathed. Empty. Tired of it all.

And he fell away . . . laid out . . . and now adrift . . .

. . . *thrown by the sea. The naked remnant of a crowd of brightly clad warriors who had shone in the sun for 100 days waiting for the winds to lead them to Troy.*

The spirited winds had finally led them.

He had had so many dusty battles to fight that his strong arms ached, so many waves that strained his oar and punished his back. So much tired hope, enough that he was tempted to hang in the water and not even try to swim. Just to hang there and wait for what would be.

He had done all he could to survive. The water pulled him away; the water pushed and lifted. The water pulled him away; the water pushed him and lifted. The breath of the sea as he rode its cold bosom. He would let the sea take him.

On the shore he could see a grove of high grown trees along the hilltop. And black rock near the shore. And bursts of greenery between. A wide winged bird floated on the air stream, just the way the warrior did in the water. But not the same at all. The bird dipped and skated. Other fliers played the wind in their suspension. The warrior just hung. Not sure about hoping. Not ready to choose the death waiting at the base of his lips. Slapping at him. Blinding him. Mocking his naked inertia.

He was about to go under. To become something other. He had stopped caring. He would not struggle. He was at the edge. No sense struggling. The sun was brilliant bright. The water had become warm. It was rocking him, almost like a newborn.

Until this time he had never understood drowning.

At the edge, things are beautiful. Vast, perhaps even infinite. . . good. . . true. . . beautiful.

She turned onto a brown path down to the shore. She sang to herself, there being no one else in sight.

Her peacefulness was what he was searching for.

He released the tension of the struggle.

He could hear her marvelously well. Beyond what should be the ability to hear.

He closed his eyes to hear even more the loveliness of the aire.

He opened his eyes as she stopped.

She had bent to collect a flower.

He could see her beyond the ability to see. Or was hope seeing? She was sure footed on the brown path, encountering no encumbrance. She wore a filmy gown that flowed, a low gem encrusted belt shaped her waist and then hung in a vee before her. Her arms were filled with brightly colored peonies, so plentiful that as some lost hold, she never saw them fall.

(He needed to remember when he awoke. He needed to remember.)

His heart rose up. His body roused itself.

He lifted his arm; she lifted her head. He lifted his arm; she straightened. He could not shout for tiredness, but he lifted his arm to cry out. She shielded her eyes and reached his direction.

He felt the motion of the wave lift and thrust him forward. Stop. Lift and thrust him forward. He closed his eyes as finally the shallow waves rolled him onto the bruising sand. She was there in the water. Her hand touched him, lifted his head to the air.

She had a beauty twice any other. A beauty twice . . . She had given him breath. He would let himself be with her.

He would touch her.

If she would have him, he wanted to touch her.

Half waking, he stretched on the top of the bed. Spent.

He didn't care what the story was. He would see all that later. What he cared about was that he wanted to touch her. He could somehow only be saved if he touched her.

Alone, he was lost.

◆

Meese's radio was in the air. The Who. Roger Daltrey. He knew this one. He had prayed with this one. How Matt loved this, their *Tommy*. He gave himself to it.

"Listening to You." Indeed.

He closed his eyes and let it fill him. He breathed the opening of the song.

The time between each lyric was . . .

He felt flayed . . . laid out and flayed. He opened his eyes and looked at the stain on the ceiling above him.

Could he ever be whole?

He laughed out loud, a dark laugh,

He had never prayed like this: aroused and singing, and laughing as he wept.

Was that what it was? Prayer?

O, my god.

Ch 17

He awoke to a brightness in his room. He had not closed his blind. He had not brushed his teeth. He had not taken his clothes off the foot of his bed. He had kicked them to the floor in the middle of the night.

He turned the clock to himself: 10 AM. No AM class on Monday. O, there is a god! He rolled out of bed and saw a lovely day out toward the river. Sunlight might restore him.

Coming back from the shower, he saw three pink notes on his door. Portland: Larry. No message. Portland: Larry. No message. Spokane: "C". Message: "Now you have it, so give a call" followed by a local phone number.

He brought the three notes in to his desk. He crumpled two of them. He would get back to Larry later. He folded the last and placed it in his wallet just before he left his room for the day.

As he opened the door, he found himself directly across from Meese in full clerical attire. Standing. Concentrating.

The priest had been thinking there silently. Perhaps staring at the door. Matt didn't know. Meese might have been using the door to focus his thought as he sometimes did. Matt moved a step into the corridor. It seemed like he was on stage, and he should take a moment to lock his door.

There were no locks. No props to help him. What had he been thinking?

Perhaps Meese had even taken the phone calls and heard that one of them was from a woman. Matt didn't know. He only knew that Meese made him feel that he needed to smile without Meese himself smiling. It was as if Meese's eyes actually heated Matt's back as he tried to find some nonchalance or even a natural rhythm for his walk down the long hallway.

Meese knew. He must. Why else . . . ?

◆

Matt did not want to phone from the house, so he walked over to the Department Office. Two profs were working at their desks, and so he said "good morning" as he made show to sort some files behind his desk. He pulled two folders and left. As he walked down the hall, he dropped the torn empty folders into the trash at the corner by the stairs.

◆

On the first floor of the Ad Building two pay phones hung on the wall. Class being in session, the phones were unoccupied. He put his coin in and dialed the number.

"Hello."

He didn't recognize her voice and hesitated.

"Carol?"

"No. This is Mickey, her housemate. Hold on, I'll get her."

He felt his jaw tremble and fixed it with his breath.

"Hello. This is Carol."

"Hey, C. This is me. I got your note."

"Good. Can I take you to dinner? I'll drive."

"Sure, I guess. Where do you want to go?"

"Surprise. Part of an adventure. I'll get you at 5 if that's OK. Corner of Ruby and Sinto."

"See you at 5 then."

"At 5."

◆

He spent the afternoon in the library. His dream kept coming to him. He remembered much of it. He pulled various translations of *The Odyssey* to track down images and nuances.

Also to remind himself.

Circe was an enchantress who lived inland but near the sea. She was deceptively dangerous and those attracted to her beauty were turned into animals unless they were protected as the gods protected Odysseus. He knew all that. He knew that Odysseus was able to disarm her and neutralize her power on himself and his men. He saw the various representations history had rendered on vases, in paintings and statuary. He saw little echo of his dreamscape in the texts or in the artistic interpretations.

Calypso he knew was a weaver, a singer, a gardener or one who fostered growth. She was an immortal and could give that gift to Odysseus. She was dark and content and lived on an island and dwelt in a cave that kept both herself and any guests warm and comfortable. She was not afraid of the sea. Likely she had spent many days of her life pulling from the vast ocean, things that floated to where she lived. She was a rescuer. The Greek words gave him overtones and colors, all of which coincided with his dream. It was Calypso he had dreamed of.

◆

He was at the corner by five, and she pulled up in a long, tan Plymouth station wagon. He climbed in. She worked the big wagon around toward Division and then toward Highway 90.

He broke into her concentration. "Quite the car."

"Gift. Price was right. It's probably falling apart. I don't have a lot of money to sink into it. By the way, I'm throwing my hat into the ring for a couple of singleton creative writing classes at Ft. Wright College. I'd love to have some predictable income as well as windfall projects and the restaurant. I'm ready to be done there."

He was by now curious about their destination. They had turned onto the Valley Highway.

"Where are we headed?"

"You'll see. "

"OK. I trust you. Let's go."

They crossed into Idaho and into Post Falls within a half hour since traffic was light that early.

◆

After she turned into a burger place along the highway, and ordered for the both of them, she brought the food to the car. He had had no idea what the dinner plan was. He must have shown that on his face.

"Adventure. Don't try to figure it out. Adventures don't figure. Just go with."

She started up the Plymouth and found the exit that would take them over the river.

Crossing the river, they entered Q'emlin Park. She parked the Plymouth and announced that they had arrived and could begin their dinner and then would be able to have a good walk. Constitutional. She winked.

The burgers disappeared rapidly. They disposed of the trash and left the car which still smelled of fries.

She took his hand. "Walk with me. This is a lovely park, and I'd like to share it with you." They began, and she slid in next to him, on his arm.

Matt watched a youngster in front of them pick up some stones from the edge of the path and toss them toward the bank of the river. The father barked at the boy to heel.

C looked up at Matt. She must have felt his tension. She reacted to the feeling.

"What is it?" They walked a while before he responded.

"My father. It was like that . . . It comes back to me."

◆

They walked silently for a while in the ambering of late afternoon.

"You ok?" she asked.

"I'm ok." And then he was back to silence for the next while.

She stopped on the path. "Remember what I said before: 'Don't feed the monster.'"

He looked at her, wondering how she knew his thoughts. She seemed to.

They walked. She put her hand in his. So many parts of him opened to the light he saw right and left. It was mottled, but it was a light within the densest patch of his unweeded, uncultivated tangle of stories and memories.

◆

She found a perfect pitch. "There are all kinds of trails and walks and views here. It's nice to get away and be ourselves."

That was it, he thought. The assuredness that comes from being oneself. Her self possession and its gentle authority.

He felt himself relax as they passed beneath the overhang of trees and strode down the walkway. They made their way to the river where she sat on a downward sloping bank, and he stood near the water, throwing stones.

At a loss, he reached back into Philosophy 101. "You know," he began after a short silence, "you can't put your foot in the same river twice."

"Doesn't worry me. I might not want to put my foot in the same river once."

"That is so you." He wasn't sure what that meant, but it seemed right. He searched for new stones.

She had become pensive. Her face was fixed in a smile from which she had departed. She gazed out over the water.

"What?" He asked as he saw her, although he continued to toss stones.

A bit startled she looked at him and then back to the water. "I found myself thinking about a piece I wrote the other day."

"What kind of piece?"

"A poem. And yes, that's a little unusual for me, but I've learned to try to listen to what my pen wants to do."

"Will you show it to me?"

"It's not a picnic poem exactly."

"So? I'd like to hear it."

"Maybe later."

"Promise?"

She reentered her smile. Her look to him brought him near. He sat with her.

"Nice word."

"What?"

"'Later.' It lets me think of being with you more, or longer, or again."

"And you like that thought?"

"I do."

◆

She tossed her one rock the direction of the water. "Have I told you about the play I'm starting work on?"

She hadn't. And she began absently to toss small pebbles toward the water and tell him the story about her handful of pictures and what they meant to her. There were the photos of Lily, her mother, of Sissy, of Random the collie who had been her favorite. Her family. Now they would become word pictures.

"Put the two together and it's magic. The squinting, innocent laughter of Sissy. Random's keen and ready exuberance. The lines of struggle, of self doubt and defeat at the edges of Lily's smile. It's all there to see immediately. Soon as you tie the least bit of story line to it. I'm going to make it a play about my family, I think.

Who they wanted to be. Who they became.

"If it's any good, would you think about directing it?"

"Of course. I'd love to do that. When'll you start?"

"I've already started a little bit. Some damn school play got in the way recently and got me knee deep in writing promos."

"The life of the artist!"

"Anyway. I've come back to it. I have a feel for it right now, and that's maybe the most important thing. We might have something by the fall. Do you have a season for the Smithson? Or could we do it in the black box?"

"Get it done, and we'll find a place to stage it. Probably the black box. The Smithson season has to be advertised really early to get interest going."

"The black box is maybe the better venue anyway. We'll just keep things small and intimate. That's the plan."

She seemed to be saying more than what she said. He looked at her, and she smiled.

He tossed a nicely flat rock, skipping it a half dozen times.

He put a skipper in her hand.

She looked at him and, smiling, put it down.

◆

She got up and brushed off the dirt that clung to her jeans. "OK. Time to head out."

He threw one last stone as she walked back up to the path. She waited for him.

◆

They still smelled the fries in the car and so started out with the front windows down and the wind sweeping the smell out of the car.

She pulled out of the lot and crossed the river, entering a small side road just before the highway. She turned into the lot of the motel. She stopped the car. She handed him a card from her purse.

He opened it and read:

> *I might be wrong, but I don't think so*
> *And if I am, I apologize.*
> *All you need to do is chalk it up*
> *To one more adventure with a friend.*
>
> *In a minute, I'm going to check us in*
> *And you can either come in,*
> *Or I'll drive us back west.*
>
> *C*

With that he looked at her and, cocking his head very slightly, he smiled. C left the car and was back out of the office soon after, waving at him with a big wave.

"C'mon."

Ch 18

She had smoothed his knotted body with her oils and washed the salt from his hair. Her hands had restored his hope, his vision — enough for him to see her cave. She had a wide loom and tapestries that hung beyond it. Her colors were more than he had ever seen. From the ceiling hung spice plants tied and drying, part of her magic he presumed.

The sea birds squawked and chattered. Two vibrant parrots watched and nodded. Her bed was wide and held him up like a thing of value. A miracle from the sea. The peonies watched from a woven basket in the corner.

He had remembered.

He woke from the dream.

On the floor he saw a hole in the half light. It was as if he might fall through the opening, fall into his lasting confusion, to his damnation. It was that dark. As dark as a clerical shirt and as wide as his very body. Only after squinting did he see the hole must be his jeans in their random landing.

The pallid light of morning seeped in at the edges of the worn curtains. The light seemed burnt and old. Used up. Reused in fact. It seemed not a new day; it was an alternate of some sort. Brilliance had been replaced by weariness. Startling profligacy by exhaustion. Ecstasy by remorse.

The night had been ecstatic. Slow discovering. Erotic. Soothingly, then electrically exciting. Sudden. Eruptive. Silent and filled with the noises of exertion and collapse.

He shifted in the bed.

He could see today that love making was not one thing.

Where he felt the urge to tear away the plain pale shirt they had given him, she had unbuttoned it slowly. And she had given herself to his careful undressing, at each opportunity looking into his eyes.

At some point it had begun.

It was not just the dark, slow, eager, glandular experience he had had in the car. It was also sudden, eruptively so, and electricity had moved up in a way he had never known. They became nakedness seen, not just touched. Their faces assenting, hands reaching to cradle, to hold. And the press. Pure nakedness to pure nakedness, resting in tight embrace.

And she had invited, and he had moved forward. She had cupped him, and he had caught his breath. He had taken leverage at her bottom, and she had pressed forward, into him. He had watched himself hold, and then, at some moment, turn her toward the wall, and she had willingly, smilingly gone, and she had leaned forward and he had come to behind her, cupping, and she had reached back for him and held him, and they had breathed impossibly fast. He had thought he might faint (even the memory was quickening his heart). And she had pushed him backward onto the bed, and they had rolled to discover each other, and he had mounted, and she had helped, and they had held each other. With their eyes, with their breathing, with their entry into what he thought must be the soul of one another, they had gripped; they had angled and found the places that pleased.

They had explored those places and shown the other.

Exhausted, they had finished and rolled away. They had never lost contact in the rolling. They had been one. They still were. As they had not been before.

◆

The adventure.

Adventures don't figure.

◆

He found himself stimulated by the dark memory of the evening. Riddled and aroused. Regretful about any of his regret.

He felt himself suddenly a fool.

He didn't know why.

He did not want to move away from her nakedness.

He was afraid to look at himself.

His breathing seemed aware of the passing of something that would never return.

He was going to have to choose something to be.

He turned to her and watched her sleep. He couldn't ignore what they had shared together. He would not ignore that. He couldn't enter the black hole in the floor and plummet into guilt.

He would not.

He owed that to himself. He owed that to her.

He would be with her.

◆

He ran his hand along the smoothness of her skin. He kissed her back. Then coming in close behind her, he cupped her breast.

She stroked the back of his hand.

She rolled over to face him.

"You liked the adventure?" Her eyes were different in the morning. He kissed her easily. They held and found places in each other.

He heard her voice.

"I don't want to take anything away from you." She pushed him back far enough that she could see him as she spoke. "I don't want to take your calling or your membership or your collar or whatever. I don't want to strip you of anything that's something you can't afford to lose. You see, I'm not sure, but I don't think you're happy. And you should be. Deeply and really. I have heard myself time and again say to you in the secret of my wishes: Be you. I think this naked man I'm holding is you."

He was listening in the silence, and she continued.

"We have something, I think. I've been with men before and never felt the connection and presence I feel with you. We have a potential, and this (she swept along his back and slowly patted his butt) is just a part, just a symbol of it. I love being with you. You spark me and remind me to work at being better. In all ways. I hope that I do the same for you.

"I'd like to be with you again because when I'm not with you, I'm with you anyway. Whatever I can give you, I'm happy to give." Her hand caressed him, and she kissed his mouth.

"End of speech." She took a deep breath. Then she exhaled it.

"OK, I lied.

"And we don't have to decide anything. I hope we can just slowly discover who we are." She kissed him again. She studied his look and knew that he had heard her.

"I'm first for the shower!"

Could he slowly discover himself to her or did he need to find an answer? Could he be what he wanted, or should he be what he had pledged? Could he hold the woman who now stood so confidently and beautifully naked in front of the mirror, or should he scratch her from his memory? Could he even begin to do that? Did he want to? Did he have to? Would that not be erasing his own self?

It all seemed so obvious and yet so complicated. This woman was part of his life in a way he never had anticipated someone could or would be.

He had never known the energy, the urgency, the fullness-making of what he had just experienced.

Could he change paths?

Should he shun what they had?

He pushed his head into the pillow. He would think on that later . . . He needed to be with C and hold her and love her. Their pledge had been made. Their connection fused.

She had changed his heart.

She turned from the mirror and smiled wide before crinkling her nose at him and walking to the shower.

He watched, attuned.

What would he say when she, at some point, would ask about him. The him she had held.

He lay back. What was his story?

He would tell her at breakfast about being raised a Catholic, sent to Parochial schools, learning the catechism, scraping his way through grammar school.

He would tell her about the revelation he had been given: seeing the young Jesuits in his high school who seemed so happy in what they were doing. He had wanted to be a part of that.

He wanted to run with them. To laugh with them. Just be part of what they were. Young men, bright with ideas and energy, in love with their teaching subjects and their call to service. He wanted to be that.

Alive was the word. That was what they were.

Real.

It was even more as he thought about it now. It was the joy they had in their work. They enjoyed helping the coaches and even coaching themselves. They liked driving buses down the hill to practice or across town to games. They kidded one another.

They knew every kid in their classes by name.

With them he could be something that he could not be alone.

◆

What he only later came to see was what should have been obvious from the start: the priesthood was to be part of that life. Priesthood with all its position and all the beliefs it represented. He had, since his ordination even, grown less convinced that he was supposed to be ordained. That's what he could share with her. It was his story.

She was helping him see himself more clearly.

◆

She came out of the bathroom wrapped in a towel and plopped down on the bed with a brush in her hand. "I want you to know something about me, since I seem to have taken the floor. I was raised in Texas, Stephenville to be exact, and would have spent my whole childhood there except my father walked off one night after having a cigarette out back. My mother started shriveling up and kept me and Sissy busy doing all daddy's chores.

"Then one night from our bedroom upstairs, we heard a different voice coming up out of the kitchen. A man was in the house.

"In the morning he was sitting at the kitchen table, looking at the paper my daddy had on subscription. My momma was fixing more eggs than we ever ate on a weekday, and the first thing she asked me was ,wasn't I late for getting all the chores done. He looked around my way. His hair was greased back. His brows were thick, and his face moved toward a smile from time to time but never got there.

"I got out of the kitchen as soon as my shoes were tied up." C combed and stopped. She had let her towel drop.

"Barker hung around off and on. Sissy and I always knew in the morning. His yellow work boots would be in the hallway." She retrieved her towel and tucked it absently. "To this day I hate the sight of work boots." She smiled, wearily it seemed.

"One night I was lying on the floor, reading the comics. He growled something at me, low enough that my mom couldn't hear it in the kitchen. He snatched the comics up, so he could read them.

"Another time Sissy and I had been playing with Random and laughing because Random had been biting on the boots from the hallway. Shaking his head, the way dogs do. That next morning Barker grabbed me by the wrist at the foot of the stairs. I was young, but I knew by the sound of what he said that those were bad words. What most people call the "F" word, I called the "K" word because it's so mean sounding." She turned and let one leg hang down.

"The next morning, my mom asked me how I got the bruises on my arm. She asked if Barker did that. I didn't say anything, but that night Sissy and I heard their voices. They were at each other.

"No surprise to me then that my summer was going to be spent visiting Gran in Iowa. She was in need of help, and I, as my mom put it, 'was getting old enough to help family in that way. It's what family does.'

"So soon after, I boarded the train and from my window watched Sissy hide in the folds of my mom's dress and almost wave. Mom waved twice and nodded." Carol ran her hand along her thigh as if straightening something that would have been there. "My mother looked so white in the sunshine. Her long sweater hung loose from the shoulders like always . . . You know, I don't think she waved to me. She just waved. Part of what a person does watching a train depart. . . Anyway, that's how I think of it. How it seemed then and still does. She was needing to be rid of me . . . And maybe she was sad . . . I really don't know." Carol turned to looked directly at Matt. She smiled again and straightened the top of the sheet.

"Random wagged, and when we started moving, followed down the platform barking and wagging, till I couldn't see him anymore . . . I loved that dog."

C shifted on the bed, and her voice changed into something thicker, heavier.

"I lived with my Gran through the rest of grade school, three years, and all of high school. We were good together. She loved me. She lived simply, but she put things away for later. She told me if I saved up as much as I could, she would help with college and make a Trust for later.

It was really Gran who taught me love. I watched her live the life she had been given and had made her own. Moments as well as things were precious. She held things as one might hold a baby bird. With a care, a reverential care. She hardly spoke a word about any of this but I watched her daily care for her life in the way she ate her food, in the way she dried her hands on the kitchen dish towel and folded it neatly returning it to its place. In the way she always touched me once at least, every day. Nothing special, but certain, nonetheless. You could count on her being there.

I saw how to find my way: surrender to loving the elements of my life. There's me and there's what I've been given. Acceptance. Valuing. My Gran showed me how to love my life. I'll always remember her and our years together."

Matt spoke up. "I'm not sure I've known love really. I know what Aquinas says about love, but in my own life . . . " his words fell away.

Carol smiled and put her hand on his chest.

"The last time I saw Gran was the morning I left for college. She stood there as I got into the cab to head to the bus. My Gran: an old skinny woman in a house dress, rolled brown stockings and black shoes, waving uncertainly. I'm sure at that distance she couldn't see me anymore.

"She touched her face. That was how I always knew she had concerns. And then she turned to enter the house. The silver screen door slammed with a noise I could almost hear. Then the round top door closed behind.

"I knew that Granny would sit in the stuffed armchair by the picture window for some time before going about her chores. That was her way. In my mind Granny would touch her face for miles as my bus rolled West."

She got up and gestured with her brush.

"My point: I know lots of things. Taught myself most of them. I don't waste my time or play games.

"I've always been by myself. I still can be. I would change that in a second if you can be with me. But if you can't, I'll move ahead. And no matter what, I'll always want the best for you. I know that already.

"There." She sat, folded up, on the edge of the bed. Then she bent over and kissed him on the forehead.

He sat up and pulled her into his arms. She had begun to tear up near the end of her Gran story. They stayed together on the bed for a long moment, and then she kissed him and shoved him away.

Matt hesitated. " I . . . " Carol waved and stood up, straightening her towel

She feigned urgency. "Now get your shower in, and let's eat some breakfast."

He slid quickly out of bed and disappeared into the bathroom. She heard the shower water start.

She shouted after him, "By the way, if anyone asks, we are the Pratts." She started to brush out her hair in front of the mirror.

"Next time you can pretend you're comfortable quickly jotting 'Pratt' on the registration."

From the bathroom, "Pratts?"

"Just came to me."

Ch 19

The drive back was in midday traffic. He played the radio, and each of them tried to sing along. She was consistently better, but he had that actor's confidence, that ability to sell.

She felt good that he had told his story on their walk. And now it made her smile as she listened to him search for notes that had anything to do with the song being played. Actually, she thought, she might have been able to write much of his story even before he spoke a word, but she loved that he would share.

"Do I get to hear your poem?" He was searching for a signpost to tell him where he was.

She was silent. "Maybe it's better another time. It's serious."

She negotiated the Plymouth through the moderate traffic.

Ignoring her, he asked, "Do you know it? Your poem?"

"I think so. I repeat poems time after time so their rhythms layer into my memory. I love that about writing them and carrying them with me."

"I'm a good listener."

She took a deep moment, deciding. She looked at him next to her. He put his hand on her leg and angled toward her to listen. He played with the trim of her blouse at her waist.

"It's just called *The Boy*. Remember we were with the water when all this came up."

"Are you going to share the poem? Or reminisce?"

Her face changed. She seemed to be watching beyond the traffic as she said one final thing. A new tone had come into her voice.

"This comes from an article in the *Review*. Every summer water accidents happen. This one caught my eye and made me stop. I guess I was ready to pay attention."

"OK. *The Boy*.

Young man I miss you
Though I didn't know your name.

I know the picnic, swim crowd that gathers at that lake.
I have seen you boys, long limbed and agile,
Proud of your hard bodies,
Deft,
Running, jumping, catching
On a level far above the blanket people

Taking off his shoes, Matt brought his feet onto the seat and watched her as she continued.

I have seen you boys
White skinned, black, toned tan,
Proud to be near-naked and loose,
Pounders and feelers of your bellies and chests,
Always in half smile.

I have watched the murmuration,
The adrenal rush past wading parents holding toddler hands,
The dive, dolphinlike, into the deep and then
The churn, sleekly violent,
Through the beach water, beyond the rope, toward the raft,
Swimming with a certain proud desperation

Aware that too slow was to lose the prize of belonging.
White water flying in the flair and flash of arms.

I have seen you boys.
You have made me smile.
At your joy in movement
At your joy in joy

You, young man, were likely one of a murmuring band
Ready to lie out on the hot boards, smiling at the sun,
Flat stomachs pulsing, sleek bellies showing
Hints of new black hair
No need of belts.

And just when all the watchers
Would have turned back to their books,
Their chips and salsa,
Their second helpings,
Your flight would start again,
Pushing, laughing, diving,
Keen to be the victor home.

Then, beachside, grabbing towels, you each would saunter
Past the blankets, past the tables, past the cars
Parked in the baking sun.

Disappearing.

This time not even realizing
That one of your number had not returned.
Had, in some chaotic kick of fate
Fallen beneath the surge
And risen to be lodged
Amid the slap of water on pontoon steel.

Until a single car
In the yellow lamplight
Told a different tale:
Not all had gone home safely for the night.

Until an abandoned ride had given out your name
And the urgency to search
The black water for a white body lost.

Just so you know,
Young man, I miss you.
I miss your joy
The laughter of your play
The promise in the unbounded length of your leaps,
The freedom you had found.

We all watched you then, taken.

I would have searched the dark water
Even though
I hadn't even known your name.

Forgive."

She stopped. Her face had gone blotchy beneath the tears that wet her face; the poem had bent her body in the resolve to finish its narration.

He could not speak. Her poem, her reading of it, had taken him. Transported him. He was silent.

He took her near hand and held it in both of his. The moment was silent as breathing. It was not brief.

The strangest thing had happened. He had found himself overcome by her poem. He did not understand how it had spoken as deeply as it had, but part way through, he had discovered he nearly knew what was coming next. He knew there would be a death. He knew the loss even before she spoke of the body rising to beneath the pontoon. It was his loss somehow.

At least it had felt that way.

"You are beautiful. Thank you for letting me hear your poem. Only a soul such as you could have written it. Thank you for letting me hear it."

"You're welcome." She glanced at him with her eyes full again. Her tremulous smile had returned.

He could not breathe for her beauty.

She loved a boy she didn't even know.

◆

"Did you like our adventure?" She wanted him to add any little detail that might please her and start a new moment in the conversation.

"C, I would go with you on an adventure like that again in a second. An adventure to end all adventures."

"To start all adventures, hopefully."

"Figure of speech."

She waited a moment before continuing. She obviously had recovered from the narration of her poem when she began, "I've been thinking of how we can stay connected. I don't want to be obvious. People are quick to sense that something is up. I don't want to hang back at the end of class or come by the office repeatedly."

"Just do that occasionally. You're a writer; write me notes that you just put on the desk as you leave class. I can pass files to you with messages. Let's be inventive." There was a note of sarcasm.

"It's hard for me to leave phone messages since anyone might answer and take a message to you. How about something like this: we could use a code of some kind. The code word would mean I want to see you."

He thought for a moment. "Whenever I phone, I'll leave a name that starts with your initial and you can leave a name that begins with mine." Even before he finished, he saw how inept the plan was.

She had seen it too. "Look, when I phone you, I'll stick the word "burger" in the message I leave. And you can do the same if you need to. "How about a burger at 5, will really mean: you up for a Pratt family outing?"

He responded immediately. "I love it. Mickey answers. I say, 'Carol Gordon: would you like a new recipe book featuring grilling techniques for your burgers?' Or: Carol Gordon: are you interested in our new coffee table book: *Rodin's Burghers of Calais*? Or: Burger King is offering your household, Carol Gordon, a major discount. Phone this number if interested."

"Keep it simple. You get carried away. And it's just for emergencies when we haven't been able to connect otherwise."

"I won't mess it up." He turned the radio off. They drove silently for just a moment.

He spoke up. "What if I throw in 'hot dog' from time to time?" He wasn't sure why he said that.

"You're going to screw up this whole code thing, and then I'll be stuck with: 'Hello. Is Father Matt Turner there? He isn't? Could you leave a message that I want to sleep with him again soon?' Do you think that will work?"

"Maybe." He smiled at the thought of Meese answering the phone down the hallway.

"Once."

She let a long silence hang in the conversation. "Are we OK, do you think?"

"I don't know. If you're asking if I want to see you and be with you, I do. Are we OK together? Yes."

He ignored the rest.

"While we're both here, let's think about our next adventure. When?"

"I have time on Thursday. No afternoon class and no class Friday AM."

"Thursday it is then. And we'll go from there. 4:30, so we have more daylight."

"4:30"

"Ruby and Sinto. One more time for Ruby and Sinto. Speaking of which . . .She showed her own affection for the dramatic. Here we are." She pulled over to let him out.

He tapped her on the thigh as a farewell and opened his door. He got out but left the door open so he could quip: "I'm hungry again; I think I'll walk over to Division and get a Dag's burger."

"Shut the door." She shook her head in mock exasperation and drove off with a wave.

◆

He watched the Plymouth drive away.

As he started his short walk back to the house, he recognized that he felt good. He was as quiet as the homes and large front yards and generous parking strips on Sinto street in the afternoon sun. His spirit was wide and open. Unbound.

She was what his life had been missing. A companion who likely even loved him for what she saw him to be. Life before C and life with her were so different. She was alive and was calling life up in him. This feeling was new, so exhilarating. He was excited even to think about her.

Her courage to follow her heart had let him follow his. Her soft confidence. Her memory of Gran. Her open-handedness in regard to him. She was letting him be next to her there in the morning sun, there on the bed. She was letting him touch her, and he was alive with her touch.

She truly saw him and he was alive in her eyes.

Her poem was about drowning and about vibrance and about youth and about possibility. Her poem was about the reverence, even for a life she only somewhat knew.

His dream was about . . .

He felt the darkness. His dream called him to stand beneath one of the huge shade trees and ponder for some moments.

In a way she was like an apparition, like one of the Greek goddesses who, as Homer told, would appear to those they favored. To direct, to inspire, maybe even to challenge. He smiled that she had entered his life path.

He had walked these streets often for his exercise, but his eyes and heart had never been as receptive as now on his walk to the university residence. She had brought that sunlight. The front yards had never seemed so wide, the sun so vibrant in the trees, the breeze so invigorating.

◆

If his heart was telling him anything with clarity, it was that she was a gift and the beginning of a new journey he had not thought to take. Just now it led him to smile at the quiet neighborhood. He turned the corner at Astor and for the first time noticed that the university's landmark spires scraped at the sky like twin tines of a broken fork. A picnic's fractured memory.

As he rounded the corner and walked past the back of the church structure, he knew something was not as he had left it. The square two story Jesuit residence hall seemed changed, seemed forbidding, somehow parental, almost admonishing him in the afternoon sun. Its appearance was more rigid, more stern than he had ever noticed.

He entered the house and stopped at the mail boxes just inside the cloister door. He had a letter. Postmarked Seattle. Marianne's return address. His first thought was Doc. Doc had not looked well at the ordination. And he had been so quiet.

He tore it open.

Matty,

Have been thinking of you.

Hope you are happy. And getting good results and satisfaction from your classes. Tough job being a teacher. Lots of apathy as well as ignorance to cut through. You have my admiration for lots of things, but that is certainly one.

What if we both had headed to the UW I often wonder. But no. I had to head for the big time, and you had the seminary thing to try. We followed what seemed best, even though there have been years of struggle that I could see in your face, and I'm sure you may have noticed the results in mine. (I certainly do!)

Put some meat on your bones, boy!

Anyway.

I just wanted to say how good it was to see you and to share some time with. I am so proud of you, my friend, for accomplishing your goal.

I think of you often and wish you the very best always.

Come by and see us. Doc asks me all the time whether I've heard anything about "Father Matt". He can't just call you Matt anymore.

I'm the one who will always call you that.

Fondly, my dear friend.

m

He folded the letter onto itself and put it carefully in his breast pocket as he took the stairs up.

◆

"So, tell me about this person in your life."

Larry was in the chair with his feet up on Matt's desk. He had apparently been paging through a script of *Our Town* Matt had been considering.

"When did you get in? I thought you had a retreat to give." Matt was truly surprised.

"Nope. That was last week. This week has been prep for retreats coming next week. You know how it is. But . . . that's not why I'm here. I'm here to follow up on a letter you sent and phone calls you didn't return."

Matt stored his jacket and sat on the corner of the bed.

Larry leaned back and put the script on his chest. "So. Who is this person?"

"A writer and a collaborator. She's working on a play I'll direct. She's very creative. You'll like her. She's smart and funny and real."

Matt felt odd putting her back into words. They failed him.

"Matt, I'm not looking for an invitation to anything." He flipped the script onto the desk. "What are you doing? Is this something serious?"

"Maybe so."

"Really?"

"Really."

"And so what are you thinking? What do you plan to do? Are you thinking of leaving or giving up your priesthood? Or is it less serious than that?"

"I don't know where all that is. But it's serious."

"So, you love her, do you think?"

"I think I do, Larry. I think she's the best thing to happen to me, probably ever."

"How so?"

"She takes me for me. She doesn't connect with me for any other reason. Not because I teach or preach or have answers — none of that. She connects with me, and I love being with her, creating with her. She sees me."

"What does that mean?"

"She sees *me*, not my collar or degree or any of that. And she . . . " Larry interrupted.

"Are you listening to this?"

"Yeah . . . She touches me, Larry. The way work and prayer and preaching don't do. She challenges me to be more alive. She makes me want to be better, to grow. Without that I have just been running because my schedule said run."

"You are such a romantic."

"What does that mean?"

"You're in the moment and out of the larger picture. Now is all. You're ready to sacrifice all for the feeling of sacrificing all; you're incendiary, combustible. That's the beauty of you; that's the drama. That's why you act and direct. Don't you think?" Larry took a moment.

He began again. "The river in Skagit, remember?" Matt nodded. "We must have stopped a half dozen times on that hike because you saw a new shade of green. You had to show me the new shade of green." Larry laughed. "You see things in life that others simply don't see."

"And that makes me a romantic?"

"It makes you a valuable person and friend. It would make you a valuable priest if you choose to continue with that. It would make you a valuable mate, if that's the direction you move." Larry fiddled with his glasses.

"You're a blessing of surprises. It's true for you like it's true for each of us: our blessing is our curse. And vice-a-versa."

Matt shifted on the bed. "I'm not sure where you're headed with this."

"OK. Let's get to things here. Tell me about being a priest. Good? Bad? What's working; what's a pain in the ass?"

Matt shifted, "Class is OK."

Larry would not be put off. "Priest. Tell me about priest."

Matt looked at him directly. "I don't believe it all, Larry."

"Neither do I, Matt. I don't think the Church should tell people lots of the things it tells them. And I think there are a lot more areas where the Church should be outspoken, and it's silent."

"It's not even that . . . I don't even know if I can tell you."

Larry swiveled the chair toward Matt. "What do you mean?"

"I mean I don't believe most of what we say in the Apostle's Creed." He studied Larry's face before he continued. "Son of God? I don't think Jesus was a savior redeeming us from the sin of Adam! I think he was an example of how we can save ourselves." Larry shrugged, and Matt continued, "We save ourselves; nobody does that for us . . ." Matt slowed and looked out toward the river before taking a breath and quietly starting again. He let the silence be.

"If anything, Jesus saves us by showing us how to make real human choices. I don't see him paying some mythic debt to set us free."

Larry was listening. "And? . . .".

"I don't think I believe in the whole Transubstantiation thing. I don't see how that can be. Bread and wine ARE the body and blood of Christ? What does that mean? And there's part of me that doesn't care."

"Is that it?"

"And I'm not the person to stand in the pulpit to tell others what things mean, Larry. I'm not. I know what I'm supposed to say. I just can't say it anymore."

Not looking away, Larry sat still for some moments.

"Here's what I think. Maybe you're being too narrow. You're wanting to reject the Church's version of things. Their language. You likely still see spiritually, just not in the way or in the places where someone else tells you to look. You need to see what you see and value it."

Matt looked at him.

Larry bent forward. "For me, here's the deal. I think the church is artificial. Not really real. I think Jesus had a group of faithful friends who loved the man they knew. They tried to capture his vision to tell others. And all their efforts eventually got turned into stories and songs and mosaics and then later, guidelines and membership and, and, and. And then words.

"I could be way wrong, but I think the message is not about being someone else. It's about being you: your best and worst, noblest and meanest aspects. To my retreatants I call them our 'poet' and 'panhandler' parts.

Matt sat still. Listening.

"Our church words: 'mission', 'apostolate', 'discipleship', 'apostle's creed' all mask the life that animated that man. They blur by trying to make clearer. They freeze an image that gets taken as 'gospel.'

"Depictions are metaphors, not photos. They are meant to evoke, not limit."

Matt needed more. "So, what are you saying?"

"You can stay in this priesthood or step out of this priesthood. Be whatever you are called to be. Whatever is your vision, your take, your response to your passion for life and for others.

I say that is what will save you." Larry stopped, letting the words sink in.

Larry sat back. "And that's what Jesus did."

Matt had turned to look out the window. He wasn't ready to speak.

Some moments passed in their silence.

"Matt, you teach literature. Literature, language, never captures the fluidity, the mutating vision of things. The Bible doesn't. The classics don't. Nothing written does. So, authors keep trying. They keep coming back to it. But words never really hold the live baby up in the air: the loveliness of the child, the softness of the skin, the motion of the weight against one's hands, the mystery of what seems and what may become.

"Language can describe but words fail. Any attempt to capture it all, that *essence*, fails. Words or even sentences should be doorways opening to the day's sun and wind. Not treasure boxes where we find and hide and hoard the same things every time.

"As soon as you think, 'This is it!' you run the risk of being stuck in the middle of stories that become sacred, untouchable. You'll try to hang on to your special phrasings, your treasured insights shaped carefully and held as carefully as the effort to support a small bird.

"Birds are meant to fly. We are meant to watch them fly. Wherever they go each time.

"When you allow things to be new, to reveal themselves, they can change and grow and become something new. Revealing themselves from behind new particular words on any given day."

"So?" Matt shifted.

"We're left believing in our silences not in our words. There just needs to be a nod. A 'look for yourself.' . . . All I'm trying to say: this may not even be about faith, Matt. Except in that trusting what you see will bring you home."

They both sat for a while. Larry leaned forward onto his knees. He looked at Matt, who was still listening.

Larry reached across and patted Matt's leg. He pushed back into his chair.

"So, it's really not about the woman you know. It's about your life as priest and Jesuit." He swung the chair around to look out the window before he continued. "What are you thinking to do?"

"I don't know."

"Bullshit. You have some idea. Do you want to run off with her? Do you just want to maintain? Do you want to retake theology classes where you got a C? What do you want?"

Matt worked at his fingernail. "Do you dream?"

"I don't think so."

"Don't think so?"

Larry shifted in the swivel chair. "I problem solve. I sense answers to things that I don't know how to deal with."

Matt continued with his nail. "Maybe it's the same."

"What are you getting at?"

"I had a dream a year or so ago, and I had it again last week. It's what's making me sweat all the time I think."

"I don't understand."

"I'm not talking filmy, ephemeral dreaming. I mean dreaming so real I sat up awake and talked to it."

"What are you talking about?"

"I dreamed that in the night a man stood there, in that corner by my closet. He was still except for his breathing. As if he was hiding there . . . or waiting." Matt was fixed on that corner of the room. Part of him was waiting to see if he could continue. "And he had a straw hat under his arm."

Larry started to laugh and then he looked at Matt. Matt was looking into the corner. This was no joke.

Larry caught up. "God, that's . . .too weird."

"In my dream I sensed him there. I couldn't make out all the details, but I could see he was breathing. And watching. I could barely see his hat.

"Are you serious?"

Matt continued, not looking at Larry so much as remembering the exact experience of the dream. "And from the corner he was watching me."

"It was dark. How could you know that?"

"It's a dream. You know things."

Matt continued. "He had on a striped blood red jacket and ghost white pants." Matt stopped.

Larry squinted. "And?"

Matt looked at Larry before responding. "He came this way a few steps, still watching me. He put on his straw hat and stood watching ... And I woke up in my dream and sat up and yelled at him."

"What did you yell?"

"Leave me alone. Get out of here." I yelled it. I didn't just say it. I yelled it two or three times, but he kept moving like he was being drawn straight to me."

"And so you woke up?

"I was already awake!" Matt shrugged away his embarrassment. "He came to my bed. If I'd reached out, I could have touched him. I could have put my hand on his side ... I didn't touch him though."

"What'd you do?"

"I sat there watching." Matt took a deep breath with the memory.

"And?"

"He sat right here where I am now, facing just like I am."

"And?"

"And then he turned his head my direction, but I couldn't see his eyes. I knew he was seeing me. I felt it. But I couldn't see his eyes. I felt his weight sag the bed. I felt his hand on my blanket."

"Then he reached up to the brim of his hat and took it off ... Larry, his head was punctured in a half dozen places, and his hand had a deep, dark puncture wound as well."

Larry was listening now.

Matt took a breath. "He just sat, and I just sat. He was looking into the dark corner he had come from, and I was watching him ... We sat that way for a long while, until he leaned forward about to push himself off the bed.

As he leaned my direction, I could finally see his eyes. He was . . . I don't know, a mixture of things. He was steely, like something had happened to him; he was disappointed somehow; he was right at the edge of angry. All of that was moving across his face. It depended on where I looked as to what I saw. His face was full of sentences he never spoke. I could feel them. Then, it was like he woke and patted my knee twice before he stood fully up."

"And then what?"

"He returned where he came from. That corner by the closet. He kept going until I couldn't see him anymore. He went through the wall." Matt took a deep breath.

"Jeez, what do you make of all that?"

Matt took his time. When he finally spoke, he spoke as if to himself. "I think it's me thinking about Jesus and seeing what I really think."

"You really think Jesus is . . . what? . . . a ringmaster?"

"No. I really think he's been made to be something he isn't."

"Like savior?" Larry was still listening.

"Maybe. . . maybe son of God. . ."

Larry's face clouded.

Matt leaned forward. "In my dream he was just a man. Just like us. No more. I got this feeling that he'd been made to dress up because he'd been made into the circus guy ushering us into the Big Top to see what we've always been told to believe and never thought we'd have a chance to see."

Larry was silent. He was taken by the seriousness with which Matt told the story. He looked over to Matt, waiting for the ending.

Matt shrugged. "I don't know . . . I just know that now the dream will sometimes come to me at Mass or at Rosary or in the middle of Benediction . . . I haven't told anyone but you. I can't tell anyone. They'd think I'm crazy." Matt took another breath and puffed out his cheeks to get rid of the story.

"It's made me look at what I'm doing." Matt hung his head and returned to picking at his nail. "I was willing to move ahead, to live with things; but that's changed recently."

Larry nodded. "So I gathered."

"I just want the doubt to stop."

Larry sighed and looked at Matt. "Likely it won't. Belief is a gift as much as anything else. And there are levels and levels of belief. Comes from our background and our vision of life and who knows where else . . . Matt, I think doubt is part of who you are. Part of how you'll touch others who doubt. My history of addiction is part of how I understand, teach and draw people. Like that.

"Here's a thought: don't ask yourself, 'Who am I ?'. You have too many answers ready for that. Try finishing this sentence: 'At my best I am'. Maybe then you'll find some rest." He got up. "You have time to come to Portland in a week? We can talk more about this."

"I don't know. I . . . "

"Take a week. Think about our little chat. Try to come to Portland next week, and we can talk some more. In the meantime," Larry moved to the bed and put his arms out, "be gentle with yourself. Think of yourself as coming to you for advice. As a youngster, fresh, but needing some direction. Have you ever tried that?"

"No."

"Try. See where it takes you . . . Here." Larry opened his arms further inviting Matt in. Matt thought Larry looked like pictures he had seen of Jesus. That stopped him. Jesus in a plaid wool shirt? He didn't know what to do with that.

Then Larry bear hugged Matt.

"I've got a ride waiting. Hitched my way with folks heading to the missions and then back to the City of Roses." Larry went to the door. "One week. See you there, my friend." He hailed somebody in the hall and closed the door firmly behind him.

There was the one thing Matt had not been able to say.

Matt took Marianne's letter from his pocket and with it came the receipt for his last meal with Carol. He tucked them into the copy of *Our Town*, like book marks.

Matt crossed to look out his window toward the river.

Jesus had reminded him somehow of his Lucas . . . There, he had admitted it.

He breathed out deeply, like a plastic toy deflating.

Ch 20

Matt didn't go to Portland. He stayed in Spokane intent on working through things. He had come no closer to finding his way. It was as if his path was constantly crossing through a scene he had been in before. If he resolved to live by his vows, he found himself up in the night, sometimes walking at all hours. If he decided he should explore his relationship with C, he was up in the night, unable to sleep, tossing with his contradiction.

C came to class. Had she not, he would still have been so distracted he would never have been able to teach. To all his students, she was a mystery observer, auditing perhaps. She always seemed to have a question that brought her legitimately to the desk when the lecture was finished. She was a serious student to all who cared to know.

He could not walk away from her. He had little desire to.

He also could not walk away from the person he had pledged himself to be.

◆

One afternoon, returning from class, Matt encountered Meese sitting in the sunlight filtered by the hall curtain. He wore his favorite or perhaps only casual shirt. Beige, almost root beer, short sleeves, without design. It was unusual to see the priest sitting on a stool, working in front of the corridor window. He seemed simply an old man stripped as he was of his clerical garb.

Matt nodded as he began to enter his room.

Meese summoned him by crooking his long, nicotine yellow finger Matt's direction.

Matt put down his books in the doorway and, leading with his head so as to be ready to hear, he moved slowly to Meese. Being so near, he noticed for the first time the chalky whiteness of Meese's hairless arms. His blemish, a single birthmark beneath the corner of his eye, and the speckling of sunspots on the backs of his hands. Dappling.

He saw, in addition, the smoothed skin of the scar at the base of his throat. The scar that had changed Meese's life.

A story Matt would love to know.

"Where do you go at night?", the older priest rasped, barely audible. His breath was tainted. Yellow.

Matt straightened before answering. He then bent again to Meese's height. "I walk. I'm in training, and nighttime is the best time for me to get that done."

Meese moved no muscles in his face except for his eyes which Matt thought must surely see through the lie. The silence became uncomfortable.

Meese nodded, apparently accepting the explanation.

Matt moved away some steps. "Be well, Father . . . This is good light to see by."

And Matt returned to his door and to his books. As he picked them up, he saw the old priest still not reading, still mulling Matt's response.

Matt put his books on the desk and began his change.

C would be parked on Hamilton St. in just a few minutes.

◆

He adventured with her in Deer Park, in Chewelah, in Reardan. They even adventured to Davenport. He had perfected his M. Pratt registration.

Their pattern was very simple. They walked; they ate; they talked further; they retired for the night. They well understood that they were not free, but more importantly, they saw that they could be. For now the freedom was contained and not wide ranging. But such understanding gave them a sweep to their feelings for one another rather than a cribbed confinement. They were still adventuring. They were not hiding and scurrying on the edge of a dangerous darkness.

At least she was not.

They had gone back to Post Falls and were part way through dinner when he looked at her over the top of his sandwich. He sometimes got so full of sentiment that he spoke. No matter what the rest of the conversation might have been.

"I love you, you know." Matt said it while stirring his milkshake.

"I do."

Carol looked away for a moment and then back. "Do you know what that means to me?" Matt smiled, waiting to hear. "In my life you will be the person who stands or sits or walks with me. And looks forward to doing that. Someone who lights up when they see me coming toward them. Who will ask how I'm doing and really want to know." She paused and wiped her mouth. She looked at him after and took a moment before speaking. "Someone who will help me see the world, and realize how wonderful my life is. Someone who will laugh with me and maybe sometimes at me and hold me and help me be stronger than I am alone." She looked at him with an inquiring smile. "Want to be him?"

"I do."

She reached across the table and took his hand, "that's what they say. And that's good enough for me. I don't need a piece of paper by the way."

"And I don't think I want to say 'forever' twice."

"What do you mean?" She understood, but she wanted him to say even more.

"My vows are permanent, not temporary."

Her eyes changed, became more serious, more inquiring. "What do you do about all that?"

"I say we finish our elegant meal and then retire to our second-floor veranda with the stunning view of the billboard and two light posts."

She wasn't wanting to let it go this time. "But really."

"We'll get there. I'll catch you up on all the dark halls of religious life. Just not tonight."

"But soon."

"Soon."

He took one more bite only. He had lost his taste for his dinner.

◆

On the way to the room he had walked slightly behind. She was so strong, this woman who had become comfortable with his life. So lovely. She was assured and clear eyed. He tossed her the key as they mounted the stairs, and she snagged it, almost without looking.

And she raised her eyebrow. As if she could always make such a catch.

They had both burst into laughter. She turned and ran up the stairs; he watched just a moment before chasing.

At that moment he knew for certain that he loved her.

◆

She unlocked the door and swung it open.

"STOP!"

She froze almost comically. He picked her up, the key still dangling from her hand, and carried her across the threshold and into the dark room. He laid her on the bed and closed the door. The dim light from the billboard washed her face with shadow as she lay there.

"Are you going to turn on a light?"

"Why?" He began to unbutton her. "We know where everything is."

He played it as a quip, and she laughed, but even as he said it, he felt the thick inkiness begin again to seep deep within.

Ch 21

The pink note had not been on his door in the Jesuit Residence. The messenger had folded it and taped it to the edge of Matt's desk. It had simply said, "IMPORTANT! CALL THIS NUMBER"

Part of him had been expecting this or something like it for a while. He had not spoken it aloud. He had not written it to Larry. But the prospect had changed his breathing as he looked in the mirror to shave. Like black smoke it had risen to blot out questions in class or conversations at the dinner table. It had choked him sometimes into distraction in front of the television and darkened his walks in the neighborhood.

What was going to be said when all this became public? What was going to happen? How could he explain himself? How would he know which people were aware?

He had seen people go through things like this. He had never truly understood just how devastating it could be to walk past a group where, in truth or in fiction, it seemed that some people must know and would whisper to those nearby. The terror of rumor. The destruction of confidence. The shunning.

He would need a shield. He dare not expose his softness, his vulnerability. That path was death.

There was only one clear choice. He needed to trust in what he felt for C. Come what may. That statement gave him courage.

That pink note was the trigger, the enemy. He found himself careening from encouragement to doubt, from fear to almost bravado. This moment was to be the facing of his fear. He would see where it would take him.

There was no other choice.

◆

The bishop's office in the Chancery was a corner office. No one else was in the waiting area when Matt arrived and presented himself to the secretary. He was expected (what did that mean? Had he already been discussed? Had it begun?). The bishop would be with him shortly.

He had not really slept. If he had dreamt, he could not remember. He had breathed some semblance of prayers as he lay naked on his covers. Nothing had made his anxiety go away. With the dim reading light on, he had noticed how much darker the stain above him had become. Darker than the rest of the darkness of the room. Only the corners of his bedroom ceiling were darker than the stain.

He couldn't read. He could only wait for it be over.

He had risen before first light and gone silently to shower. All things: the hallway, the bathroom, the shower, the lighting, the air itself, seemed alien. It seemed he had never been here. Here, where he had been daily for more than a year.

As he lathered he found himself slick with opprobrium. The sting of the soap became the sting of his own censure. Drying, he noticed a slight shudder in his body. He had held the towel to his face for the longest while.

Dressed casually, he went down the stairs to the refectory, where morning had not yet entered. He switched on an array of florescents, grabbed a box of cereal and entered the swinging door to the kitchen. He poured milk and tried to eat standing. He began to shiver instead. He put the cereal bowl aside.

He left with the lights still burning.

He didn't care to say Mass this morning, but he entered the chapel to sit. This solitary vigil was what he had done in school when others were in the hallway copying homework. He had done it in the Novitiate in the latest hours of the night. He had made such a vigil the night before his ordination. This was what he had not done for the longest time.

Sitting in the hardness of the pew with his hands out, opened, to either side, he felt a kinship to the sagging figure suffering over the altar. This was a plaster semblance calling up contemplation. Christ had been real. Did not have plaster hair. The spikes actually worked a deep pain into the soft places at his temple. Christ had nothing to do but try to catch his breath. Christ was not going to be able to push up against his own weight much longer. There was no way out. He was pinned. Exhaustion is in the will . . .

◆

Improvisation would not save Matt now. He tilted his head back heavily.

Exhaustion is in the will . . . alongside endurance.

Choose.

There must have been times when Christ was beset by fear and quaking.

Matt felt a weight that made it difficult to breathe.

How different he felt from the times when he was with Carol. He wanted to talk to the figure and ask if He had ever had a Carol in his life. If He had ever felt the touch of someone who knew him: all of him. Who held Him to her through the night. If He had had a Carol, how awful His death was.

Matt knew full well that had he spoken his questions aloud, only silence would have followed. He was not alone in that.

It seemed true for Christ and himself, both.

How different from what Matt probably should be thinking, from anything he had considered before.

Matt felt only empty silence in his hands. Only resignation in his breaths. Only the darkness with the red sanctuary flame burning.

Matt's body sagged in the pew. The darkness compressed him. He closed his eyes. He was exhausted. Hanging on.

◆

The back doors opened with a muted crash as someone bustled in and turned the chapel lights on. The entry woke Matt. Fr. Merriman made his way down the main aisle and disappeared into the sacristy.

Matt nodded to the statue at the lowest part of his genuflection and left.

◆

"The Bishop will see you now." He wondered what the secretary knew. If she knew why he was here. The dampness behind his collar threatened to raise it awkwardly out of place.

The office was surprisingly small and simple. A wooden chair faced parallel to the front of the desk, and the bishop was just finishing with placing a second chair to face the first. On the desk a small statue, seemingly of Jesus, faced away. Book cases lined either side of the room giving it the weight of authority. The window was draped. Only a filtered light fell onto the desk area.

Finished, the bishop gestured to the wooden chair nearest Matt. Matt sat, hands in lap while the bishop crossed to his desk and retrieved a file folder. He returned to his chair.

"Fr. Matthew Turner?"

"Yes."

The bishop looked at him briefly, as if Matt had already said something inappropriate.

The small man read the documents and worked to clean something out of his teeth. Finishing the paper, he looked out, tilted his head back and peered through the bottom of his glasses, still cleaning out something. He resumed filing through the papers.

"I've called you to this unusual meeting since your Superiors are in the Far East for a week. My feeling is that this could not wait. I have spoken to your Provincial, and you will be contacted by the Province on their return.

"Father, there are some reports here. I see you are obviously a member of the Society of Jesus and applied to the university, that you teach the classics and direct stage productions along with your priestly duties."

"Yes, Your Excellency."

The bishop sat momentarily silent, observing.

"I see you are taking on a role from time to time."

"Your Excellency?"

"M. Pratt? Was that one of your roles, Father?"

"Excellency?"

"Explain, if you would."

"Your Excellency, I can't."

"It was a role you played though, unless I'm mistaken." He shifted to put the file back onto the desk. "Father, the clergy has very little privacy. We are public figures. You seemed to know something of that judging from the fact that this report came from Idaho.

"As public figures, we never know when we are being seen by someone who has seen us before. In class, at one of our plays, at a Mass we said, wherever. As public figures we encounter judgements then that people don't quite know what to do with if they see us in compromising situations. Does that make sense, Father?"

"Yes."

"This confusion is sometimes referred to as scandal. Scandalous behavior." He squinted at nothing Matt could see. The bishop was disturbed. There fell a long silence.

The bishop folded his hands on his lap and sat, still, for an longer while. "I don't understand."

"Excellency?"

The bishop shifted, leaning forward. "You took the same vows I did. True?"

"True, your excellency."

"Not a year ago. Not six damn months ago, for godssake, you put yourself on the ground in front of all of us and begged for ordination. And all of us there believed you and blessed you and set you up to lead us." His color was reddening. "You were made a leader of the Church, representing us all." He sat back.

Matt was silent.

"What the hell is happening?" It seemed a question that reached beyond Matt.

Matt blinked at the question and studied the carpet by the bishop's chair.

The bishop searched for his words.

"What if you were to hear that I was . . . 'sleeping around?' What would that do to your . . . "

Another long silence.

His voice trembled as he spoke, "Son, I stand humbled and encouraged (do you know the meaning of that word?) *encouraged* by young ordinands dedicating their lives to service in the Church. *Encouraged* to be with them, to have them be with me.

"As much as I was encouraged, I am now disheartened," he whipped his red cincture across his thigh, "though that is no consideration of yours . . .

"Do you understand . . . ?" He was truly angry. He was sorting what he could say.

"Son, you are the third priest in the last five months to come before me for a serious reprimand and decision . . . "

He seemed to chew on the gristle of the issue.

"Serious. Involving . . . Not all of them newly ordained either. Scandalous behavior! And these are not frivolous, nit-picky complaints . . . Our people are being scandalized by these behaviors. People deeply and properly and rightly distressed by their clergy." He pounded every word. "Things that I . . . "

Matt could see the tremor of the bishop's aggravated heartbeat pound at his cassock. He thought the bishop might even be on the edge of tears. "I have to be frank with you, I do not understand. You have no idea how these blemishes turn people away from their faith. They are bewildered or alienated . . . Shaken at the very least." He considered his words while shaking his head before gathering himself for a new question.

"What's going on? Do you people know the meaning of the word swear? Did you mean what you said?"

Matt nodded mildly.

"Well, it doesn't seem like it . . . and I sure as hell do not understand. You have had special training. It's not like we just up and ordained you. Any of you."

The bishop crossed to the veiled window as if to look out for his answer. He stood for a long while.

Matt did not look away from the carpet.

The bishop turned. "Do you have anything to say?"

He came back to stand in Matt's silence. His anger was subsiding. "I will never understand how someone sworn, *sworn* . . . to a life of holiness and service can be so selfish.

Matt absorbed the accusation as just.

Matt looked at him, and oddly it seemed that the bishop was the one in anguish.

The bishop seemed for a moment to have something further to say but instead moved to his chair and sat back down.

There was another long silence as the bishop waited for something.

His voice and his manner reemerged, changed.

"Father, there is no use for scandalous behavior in the Church. No matter the explanation. *No matter!* . . . The Church wants to avoid scandal at all costs. It shakes the faith of the parishioners."

"Yes, Your Excellency."

The bishop worked as if trying to get comfortable in his chair.

"Do you contest this report that you registered and spent the night with a woman in . . .", with the last of his consternation he reached toward the desk to retrieve the file.

Here it was; he would face it. "I don't contest the report, Your Excellency."

He looked at Matt as if he would burn a hole. "And what do you propose we should do?" The two looked at each other in the pause.

The bishop shook his head. "No. Before that." He settled and found a new pitch for his question. "Before that . . . Do you even love this person?"

"I do, Your Excellency."

"Of course you do." The bishop took a long time. Matt could see subtle changes in the bishop's face. The man rocked a bit. It was almost a musing when he finally spoke. "My apologies."

Matt nodded.

"Love is what our lives are to be all about." His tone was flat, academic. "Love is what we are supposed to be engaged with. Not lust. Lust is temporary: 'Me', not her or us. Lust makes few plans except to repeat itself." He stopped and thought. "Love. Love is about the other person, really." He shifted. "To an observer, it's hard to distinguish the two. But that is of no matter here. You should not have been . . . " He drifted off.

"So we have a goddam problem we never should have had. One that needs addressing, you see?"

"Yes, Excellency."

"Good." He folded his hands after sweeping something from his lap. "You need to make a decision, Matthew." His body had changed. He was looking directly now.

Matt met his eyes.

"In present circumstances in the Church, your choice must be the priesthood or this person. Which do you love the more or maybe better, which choice seems to be what you are being called to? . . . Make sense?"

"Yes, Excellency."

"But dammit, man, we cannot continue as M. Pratt and Reverend Father Matthew Turner simultaneously. Just cannot do . . . Do you understand this time?" He looked away, shaking his head slightly. "So, within two weeks, after you have had a chance to meet with your Provincial, I want you to tell me in written form, your choice. Pratt or Turner."

"Yes, Excellency."

"And, as the shepherd of souls, I need to tell you the following complications: Should you choose to stay with your calling to the priesthood, you will be transferred, and my report on this matter will be sent to your new bishop. I will ask you to break off all communications with this person. No matter what we think, these situations become quite destructive if scandalous arrangements have room to continue. All communication is to be avoided. All. Do I make myself clear?"

"Yes, Excellency."

"Should you choose, on the other hand, that your calling is to be with this person, you must tell me that, and we must consider what to do in that regard. We will inform the Society of Jesus in any case, and we will seek the solution that gives you some protection for your reputation and clarity for your future participation in the Church as a lay person. No need to go into all that now."

"Yes, Excellency."

"So. Two weeks from today. I will be expecting a letter on my desk. Agreed?" Matt nodded. The bishop turned and reached for something on the desk. He turned back. "And in the meantime, please, no Post Falls."

Matt sat up in his chair.

The bishop started to unfurl his narrow purple stole, then stopped. "Father, would you desire for me to hear your confession? . . . You may already have taken care of that."

Matt nodded again and sat forward in his chair as the bishop kissed the stole and placed it behind his neck and draped it over the chest of his cassock.

"Bless me", Matt began. "It has been some time since my last confession. In that time, I have failed to be diligent with my prayer life almost daily. I have often lost my patience over things too small to call for anger. I have broken my vows by sleeping with a person nearly a dozen times." It sounded sterile. To make C an anonymous anybody violated who they were together. It was a betrayal.

The formula continued. "For these and all my sins I ask forgiveness and true repentance."

"Act of Contrition, please."

Matt began the words he had said since a small boy. As children they had been marched across the street to the church and sat in the pews waiting to go behind the heavy velvet curtains on either side of the priest's box.

"O my God, I am heartily sorry for having offended Thee. And I detest all my sins because of Thy just punishments but most of all because they have offended Thee, my God . . . " Matt stopped. He had heard "detest"; he had heard "offended". He did not detest; he had not offended. He shifted in the chair.

"Your Excellency, I can't continue." Matt stood. "Thank you for your kindness and understanding. You are right about our mission being love. Thank you for extending that to me."

"I'll have the letter from you by this day in two weeks."

Matt nodded and went to the door. Turning he saw the bishop very carefully folding his purple priestly stole and nodding almost imperceptibly.

Ch 22

That afternoon Matt was methodical in the extreme. He approached the Minister for $100 on the pretext of helping with a retreat in Portland. He found a set of university envelopes and wrote a letter to his Dean. He asked for a recommendation. He phrased it as updating his file, but soon the word would get around that something might be changing. Matt would need to have everything in order so as to give himself immediate freedom of movement.

He put out the stationary for a letter to his superior, the Provincial. This note would be more difficult.

The sheet was blank white, waiting for him to find words to express his change, to try to capsulize his essence, to request release from the life he had pledged himself to follow.

His life of service.

What had happened really?

So much. The clerical clothing hanging in front of him was the same set as when he took his vows years ago. The vow crucifix at the end of his desk was the same cross he had prayed in front of for years. The simple bed, the bare wall, the meager closet: all that was still fine. He could live like that. Simply. Humbly.

He could live on a class schedule, teaching young people things that he felt they should know. He could find fulfillment in directing actors and discussing points of the classics with those who came with an interest. He was well suited.

He hesitated over how to express the issue.

He began.

I have lost something . . . The brotherhood that had seen me through so many years of study had become diluted by folks' departures. Only four of them had eventually made it to ordination. Now it would be three left from the twenty one who had begun.

I have lost my brotherhood. At the beginning they were a hearty band. For good or ill, they were together, making sense of things by being together. They were not isolated or left alone in a hallway of closed doors.

He looked out the window to the parking lot and the campus and the flow of people moving to or from.

The brotherhood had become *myself here, one person in California, another off to the mission in Africa, another away on loan to administer at Boston College.*

His brotherhood had become *a residence half full of closed doors, a collection of self involved men who rarely enjoyed time with one another and had meals spent essentially in silence.*

And, he thought but did not write, Meese.

Moreover, Matt continued, my *priesthood is riddled with anxiety,* my *faith has become eroded,* my *ability to profess the truths held by the Church impossibly broken.*

He had tried, he continued, *for fourteen years to make it work.* It had *finally become clear that it was not bringing him life, this calling.* He needed *to step away.*

That, reluctantly was the truth. That reluctantly was what he had to communicate this day. That finally had come to be clear in light of his recent ultimatum from the bishop.

He was *in need of change.*

Please begin the process by which I might be returned to lay status.

That is my sincere and considered request.

He put his pen onto the paper and pushed back.

The view outside was still the same. The hallway was silent. There was no sign that he should consider. Nothing new.

The silence.

He bent toward the desk and signed the letter.

◆

He was certain there would be a long process that was just beginning, but that didn't shake him. He knew that he had already distanced himself from the priesthood. He had also become clear about his life within the Jesuits. He was not alive here. He was already disconnected, afloat, loosed from many of the ligatures that had bound him, so that now he was strung up by the ones that remained. Hung out to dry.

If this were a journey, his raft had been broken apart by the repeated heave and muscularity of the sea. He was overboard, stripped naked and holding on.

It was time to struggle toward life, not just endure.

He just needed a thin fabric of hope.

The rest was paper.

◆

As Matt opened his door, Meese was right across the hall, watching. He had not been using Matt's door to think, the way he often did. He was watching the door, waiting.

He was in the middle of a cigarette, smoking almost like Bogart in *Casablanca*, letting the smoke rise to his face, closing one eye in response.

Using this as his cue, and in his best Claude Raines, Matt smiled and gave a vague, perfunctory salute. He tucked his letter beneath his jacket and turned to go.

Meese's hand went up. It stopped him.

"Busy day." The whisper was unmistakable. What was less certain was to what Meese was referring. There was a moment.

Matt nodded, saying nothing. He smiled evasively and made his way to the stairs.

Just before descending, Matt glanced. Meese was still standing in the same place, smoking.

◆

The first floor was as quiet as his. Matt placed the letter in the outgoing box. He turned it face down and put others on top to hide his.

He would be gone before they took the mail out.

He was safe.

When he returned to his room, Meese was gone. Matt's door was open, which he didn't remember doing. There was a faint odor of smoke.

Meese's door was closed.

Everything was in order. Matt closed the door and opened his window a crack to air the place.

Yes. It was time. He was doing the right thing. He felt more and more certain.

◆

Still he would have time to take a week away, just to live with his choice. To walk in these new shoes. That seemed important. He needed to feel a consistent peace about his new course. He needed a confidence that after fourteen years he knew how to be someone other, a lay person, on his own.

He would type a posting for the door of his classroom, so class would be cancelled; he would let Carol know that he was going to be away for a week; he would catch a bus to Portland. He had better phone KT and ask to stay for a couple days. He could connect with Larry when he got there. He needed to think this out and see that he was being sure footed.

◆

Mickey answered. "Hello."

"Mickey, this is Carol's friend Matt. Is she in?" Mickey strained to hear her TV program.

"Nope. But I would expect her for dinner around 5."

"Could I ask you to leave her a message?"

"Sure." She searched through a mess of papers to find the notepad. She tore a triangle corner off a piece of nearly blank paper. "Getting a pen." She put the phone down and, watching the TV intently, made her way to the hall table and grabbed a pen from the drawer. Back at the phone. "OK, man."

"Tell her that I have been called away and that I will be gone for about a week but will connect with her when I get back."

"Will tell her." Then a silence. Then a dial tone.

Matt hung up.

Mickey quickly scribbled the note as she hung up the phone: "Mark gone. Will connect." She would put it on Carol's door once her program was over.

◆

The Minister suggested to Matt that the next time he was in need of money, he not wait to the last minute. Lucky for him, he was told, there was enough money for his needs this time, but in the future, a heads up would be appreciated. Matt walked into the hallway, tucking the money away and thanking god he would not be treated like an adolescent much longer.

Back in his room, Matt finished his letters and put them into a file which he stacked in the file holder on his desk. He pulled a gym bag from the back of his closet, stuffing a week's worth of clothes in it. Finding his pair of jeans and his tennis shoes, he dressed for the trip.

He surveyed the room. He took his clerics down from the curtain rod where they had been hanging and, putting them into the closet, grabbed his light jacket and a cap.

When he shut the door, he listened to the solidity of the sound.

Meese's door was still shut. Just as well.

◆

The bus station was not crowded. A few folks sat in the pew-like benches. A body with a backpack was stretched out along one of the pews, and two people occupied the opposite side. Matt went to the ticket window.

He could get to Portland in 8 hours, depending. He could get there in 6 if he wanted to spend for that. Or, he could take the slow bus for 9 hours.

He had not thought this through.

So, working back from an arrival time of 8 AM, he asked if there was a bus leaving around midnight and arriving in Portland at 8.

"Round trip, sir?

"Yes, round trip."

The woman ran the ticket without responding to his question.

"$50 please." Matt counted out three twenties. He took the $10 and the ticket.

"What time does that bus load?"

"It should load about twenty minutes before departure."

"And what is the earliest time to load?"

"Depends on when it arrives in the station."

"Usually. . . ?"

"Depends. Lots of things affect a schedule. Got to get used to that." She adjusted her glasses and looked at him with one eye shut.

"Can you tell me, is there a place nearby to get something to eat."

"Depends." She tapped a small set of papers into order. "Depends on what you want. There's Rick's across the street. There's burgers on the corner. There's The Walnut two blocks down."

"Recommendation?"

She gawked. "Sir, there is a person behind you."

"Thank you. You have been helpful." He wasn't exactly sure where the line for sarcasm began.

Matt wandered to the doorway. The sky was heavy with dark clouds; it was threatening rain. The round clock over the exit at the end of the room read 6 PM. He had nearly six hours to kill before departure.

There were cheese and crackers in the machine, and another had coffee or hot chocolate.

That was alright. He had plenty to think about.

◆

The bus hurtled through the night while he looked into the dark rather than at himself in the mirror of the window. It had been a long day after a short night. The fear of his meeting had shaken him, had, in some dark alchemy, poisoned all his workings. And then the unseen, the unanticipated refusal to detest what he and C had been making together. What a sudden moment of assertion. How unlike him. Assertion. C had wakened something in him.

He would give the decision some days to settle, but he knew where he should be. His dreams had told him. How could he walk away from the woman who had pulled him from the sea into which he had plunged? She had washed his hair free of salt and worked his muscles with her oil and strong hands. And the sea birds wheeled and cried, and the breeze cooled him from the sun. He had been spared. How could he leave? And how could that be selfish?

But he also didn't want to make a second pledge as flawed as the first.

How was he going to be able to explain it all? How could he speak the quality of what he had with Carol? How could any man in a restaurant, in a depot, on a bus explain salvation? If the sagging figure in the chapel could never make it clear, then how could he presume?

How could any man?

◆

The bus settled at its last stop, and weary travelers worked at muscles and staggered slightly into the center aisle to depart.

In the depot he waited in line to make his call. It gave him time to actually arrive.

"KT? Good morning . . . This is Matt . . . It's OK. Everything is OK. Look, I know this is unusual, but could I stay with you for a day or two? . . . I had a chance to get away, and I thought we might like some time together. . . No, I'm already here . . . Here, in Portland . . . I know. Surprises me a little too. Anyway. Do you have time to see me, or can I stay with you, either one? . . . O, great . . . No. I came on a bus. But I can get a cab . . . Well, I'm downtown at the bus sta . . . O, OK. . . No, I'll be fine. I can get a cup of coffee. I'll meet you then."

◆

Half way to KT's he realized cab fare would have taken much of his remaining money. KT's home was in an adjoining community. She lived in Raleigh Hills. Her home was on a sloping hill among tall evergreens. Behind her newly mown yard stood a handsome fence and even more trees. A cool, green refuge, both front and back.

His room was in the back; the bathroom down the hall on the way to KT's room in the front of the house. The kitchen looked out over a half deck and the yard behind.

She must have made fresh coffee while he was changing and freshening up. A hot cup was waiting on the table.

"Still like milk in, right?"

"Still do. Thank you."

They spent the morning moving around the obvious. Something had prompted Matt's unexpected, hastily planned visit to Portland, a city he had not visited for at least a half dozen years, at least since KT had been in this house.

She showed him her tea cup collection displayed behind glass in the built in. She lit the fireplace with the expertise of one who relies on it daily. She sat next to him and showed him her albums of family photos: mom and dad and the relatives in Bemidji and those in St. Paul and those in Sioux Falls.

He thought of Carol and her play about photos. She would love to be here.

He told KT his realization made during the trip: He had been an awful brother and had been so wrapped up in playing pranks on people and on her in particular, that he was suffering the guilt for it now. He recalled the little house where they spent their youngest years, where the two of them had shared a room, and he had made eerie noises in the night and taken great delight in hearing her call for her dad. He apologized. She didn't remember that at all.

It finally came time.

"So. What's up with you that you would grab a bus in the middle of the night and show up in Portland to phone your sister?"

"I needed to get away and evaluate."

"Evaluate?"

"Not trying to be evasive. My life. See, I've discovered that I'm not perhaps best as a priest. I've been struggling with that for the better part of this year."

"Almost since your ordination then."

"Almost since. It's odd. I had thirteen years to test my choice and for them to test my mettle, but neither one of us was thorough enough it seems. I don't think I'm well suited to be a priest."

"When did that first appear?"

"A while ago . . . When I started hearing words that I had trouble saying with any faith that they were true. And there were signs of resistance to how the Church feels on some issues."

"Well, I'm with you there, I suspect."

"And then I met a person who switched on a light for me and has begun teaching me things that have changed my ways of thinking."

KT sipped at her coffee. She smiled slightly. "I always wondered how you could do that, Matt." She put her coffee down and leaned in. "I remember mom saying she didn't understand how a man could live without a woman. I always asked, how about a woman living without a man? She wasn't ready to go there. And I think her notion was from dad's being a young man in the Navy where being without a woman was such a focus. But anyway, she never quite understood what you were doing by going celibate."

Matt sat silent, looking at his coffee, waiting for words to appear that would represent and not trivialize his feelings for Carol.

"So you met a woman."

She had hit it right on the head. The predictability. The trivializing. He reacted "'So you've met a woman?'" He tried to slow down to calm himself.

He paused a long while.

She could see his frustration and allowed the silence to sit between them. "I'm sorry," she said finally.

He looked at her. "I need some time to sort things out. And to walk." He looked down and then up from his coffee. "And to have time with my Sis."

Unsure of exactly what she had said but judging that she had time to inquire further, she offered: "Thanks for coming here. There are lots of places you could have gone." She put her coffee down and came over to hug him, awkwardly.

"What say we get some lunch?"

◆

Talking about Carol wasn't difficult. In fact, he restrained himself. He told of their shared interest in theater, of her love of the outdoors and of gardening. He told how C treated him as an equal, not someone above her or different than her. He loved the connections they had made: the disclosures, the laughter, the honesty. He told how C seemed to understand and was teaching him by her freedom how much his training had limited him. C had called him to come out of his dark hallways into the bright air.

KT had listened and quietly stirred. She had come to smile during the litany of virtues. "You are smitten, my brother." And then after smiling at his face. "It's nice to see you so happy."

"I am happy. I just have to be sure of what I'm doing this time."

"What do you mean?"

"I thought I was going the right direction last time. I spent more than a dozen years coming to the wrong conclusion, stepping into the wrong myth. I don't quite trust myself."

"I think you do. I understand your hesitancy, but I think you know what you want. You wouldn't be here otherwise. You would be at the Jesuit House on campus, trying to relaunch your shaky canoe that had run aground.

"But you're here." She continued half joking, half very serious. "I'm to be your guide, I guess, and you have a mandate to explore. Your heart has given you that.

"It's true, little bro. You already made your decision and are just waiting to see what it feels like, where it takes you. Maybe you want assurance that there's a trail to follow . . . There is no assurance. It's an adventure. No trail . . . Trust me on that."

Matt heard his sister and felt restful in her acceptance of his story. "It's always good to talk with you. I've passed by too many opportunities."

"No apologizing. Now is what's important. My love for you has always been there, even when you were preoccupied. No problem. You are my brother." She sat back in her chair.

"So, have you taken any steps?"

Matt told her about his letters, his sense of possible scenarios.

"Have you talked with . . . ?"

"Carol."

"With Carol about all of this?"

"No. I was . . . "

"God! You are such a male! You need to talk with her and tell her what you're doing and thinking. Even if you don't know what the hell you're doing."

"I wanted to talk to you and Larry before taking the next step."

"And you didn't even think to include her in all your planning about your future life? You have a lot to learn my dearest brother. This is not to say that I'm not glad that you've come here to be with me." She picked at her bracelet. "You'll miss Larry, by the way."

"How so?"

"He's gone for two weeks. Giving a ten day retreat in Kamloops. I don't think you can even phone there unless you got an inheritance I don't know of."

Matt stirred at his coffee.

"Matt, you already know what you want. And what you don't want. My understanding is that even if this woman were not in the picture, you see a truth: you're struggling to live a life that doesn't help you thrive." She stood alongside her chair.

"You'll be able to start over. I'm here to tell you. You'll thrive in this adventure."

Matt thought it was strange she should select that word.

"Even should this relationship fall apart, you'll be fine, little brother. I didn't get to be a guide by sitting in the village, poking at a fire, trying to get some heat going. And you have good instincts." She pointed at him. "That's what brought you here."

Matt inquired: "Are you happy? Living alone, I mean. Is it hard to live without companionship?"

"Probably. I don't live without companionship. I have lots of friends and do lots of things that I'm absolutely positive about doing. I'm gone a good part of most days, except when my brother comes over.

"Yes. I'm happy. And no matter what twists all this takes, you'll be fine. There are as many lifestyles as people. You'll be called to create the one that's right for you. Not walk into a prefab. I discovered that long ago. On one of my expeditions."

She sipped the last of her coffee and stood.

"You'll find your way." She ruffled his hair.

Matt sensed there was more. He didn't want to press her.

Ch 23

Carol sat on her bed. She had had no luck at all. The sign on his classroom door just said that class was cancelled. Her calls were apparently posted as usual, but there had been no response. She had gone so far as to venture into the sacristy at church to see the schedule for Masses. He was not on it.

Mickey had already left for Sandpoint when Carol had returned two days ago, so if there was a message, Carol had no idea. The partial note she had found on the dining room table was from Mickey to herself about Mark being gone. She had no idea what that was about. He must be Mickey's latest.

She rocked on the quilt. The clouds were coming through from the south. Unusual to see them come that direction. Was it a sign? She didn't know how to read it, if there even was anything there to read. Could she trust the universe to honor her love?

She felt as if she was locked in her tiny cavern of a room with little hope of escape. The unusual dark chill of melancholy dulled every color that usually warmed her day. She found herself rocking as if the gentle motion would keep her hope alive.

She pulled a shawl over her shoulders just as she had seen her mother do many years ago.

Ch 24

His sis had left him tending the fire. She had trundled off in her rabbit slippers and fuzzy robe. She hated to leave a fire unguarded. He had the duty.

The day had been a good one. They had laughed together, had good talks and a nice walk up through the wooded area behind – an overlook which, if you looked one way and ignored all the traffic and the strip mall in the distance, gave legs to her explorer myth.

If you looked the other direction, you saw KT's home huddled among the evergreens.

He had sat on the hill watching for the longest time after KT walked back down.

He had seen her come out of the trees and into the yard. She had entered the back door and was gone.

He too had been gone. Had been away from the expansive silence of the woods and had struggled to find his life in cubicles and rows of rooms. Had searched for answers down the hallways and in the backs of chapels, visiting after meals. The seminary had been something apart. Its lessons in some way artificial.

Like a bird loose in an attic, he had banged against the joists and the cobwebbed crossbeams. He had even thrown himself into the acrid curtaining and struck time frosted glass. He had been knocked down from his flights. He was then where he didn't belong.

To be what they asked for and for what he seemed to need, he had made every effort trying to succeed.

He had been exhausted.

He sat now above the belt of trees and considered what he could see. In the trees he had been shaded and cool; on the hill he sat in the sunshine. He looked onto the yard and KT's little house.

In the trees there is always a way. To somewhere. You choose. He felt the conviction rise. In the trees is where the bird should be.

That choice had hardly ever happened in the hallways of the seminary. A hall had led to a corner, to a doorway, to his room, to his desk by his window. And, more often than not, he had consigned himself to sit in a chair beside the window in the room at the hallway's end. He had opened up a book to explain what lay beyond and within. There was preparation to do. He must become a man for others.

But as he considered his avatar, he could now see that in studying to prepare himself to help others to embrace their faith, he paradoxically had removed himself from engagement in his own life. He had abandoned them and himself.

Freedom was in the trees.

Because of Carol, he felt that he was perched miraculously on the edge of the broken glass window. It was time to fly into the moving air, toward the trees.

◆

Matt shifted. There was a richness to the moment. He was here, at home with his family, in a place where he was welcome. No matter.

A flame-hollowed log collapsed into itself.

The scattered remnant of the fire mesmerized him and folded him into a contemplative shape. He couldn't look away from the destruction. He couldn't stop the questions: how did this happen when so much was in place to prevent it? Had his life become rubble? How had he lost the ease and the confidence that he previously had as a given? Did any piece of cinder still burn? What could be salvaged? Anything at all? Or was the future about moving away and starting over? And did Carol want to go walking?

He had lived the last dozen years with everything as a given. Each year had been planned out: Learn to pray in this building; start to study at this school; study and finish your philosophy major here; pursue an advanced degree, your choice; work in a school here for three years; go here and study theology for three years; teach here in your extra year, proceed through ordination and be assigned to ministry.

And through it all he had felt called to be with the others. He had felt supported even when his prayers were met with silence. He had felt that it was about the struggle, and he had been willing to do that since everyone else seemed to be having the same trials and even the same spiritual mile markers (consolation, desolation, spiritual dryness). And some would leave, but he would not. And others would go a year later, but he would not; and a few of them stayed and grew confident that this was it. They were it. They would make it.

Even if it took an extra year.

And that communal march forward had assured him that he could be a "man for others", could live this religious life, could weather the storms — everybody had storms. You just stayed honest about your struggles. He had been. Mostly anyway. And then they got severe, but by then he had self-analyzed them as an anxiety about the finality of ordination. Like the shakes before a wedding he was told.

◆

And now he was watching a fire die in a small dark house outside of Portland.

Nine hours away was the remnant of his former life: Carol and his classes and his theater program and the Mass schedule and meals in the refectory . . . Or dinner from machines in a bus station. Was that what the future was going to be like? He was anonymous there. Even to himself. And what did people do?

He wasn't fully confident of everything yet, but he was more sure of some things. He had been shown something. She had opened the windows to his stale room without once touching them. The breeze had set him to dreaming again.

He would leave his acrid attic perch and fly to the trees.

Ch 25

Carol had dived into her work. She walked in the mornings to clear her head, and when she returned, she pulled out some notebooks and started circling names and jotting memories that seemed appropriate to her play. Her focus was still taking shape, but she was used to that.

The story had something to do with how much we can ever know about a person. She was interested about what happens to our perception of them when they get stopped in time as happens in a photo or a memory. How can one put Humpty back together again? Something there was calling for her attention. Betrayal was in there as well. She just needed to find the key pieces and listen for what those pieces had to say.

Was it her father that prompted these thoughts? Or her mother who had let her go? Or others who had betrayed her? She would need to carry that for a while.

She had never written any long fiction. Her longest piece had been the one act Kauffman spin off. She could do better.

Mickey had returned from Sandpoint, and while "Mark" was still a mystery, Mickey said the note had been called in for Carol. It just didn't make any sense. Mickey would not likely make that mistake. More to the point though, Matt had evaporated. Something sudden must have come up to have him disappear without a word.

She felt more confident today that she would know something soon. In the mean-time she had work laid out all across her bed. She found that to be a good device. Until she put her hands on each thing to put it away for the night, she could not clean off her bed. So each piece had a chance to come into her subconscious and rise into its own ghostly meaning in her sleep. She loved that about writing.

Even the weather had settled. In the afternoon, no more storm clouds were blowing in from the southwest. No more pushy wind to pry at her sliders. She was warm and bright and content that good things were about to reveal themselves. After all, had Matt not wanted to see her again, he would have been man enough to say so in one way or another. She felt strongly about the man she had come to know, had come to love. The word came cautiously. She had never said it to Gene. To Matt, she had only said it over burgers and with the promise of extended time with him. There was danger, excitement, freedom and commitment in that most common and yet radically essential word. Her statement of her love had never been conversational. It had always been revelatory. The importance of that word and her feelings for Matt were not just in her head. Her body was certainly being clear.

She thought about the Martha Graham quote: "Movement does not lie." Her body was telling her to walk into the mist that her mind had not fully blown away. She was not just saying words. She was bringing herself to the light and into the air for him to see. And he was touching her. And completely. Her body knew that, knew him.

He would be back to her.

Meanwhile she would build a world. Or start to recall and treasure the feel of her former collie's thick coat against her hand. She would see.

Dreams would tell.

Ch 26

So he was off on his adventure. The word made him smile. That the two most important women in his life had both referred to his future in this way was somehow exciting. It meant a validation of sorts. The universe was behind all this, or in front of it, or something.

There was lots to discover about the "universe."

His visit had ended well with a day of play in the city. He had discovered that KT had her own path calling, that she and Larry had "crossed paths" at some point but were now walking parallel. He had grown to suspect the truth of her disclosure during their conversations. She was ready, not only to listen but to confide.

He had more to learn about love. And the search to find its path in one's life.

He loved his sister.

She had handed him an image that he loved. Talking about dreams, she had told him, "It's good to have a dream. You walk along and its hanging behind you somewhere, so you don't really see it. Like a kid's balloon on a long string. And then somebody says something or other, and you glance around. And see, it's still there . . . Yeah. I really do want to do that special thing one day. I do."

He would remember that. And her readiness to listen. His guide. She was worldly wise, his sis.

◆

He left for Spokane by way of the Dalles. On one side, the wide silent power of the Columbia River and on the other, the white arrowhead of Mt. Hood. Pointers and pushers. Was the world really filled with that? Were there signs? He suspected that his imagination was sparking.

But if prayer sought answers in the dark of a chapel, why couldn't imagination in the light of day?

He remembered when he was 16, he had taken his visiting cousin out for fishing. They had decided to camp up by Port Angeles. In what seemed the middle of the night, they had folded the tent and bedding into the back of the car and started out for the boat ramps. His little aluminum boat was only 16', but they should be fine with all the other folks out there. He had a depth finder, two full gas tanks, and his Evinrude. They would be bringing in at least a salmon apiece. The news was that the Silvers were running.

Matt pushed into the bus seat, remembering.

The water was black, and they sipped at their coffee and held a thought-ful silence. Two or three other small boats had slid out at the same time, green lights on their prows, pushing through the predawn, all silent, all slow, past the sterns of the white yachts that would not be moving for some time, past the yellow arc lights showing the piering, past the Coast Guard light and off into the open water of the Straits.

He opened it up and headed out from the light, north. The other fishermen had raised a bright wake as well, and though he had charts, he had followed the others at a distance, judging that they knew what they were doing.

When he fished back home, he had always been in view of land. Wherever the current had taken him, he still had his bearings. That morning he had checked. He turned and could still see the Coast Guard light. Land. The others had sped off, and so he decided it was time to put their lines in. He slowed the Evinrude, and they put the herring onto the hooks and dropped them in, one to each side.

The first of the morning light had begun to wake the sky. They made pass after pass west, then east; west, then east. They no longer needed the Coast Guard light; they could see some of the shadowy distant shoreline.

As they made another pass west, he noticed a fog bank to the north. And as they completed their drift east, it was upon them.

One of the first things he had learned about a boat on open water is that it's very easy to lose sense of direction. His compass had always helped as needed. He had reached into his pocket. He still recalled the feeling: his compass was missing. He had had it, but somewhere . . . perhaps in the night? They could no longer see the Coast Guard light. They were drifting. They were in a fog bank that showed no signs of dissipating. The cousin had pulled in the lines.

Matt had felt the change in his alertness. Then he had an even worse feeling. He had no idea how far north or east they may have drifted, and the Straits are a major shipping route coming in and going out of the Pacific Northwest. And they were in a 16' aluminum boat. He had tugged at his life preserver.

At some point a cubby outboard sped past. He had heard it before he saw it. The cousin had perched like a trusty retriever, leaning forward on the bow. They tried to follow and hoped for the best.

Luckily enough the cubby had headed the right direction and led them to within sight of the shore, and from there, they had limped to the harbor, confidence crushed, but happy to have survived.

And how was he to find his way now? He had lost all the tools he had used for years. Where would the journey take him? He had always thought he knew. But all that was soon to be gone. What were the signs that he was headed the right direction? Was KT right? It was an adventure. Trust the outcome.

He watched the Columbia as the bus moved through the Dalles. He began to drift away. He felt he was in a whirlpool now rather than near a river. A compass was useless. Had the lost compass been a sign? Had the cubby been a sign? What were the signs today? Was the river, the bus ride, the mountain? He could see for the first time why people chose a life that had certain certainties.

He shifted and watched the river, its illusion of stillness.

He closed his eyes.

In the near dark he felt himself being spun, spun and dropped, spun and lifted again. He was drenched and holding mightily onto his little boat. Sickened with the spinning, pulled deeper into the whirlpool. Washed into submersion. Breathe! If you know it's coming, you can prepare. Grab even a portion of a breath and hold on.

But he didn't know what was coming. From where? When? What would be left of him when he finally would be spit out? What would be left of him?

He tossed in his seat.

He heard his Evinrude and a deeper thrumb, a thrumbing that entered his hands as he held onto the ribs of the tiny boat. A thrumbing. The shipping! The thrumbing. Up his arms, along the seats to his butt, through his genitals, up his back and even beyond him out into the fog.

He had nothing left. His cousin was gone now; did not want to finish with him; the poles had been swept away, out into the whirling. The Evinrude was torn away, still revving high. He held. No balance. No control. The fog swept in more densely and the thrumbing bearing down! Nearby, he heard the breaking of water! His hand slid away! He could feel it coming! He tried to set himself!

He woke.

The wheatlands. He recognized the wheatlands. He knew where he was. He was nearly home.

His breath came short still, reminding him of the journey he had begun. And the dream. And the balloon diving somewhere behind.

Ch 27

He rapped on the door. A bare footed young woman answered, hair pulled up and tied off, in a loose sweatshirt and pants.

"Hello. Is Carol in?"

"I just came in actually, so I don't know. I'll check." She disappeared up the stairs, leaving him standing, the door open. She loped back down a moment later, taking the stairs two at a time.

"Come in. She'll be right down."

He entered and shut the door himself. The young woman had ridden her imaginary steed into the front room. He followed to the entry arch. She picked up a cigarette from the round green glass ashtray already packed with greywhite butts. She didn't sit.

Whatever her situation, she was taken by the TV as if her graduation exams would be selected from this melodrama. Commercials came on. She watched no less intently. *All My Children.*

The room was furnished sparsely with a sofa and two mismatched chairs, a coffee table for the ashtray it seemed. An oval area rug. In the adjoining room a dining table teemed with sprawling piles of books and papers.

Fingers went for his ribs.

He grabbed at her wrists and spun. Carol laughed and kissed him quickly.

She spoke immediately. "I need to listen to you, not to TV. Do you want to get a coffee?" She opened the door even before he answered.

"I do."

"Let's go then." She shut the door after he exited onto the porch.

"I can't walk there." He looked around, deciding.

She looked at him.

"Do you have gas in the Plymouth," he asked.

"Sure. It's In the garage." This mysteriousness had slid a film of concern down over the joy of seeing him. "We can cut through the yard."

The old Plymouth complained momentarily before it started up, leaving the two of them in silence.

Carol drove onto the side street. They drove down Sharp St. in the clear light. She, ordering her questions, and he, feeling he must wait.

As they approached the diner near the end of the block, he spoke up.

"I'll pop in and get two to go."

"What is all this?"

"I'll be right back."

She was tempted to say that she'd heard him say that before, but she held off. "Silence is the bitter part of valor" she thought.

With coffees in hand they drove up South Hill and over to the viewpoint where they had spent part of an evening. He scanned the valley and the bridge and the tavern where he had gone with Larry.

They parked.

Swinging her leg up onto the seat, she turned to him. "So, what's up?"

He could hear a tremble.

"Not sure how to start this." He put his hand on her knee. "I love you."

She smiled and then moved her coffee cup to in front of her mouth. He knew immediately that he had chosen wrong.

"Don't worry. This is mostly good news I think. We just need to talk it out."

"Fuck, Matt! Just say it."

"Four days ago, I was called in to see the bishop. Someone had seen us in Post Falls."

She heard him.

"He told me to make a decision and told me not to see you any more if I was going to stay in Spokane."

"Really? Am I like the fast girl in school or something?"

"No. In his mind, it's about scandal. I told him I'm serious, and this isn't some fling."

"What other choices are there?"

"Stay a priest and be assigned somewhere else, or not stay a priest."

"And so . . . ?"

"Carol, I knew my decision even before I got up from the chair. I came to the house and wrote some letters to people who need to know things and called you to say I was going away for a few days."

Carol shifted. There it was. Matt was "Mark". Thank you, Mickey!

"And then I took a bus trip to Portland and spent time with KT, my sister. I told her all about us and about my need to make a choice."

Carol's eyes were looking out the windshield as she listened. She sipped it all in.

"I'm no longer going to be a priest."

"Why?" She asked after some delay.

He laughed.

"No, really. Why? This is important."

"OK . . . I'm not alive there . . . Not good . . . It's the wrong role." He turned even more directly toward her. "C, I can touch and help people see things some other way . . . in a classroom rather than in the pulpit having to say things I don't believe . . . Being a mouthpiece for the Church is not it."

"Not as it is now. Or as you are now. But that could change . . . You spent years to get where you are. Can you just walk away? What will you walk to?"

He was calm. He felt sure. This was good. The journey had begun.

"I'll teach; I'll direct some; I need to help people. That can still happen." He rubbed at the back of his hand.

They sat for a moment in the silence.

"That's the way I know."

Somewhere near, over the ravine, crows scolded or warned or laughed or . . .

He looked toward their sound. "I'll be with you if you want to be with me."

Silence resettled in the car.

She took a deep breath before beginning. "What if I said I can't do that?"

He sat for a long while. He looked to her as she watched the road out the windshield and held her coffee like a place to hide.

He looked away.

The valley below seemed oddly primitive. The road hidden by all the trees.

He took his time. When he spoke, his voice had become subdued. "I still need to do this. Everything's telling me that."

C turned to him. She looked at him for some time in silence.

He faced forward, as if steeling for a blow. He spoke. "Say something."

"I love you too, Matt. I'll be with you if you want to be with me. I only ask you one thing."

"What's that?"

"Don't hide from me. Don't keep me in the dark. Don't make any more decisions on your own from this time forward without us talking things through first. Promise?"

"I do."

She put her coffee on the dash and slid over to him. He brought her to him and held her. The silence had broken. She was crying in his arms.

He looked at her face. She turned it away and then back.

"I thought I had lost you. I thought you were gone. And you puzzled me when I first saw you today. I went from excited to scared. Then as I listened, I began to be afraid for you if you hadn't thought things through yet."

"Trust me," he brought her hand between his. "I've thought about all of it and about us for hours and hours and talked about all of it and about us for hours. I'm doing the right thing. This is the right thing."

Just then a car drove by them honking. A young teen leaned out of the window and yelled, "Get a room!"

Without even looking C flipped her finger at the disappearing car. Matt laughed and wiped the tears off her cheek. He gave her the handkerchief.

Her defiance was something he admired.

He turned her face back to him. "That's not a bad idea you know."

She wasn't listening. "What about all that bishop stuff?"

"I have a letter going to him tomorrow. C, I'm really not much concerned after that. But we need to think into the future. I just want to know, and I hope beyond anything else, that you're with me."

She looked at him. He could see her resolve, the tremulous fierceness of her hope. She gave him her face, all the vulnerability of her openness, the breath of beginning. She took time. Looking . . . She nodded. "I'm with you."

Beneath her tears, she smiled.

He bent in and kissed her. How soft her tears had made her face.

It was as he had hoped it might be: saying the words made things real.

Ch 28

He didn't go home that night. Nor the two nights after that. He had stopped by the residence to get a change of clothes, but then he had immediately left.

His letter had gone to the Provincial and to the bishop. His letter had gone to the Dean. He had received a sealed envelope from the Dean in his faculty mailbox when next he checked. It seemed that all was well. He was being replaced by another part time instructor, and he was thanked for his work with the department and the university. As he had thought: he was expendable. He would read it again later. A letter of recommendation was included.

The Provincial was still travelling. They would settle things later, it seemed.

The bishop had sent nothing.

◆

He still knocked at C's front door, even though she had told him just to come up when he returned. Mickey didn't even greet him this time. She opened the door and ran back to the TV. He closed it for himself.

He wouldn't worry about entering in the future.

"Come." Carol was standing in front of the sliders cradling her cup of tea, looking out over the trees. The afternoon was a breezy one, ruffling the leaves still holding onto their branches on the maples below. The last of the hot sun. Changes.

Matt put his bag in the corner and sat in her desk chair. He looked at her and began to laugh.

"OK."

He surveyed the room with a single rock of his head, "Or how about I put my stuff on the landing and sit on the top stair during the daylight hours."

"You're right. It is a little crazy. Two adults in this tiny space. It makes me feel like I'm back to being an undergrad. Not that I had guys over that much . . . Stay tonight, and we'll figure things out after that."

"I can get us food if you want. I still have some money."

"Let's just grab something and go to the river."

◆

They made their own place. Just off the Loop Hiking Trail, they put down a blanket and their simple meal. They had come here before to be higher than the Jack Pine, looking out over the width and bend in the river. It was peaceful even with the breeze putting them just on the edge of chilled. They pulled at coats, and after they had eaten, he moved to behind her, so he could shield her from the breeze and so that he could get as close as possible, his head near hers. They were quiet for a long while before Carol spoke.

"Beauty leads us on. Don't you think?"

"What do you mean?"

"Just that. Beauty brings us to see some kind of specialness that we don't see every moment. The specialness of the most simple or the most expansive of moments. . . Lots of my poet friends talk about it."

"Given attention, the world is full of grandeur. It's sacramental even." She stayed settled looking out.

"When they talk about it, they mean it is itself but shows something beyond itself. Sublimity. Some say divinity."

They were quiet. He was formulating his question.

He asked. "Do you believe in God?" Carol laughed once in her throat before responding.

"I do. I think. I know I believe in the beauty of the world." She shifted more closely into him. "Do you remember what you said after I read you my poem in the car?"

"You mean about . . .?"

"About the 'soul' that created it."

"I remember."

"Well, that's how I find my way to what I think must be God. I look at the beauty of the poem and marvel at the vision of the poet."

He shifted to hold her more tightly.

In the short silence he could nearly feel the God question rising in her; it was going to be his turn to answer. She asked, "Do you?"

"I do." His answer had been slow to come. She heard him.

"But?"

"But. . . that's it. I don't believe in much of the rest anymore." They sat in a silence for some time.

"That's fine." She pulled his arm around her. "You have what you need, don't you think?" He had not thought of it like that.

He took time.

"I do. I have what I need."

◆

She took his hand and leaned into him. They watched the river flow and recounted the times they had been together, each with its own moment of comedy or memorable complication. Before long the sun lowered, and the chill increased. They walked back down to the car.

The house was empty when they returned. Mickey had left a loopy scrawled note on a full piece of paper just inside the door. "Sandpoint 'til Monday."

"It's very strange living with Mickey. But it's worked for what I've needed." Carol went into the front room and immediately took the ashtray in hand and disappeared into the kitchen. She stacked the books as she came back by the dining table. She shuffled all the papers into one ragged pile and then continued to straighten them before placing them near the books. He still stood near the arch and watched her.

"OK. Now I can at least pay attention to something else. Have a seat." He chose the sofa; she joined him. The silence in the house was strangely like the silence at the river, without the breeze. It was full and comforting. It let all other things fall away.

Carol got up after darkness fell and moved to pull the blinds in the large front window. Matt opened the screen on the fireplace and began wrinkling paper for the fire.

"Shit!" She sounded as if she had dropped something precious.

He turned to see her flattened against the wall. She looked as if she was hiding in a kid's game.

"What?"

"Nothing." Keeping her body behind the living room wall, she reached to pull awkwardly on what seemed a temperamental shade.

"This isn't a real house. A proper house. This isn't it." She then crossed to the back of the sofa and offered her hand to let him know she was ready to head off to bed.

He followed her up the stairs to her room.

He did not ask what had distressed her and led her to get upset.

And she did not say.

◆

The days alone in the house gave them the time they needed, time to themselves. They had time to be quiet; they had time to talk; he had time to sit on the countertop while Carol made pasta.

On the second afternoon, he had taken two hours to mow the back yard with a push mower and had raked it all up. He had come back into the kitchen and hugged her, at which she turned her head away and pointed to the stairs. He tossed all but his underwear into the washer before going up to shower. She had waited five minutes, and then, sneaking into the steam filled bathroom, stole his sweaty underwear and turned his water to cold. He had screamed; she had laughed and run down the stairs squealing like a little piglet. He had come naked and dripping to the top of the stairs with the threat to get revenge, and she had gone into the kitchen holding her stomach, convulsed with her laughing.

Falling asleep in the relaxation of an embrace, they slept comfortably in her narrow double bed.

The next day she had dusted the entire downstairs. He had washed down a kitchen floor that perhaps had never been scrubbed since the linoleum was laid. He had tacked the loose carpet on the staircase and after nightfall, they made a fire and covered themselves with a blanket in the flicker. Later they spread the blanket down and made love in front of the fire.

He brushed her hair off her cheek as she rested her head on him.

"What should we do?" He asked it without any urgency.

"What do you want to do?"

He responded after just a moment. "I think I want to move. I think I want to head west. I think that, like you, being near water is something I would like to do."

"So how do we make that happen?"

"But is that what you want?"

"Matt, I don't care. Us being together is more important than where we are or even what we have to do. I think it's time to access the Trust Gran put aside for me. That'll give us the freedom to search for what seems best. I let it stay making money to this point because I knew I was in temporary situations about my work, about my writing, about my life, really." She played with the hair of his chest.

"We can rent, and when it seems right, we can buy. I have enough to get us going."

"C, be patient with me. I probably hide this really well, but just so you know, if life were school, I would have been held back each of my first twelve years. Slow learner here." She pulled the hair on his belly.

Grimacing and taking her hand away, "You're lying on the chest of a man who has had to ask for movie allowance and miscellaneous spending money for the last dozen years of his life. Whatever I made teaching went back to the Order. I have no money. I'm starting from a dead standstill."

Carol shifted. She rubbed his belly and hugged him. "We just need to trust that we can make this work." She patted him. "I trust that."

"I'm going to write a friend and see if there might be a place for us to rent in Seattle. Yes?"

"That's fine. I think I'd like it there. Renting is good until we see how it suits us."

"Us." He stroked her back and held her to him. He watched the fire. "I can't believe that we're starting out together. We don't have to hide or sneak or pretend."

She sat up and straddled him with mock urgency. She was beautiful in the firelight.

"Does this mean death to Mister Pratt?"

Laughing, he ran his hands along her thighs.

She looked at him, waiting. Then both of them in falsetto: "O, no!" Their laughter brought her down to lie on him.

He could hold her like this forever.

Ch 29

Marianne,

By now you have probably heard that I'm stepping away from my life as a priest. I suppose that you and KT have talked about that. I hope she has helped you understand.

I'm ready to move out of Spokane and to head west. Seattle is the chosen destination.

Does your father still have some properties in the Seattle area? If so, might you have an opening in a rental situation? I'm not picky about where the property is. Safe is always nice.

Let me know what might be the prospects for a rental. House preferred, but apartment can work.

Hope all is well with the business and with your life. Give my best to Doc and to Elizabeth. Hope she is feeling better.

Looking forward to hearing. Heading to your city in the next couple days and will phone you when I arrive.

Matt.

Ch 30

Matt waited a day and then took time in the afternoon to go to the Jesuit Residence. He drove the Plymouth the few blocks and parked. Hopefully he would be able to remove the trunk on this visit. In the afternoon he was also least likely to find a number of priests in the hallway. Least likely to have to do any unnecessary explaining.

Meese was likely napping.

Near the flowers and the sign identifying the university was a fountain. Four feet tall and with one large tier that caught the spilled water. That was what he heard as he walked after parking the Plymouth. It seemed unusually loud today as its water sprayed in impulsive, energetic leaps and tumbled into the larger level below. For the first time he saw its crystalline exertion. It seemed nearly alive in its expansive leap upwards and fall into the broad catching pool. Momentarily he stood mesmerized.

He had never understood how that fountain fit as a symbol for a school. Meant as a reminder he guessed. Of? . . . The boast of abundance perhaps . . . But that was nothing for him to be concerned about. He was leaving.

It would spray on.

◆

As anticipated, the hall was empty. Meese's door was partially open as was the window behind the sagging curtain which was moving slightly in a breeze.

Matt entered stealthily. He closed his door as silently as possible. He would not take long.

The steamer trunk was in the middle of his room as requested. He had lost the key some moves ago, and so the brass clasp hung open like a tongue. He chuckled and decided not to take it personally. The trunk had been scarred with all the moves over the years, but it had travelled well with him. His mom and KT had bought the trunk as their contribution to the success of his choice, his vocation. Remembering them made him smile at the old piece.

He made short work of stuffing his life into the beat up trunk. Books, notes, clothing, junk from the desk.

He closed the trunk and did the clasps.

◆

He was able to escape the room without raising any apparent interest.

◆

The elevator to the basement storage area let him off next to the handcart and dolly. He kept the elevator door open and wheeled in the handcart.

Back upstairs, the trunk needed to be upended to go out the door, and he heard the miscellaneous pieces cascade as he hoisted the trunk onto the cart.

Had Meese heard him?

He waited some moments and then pushed into the hallway.

◆

Outside, where he had parked, he was able to lean the trunk onto the back gate of the Plymouth. Enough so that he was able to slide it into the back of the wagon.

He shut the tailgate and returned the handcart to the elevator doors.

As the doors opened, Fr. Hopkins started a bit, but smiled. "Going down, Father," he asked.

"I am . . . " Matt responded. "We'll ride along with you." He wasn't sure when he and the dolly had become a "we." It amused him, this secret joke of his.

"Moving in some furniture?" the old priest asked.

"No, just shifting things around a bit."

They arrived at the all but unlit basement. A gray, lifeless room with light from one narrow basement window only. Cool as a morgue and dark as a mausoleum.

Fr. Hopkins felt his way past the wood and chicken-wire cells built for bulky or seldom used personal items. He sorted for a key and unlocked his cell as Matt returned the cart and boarded the elevator.

"I'm turning the light on for you, Father. Take care now."

"Bless you."

He would never want to be anything less than kind to these men. They were all good men and committed. They each had something for someone. Just as he had had. They were able to actually live the life more bravely than he had been able. They were to be admired, these men. Perhaps he would write a play about them. He could make it dashing.

He closed the door and took the elevator up.

He walked back to the Plymouth. As was his habit, he glanced up to his room. What used to be his room and would now return to the market for a different short timer.

Someone new for Meese.

What a story that was.

◆

The curtains to his corner room were open. As usual they were the only ones on the entire floor that were. And in the closest window to the corner he saw a figure begin to emerge. As if rising to the surface of water. The plain beige short sleeve shirt told no lies. The figure became more and more clear. Matt watched as if he were taking a final photo.

He couldn't tell if the figure was about to wave or watch.

A last look before turning to the Plymouth showed the watching figure behind the pane: both arms out and up. As large as life.

Meese.

Matt felt a pang his breath didn't erase. He was certain he didn't understand what was happening.

But it was time.

◆

The Plymouth looked oddly like a hearse. The steamer trunk, a casket. He became the mortician as he slid into the seat and started the car. Looking in the rearview mirror, he saw his history behind him. It would be good to find a basement anywhere to store that black trunk.

He didn't glance up at the window as he pulled away.

That balloon had become a load to carry.

◆

Meese watched from the empty room.

The long station wagon pulled out of its space and at a funereal pace moved toward Boone St. It turned right and disappeared behind the structure of St. Aloysius church.

That was the last of that.

Minus the vibrancy of one's things, any room is stark. These rooms, with their institutional green paint, simple monastic furniture, cold metal bed with its thin mattress – these rooms were barren. How much investment it took to make them vibrant.

Too bad.

◆

Meese had left his own door open. He needed to laugh to himself at the welter of life strewn across his view of his overfilled room. His boxes, of course. His desk with papers disorganized to any eye but his own. His books and above them the photos he had become almost blind to: he and his parents: Florence and Albert. Before they moved across two states to live in Seattle. He and his high school team with the Missoula, Montana City League High School Basketball Trophy. He and Bob. And the marching band that he had played sax in before the accident. He tried to recall the moment of the photo, looking up from the field into the glare of stadium lights, smiling broadly on command. He thought he remembered that he had joked to Bob just before the photo. In the photo Bob's head was just beginning to dip away to shield his laughter.

"Good!"

He recalled how he and Bob had been Jerry and Bobby. Names like long pants. Names become more formal with age, but the thread first unspooling at childhood continues along. Always. Jerry and Bobby in the driveway with a basketball. Jerry and Bobby in band. Dueling saxes. Jerry and Bobby. Always Jerry and Bobby. Always in competition. Always finding a way to even the score with each other.

And that afternoon they had been headed to the garage to make belts for themselves when Bobby had pushed, and Jerry had shoved, and Bobby had returned the favor, and Jerry had tripped in trying to reach him and had fallen.

The immediate pain. He had never seen how the leather punch had pierced him at this throat. Bobby had been on him immediately. Holding him and crying out. Albert had left his work on the truck and Flo must have hurried out of kitchen's back door. Such was the alarm in Bobby's voice.

The accident. After which he had never been the same. After which Bob had never released himself from blame.

Meese sighed and dusted at the photo, returning it to its place.

◆

How young. So many bright futures yet to be written. He stepped past one of the boxes, sliding it with his foot.

So many pasts.

Why did he never look at these photos any longer? They might as well be stored in his dark trunk in the closet as out in plain view. Hidden in plain sight.

Whatever had led him to place them so prominently above his books had changed in some way. In what way?

He sat. The swivel chair turned as if directed. As if it had a mind to.

The rumpled bed. The windows he had not looked from for . . . Blinds closed. Absently he reached across the desk and without looking found his ball to accompany him in his survey.

At the foot of the bed, the vertical vase table with his saxophone in the stand he had had made, undusted, its dark case just below.

He remembered his father's voice at the accident, "You'll be OK. Don't touch it. I'm taking you in right now."

He had tried to find a place where he could draw full breath. He had felt the choking fluids in his breath; he had thought he might . . . His breath came short at the memory.

In the car Florence had held him and smoothed his hair as she nearly imperceptibly rocked. Albert must have driven way too fast. It seemed once that the car might lean too far; he said words Jerry had never heard him say to get slow traffic out of his path. "Albert!" She must have reached to him, but then she was back to smoothing.

And then the flurry of voices and the lifting and the gurney and the rush and the jostle of the ride over the concrete.

He had seen Florence watching, her arm around Bobby's shoulder and smoothing his hair.

And that was all he knew.

They were playing. Bobby had shoved at him while Jerry had tried to twist away. He had fallen. (On the leather punch of all things. How stupid he later felt.). And the pain at his throat and Bobby yelling for Albert.

He looked down now and saw that he was squeezing repeatedly at the rubber ball. As if he were bringing air to a lung, as if he were inflating the memory that he had so well emptied of life.

He would no longer play on high school teams; he would no longer stand joking for photos with his bandmates; he would never be called on to recite in class. He would be fine. He would just be different.

And Bob would be different. He could never let go of the blame.

And from time to time Jerry caught Florence looking at him, and he wondered what she was thinking. He tried to pay it no mind.

They had never talked about it.

◆

Meese without malice threw the ball at the open doorway. It did not come back off the far wall but ricocheted and wandered somewhere down the hall.

Isn't that the way?

He would get it later. After all, no one lived near him any longer.

Ch 31

Matt wasn't sure whether he actually slept.

There was an excitement to his breathing. He was going away. This sleeping in narrow beds may soon be over. The need to claim a false identity was done. Father Matt would be no more. M. Pratt would vanish.

He would be going home. He was headed to the trees.

◆

They had packed the night before. Carol was smart; she didn't even leave the drape closed after they retired. Expectantly, they rose with the sun.

The day had all the excitement he remembered from childhood. A trip, a car ride, a breakaway. An adventure.

Heading who knew where, to begin.

◆

She had packed the Plymouth the previous afternoon, and with her stuff and his, the old wagon stood a bit lower but was full of gas and ready for the journey. Like the Old West, she thought. Striking out to the new land. The new world.

Had they been sailors of old, these two would have proudly entered their weathered craft and set out. She would have to decide how to think about them.

◆

Each of the Western states have wildly differing sides to them. The east is dry and more extreme in temperatures; the west is more damp and more moderate. They would be crossing the wheatlands and the immense and darkly sweeping Columbia River. Then they would begin the climb up the Cascades and then down and through the western foothills into the lush western side. The drive would not be especially long: five to six hours. They were in no hurry and would have lunch along the way. That lunch basket was already packed and behind the front seat.

Carol started in the middle of the front seat, leaning on Matt. She leaned toward the dashboard to watch as, with their turn at the end of the alley, her house disappeared. She held the ancient role of navigator in her lap. The map was never far from her, though Matt knew the drive was simply to follow I 90. Their plan seemed perfect. There was so little traffic this time of morning, in the neighborhood he had only seen a few cars out on the road. Ironically one of them came from their alley. What were the odds!

But . . . He *was* the first car out of the alley. He loved being first in any line of any kind. It made the day even brighter; he smiled.

As they moved out of town, she kept her feet against her door and her back against Matt as he drove. Out her side window Carol watched Spokane pass by, like a movie.

She was also master of the radio, responsible for tuning out and tuning in. She would stop at any station that promised a strong signal and that played music she could sing to, if only for a few words. Matt just drove.

She suddenly found it: a distant, clouded singer but recognizable to her ear: "David Essex. I love David Essex." The weak signal became static.

Carol pounded on the dash. "Shit."

Matt laughed. He hadn't known any of the words anyway. She turned the faded radio off. "If you can't get a clear signal, it's time to quit." She kept the song with her as she "danced" for a while as Matt drove on, enjoying.

She had picked some daisies from the yard and now wove them into a coronet. When she had finished, she showed it to Matt, and then twisting the rearview mirror to see, she had posed in a variety of angles to assure herself that she was lovely as a queen. She was. They both agreed.

Matt had readjusted the mirror.

At the Vantage Bridge, crossing the Columbia, Matt held firmly onto the wheel since the side winds were blowing violently. He was alerted as he watched a VW bug get blown suddenly from the outside to the middle lane. The driver had corrected back to the outside for safety. Matt had slowed. Carol had become quiet some miles before and had curled sleepily against her door. Matt had quieted the radio as he held the car in its lane across the windy bridge.

For the first time since they had been together, Matt felt a kind of immediate responsibility. She was sleeping innocently now, with her daisy crown at an angle. She was beautiful. He looked again and then again. She was snuggled into herself and the seat and the trip. She showed only the remnant of the last song, a yawn and a smile on her face.

He was her protector, her partner. He was leaving Spokane with his arm around Carol Gordon as he had told KT he would. He had seen that as a loving image of the two of them. This moment showed him a protective side of that image. His dream was more than he had known.

She had given herself to him. She could rest easily as he steered the Plymouth along the interstate. She would go with him. This was what "going with" was like. He liked the feel of that.

He had been so wrapped in his thoughts that he had not noticed the traffic moving behind him onto the Interstate. There was no reason to note it really.

Other than the steadiness with which the trailing car shadowed his own.

This pattern drew Matt's eye.

If Matt passed someone, the blue car passed as well. When Matt turned into the slow lane, so did the blue car. An unexpected tandem was happening. It seemed as if the blue car was linked to the Plymouth, bound to it in some way.

Matt turned into a Rest Area. Carol shifted in her sleep and didn't wake when Matt left the car, taking care to lock it. The blue car had also exited but had parked near the entrance of the lot, almost as if waiting.

When Matt exited the restroom, the blue car was still in place. He could not see a driver.

He started the Plymouth watching in his mirror for what, if anything, would be next. Carol was still lying across the bench seat; she had shifted once after he closed the car door and begun the engine. It was best she slept.

Matt cleared the parking lot and exited, merging onto the Interstate once again. Nothing was behind him. He watched as long as the traffic allowed.

Nothing.

He wondered what he had thought was happening. How foolish he could be. Imagination! There was no reason to think a car would follow him purposely. Why would a fast, nimble, muscle car want to follow a slow Plymouth station wagon? The silliness of the prospect led him to laugh. He pushed the Plymouth forward.

Suddenly alongside, matching his speed exactly was the blue Chev. The road was clear enough for the Chev to pass, but it seemed the driver wanted something else. He wanted Matt to know he was there. The dark windows of the Chev kept Matt from seeing anyone inside, but whoever was driving seemed to be having some fun with this game, whatever it was.

If Matt slowed, the Chevy slowed. Accelerated, so did the Chev. Matt waved him to pass. The dark windows stayed steadily alongside. The road ahead was clear of traffic. There was no reason for this to be happening.

As he was trying to determine what to do, Matt felt the change. The tinted window began to roll down. The blue car stayed steadily with his own. Leaning across the seat to bring the window all the way open, the driver revealed himself. The revelation still left Matt puzzled. He had never seen this person.

He was a young man. The wide bandage patched totally over the one eye made him look broken and poorly mended. Matt did not know him. He was not one of Matt's students playing a game. He was not someone from the tavern or a cast member who had spied him on the road. Matt would have recognized the broad grin and the intent stare.

The other driver pointed at Matt. There was a kind of menace mixed with playfulness that Matt did not know how to read. "You!" he seemed to be saying.

"You!"

Something totally obscure was hidden behind those punching, pointing gestures.

The other driver jabbed, pointing his finger accusingly. And then he pointed to his patched eye. The move made Matt question.

What was he meaning?

Matt felt Carol sit up to lean alongside. She looked to the parallel car. "Shit!"

"What?"

"Gene. That's him. That's Gene!"

In that moment the face of the other driver changed. He shook his head savagely in the direction of the Plymouth. He pounded a fist on his steering wheel. He twisted his steering wheel erratically from side to side.

"Get away!" Carol pushed herself forward to scream across Matt.

Matt couldn't tell whether she was speaking to him or to Gene. "Get away!" she repeated.

The face in the Chev seemed ready to explode. He shouted something at Matt or at Carol and twisted suddenly back and forth, slamming his fist down onto his dashboard.

Two cars, Matt saw them now, had come up behind, anxious to move past.

The Chev pushed right as if it wanted to crowd the Plymouth off the road, but missing, swerved nearly off the road, and then, after veering left again moved crazily right. Matt pressed hard at the throttle. Feeling the limits of the Plymouth, he braced for the impact from the crazy car.

But then, as suddenly as it had begun, it ended.

The blue car was gone. No longer alongside.

Matt watched in his sideview mirror as the Chev spun once and raising dust with its exit, spun back onto the highway and then again off as following cars dove right and left to avoid the spinning blue car disappearing into the dust of the median.

Carol was on her knees watching out the rear window as Matt slowed. "Keep going. He's OK. Keep going."

Matt looked in his mirrors. The road was crazed with scattered cars and in the median the blue Chevy sat in the midst of its own smoke and dust. The back window broken from its landing impact; the silver primed hood sprung awkwardly.

Gene would not be threatening anyone on the road for a while.

◆

They had been silent for some time. And then Carol shifted. "I thought I was rid of him. I guess I wasn't. What a mistake that was." Matt wasn't certain what she was saying. "Sorry you got mixed up in that."

Matt waited for her explanation.

"Remember I told you about Gene and how crazy he got when he didn't get his way? Well, that was him. I don't know how he thinks I would come back to him."

"Would you ever?"

"Matt, you saw him. He's a crazy man. He was sweet and . . . when we first were together, but that was an act . . . then . . . " Carol stopped. " I told you all of this."

"Well, it seems that he was still on the look for you. Quite the resourceful stalker. But I think we can safely say he's part of your past. Thank God."

"I hope I never see that face again in my life."

"Chances are, C . . . You should be fine."

Things fell silent.

"Where are we?" Carol surveyed the change in landscape.

Matt took it at face value. "Still on I 90. We'll be half way home soon."

"That's good." And she had fallen silent.

Matt watched the highway ahead. Traffic was light. They would be over the mountains soon enough. He had driven this road on much more difficult days. So much depended on the weather and the number of trucks making the crossing.

After a time, Matt glanced over to see Carol asleep in the corner of the seat. Her daisy crown had fallen into the foot well.

◆

By Ellensburg, Carol began to awaken. For a while she simply sat up and watched the highway. And then she toyed with the radio but soon turned that off.

He would let the encounter go.

Driving had let him grow silent.

This was a homecoming, this return to the trees he had known as a youth, to the intense forests that led to or from Snoqualmie Pass. It was a sign. A landmark in his journey. He was coming to a place he had not been in some time, and it was lifting this trip to an even more momentous meaning. He would be free here. These were his trees.

His mood began to change.

The Pass itself was clear. Traffic moderate. They had been fortunate to have it work out like this. Snoqualmie Pass could be slow and treacherous. All things were working for their easy passage. No complications.

Coming down the west side of the Pass, Carol was transported by the views that opened up and sped by. Matt was glad to see that she had put the incident behind her.

She laughed. "This is not Texas. Not Iowa. And it's not flat Spokane."

True enough. This was a forest land like nothing she had ever entered. Hill after hill after hill of deep green forest stands.

He could almost hear her thinking. Taking it all in.

He turned on the wipers as a misty rain began fogging the windshield.

"So. Do you think we made a good choice?" he asked.

She gazed out the dry side window for a moment before turning to him. She put her hand on his leg. "We always make good choices. It's who we are."

Coming off the mountain, they sped past North Bend, and he felt himself becoming more and more excited to be coming home. Bellevue. Lake Washington Floating Bridge.

"This is a lake?"

"Yep. This is a lake that connects to another lake that connects to the Sound that connects to the Straits of Juan de Fuca and then right to the pounding waves of the Pacific Ocean. You're not in Texas anymore. You wanted your water; you got your water."

"I love it."

Exiting the bridge and turning onto I-5 north, he drove beside the city on the freeway as C leaned forward in her seat.

"O my God, this is a real city!" She put one elbow up on the dashboard and her left hand around the back of his neck.

He loved her.

"Is that the other lake?" she asked pointing toward two ferries moving in opposite directions.

"Nope. That's the Sound. Think of Washington as a right-hand fist with the thumb out. What goes in the webbed part and all the way to the top of your thumb is Puget Sound. Lots of islands and ferries that run between. Lots of long drives. Lots of places to explore.

He swept his hand grandly.

"Welcome to my old home town." He wished it were not raining. But then . . .

He passed by the Lower Woodland playfields where he played soccer and baseball and smoked his first cigarette, then Pitch and Putt golf where he had made a firm youthful resolution never to be lured onto a golf course again. The east side of the lake where the beach was always crowded in summer, the wading pool. She was rapt. C was silent in the face of this city. She could hardly look at each new thing quickly enough, since she had not exhausted the last attraction he had pointed to.

They found a motel up from the lake. He turned the Plymouth into a slot for parking and waited while C registered them and flagged him to room 8.

He would unpack the car later. It was time for a stretch and a shower.

◆

After eating out and watching a very fuzzy and occasionally rolling picture on their black and white TV, they closed down for the day. She was asleep almost immediately. He didn't fall asleep even though, and maybe because, he was tired from the drive. C's breathing next to him gave him enough respite from the highway. He could ride on that.

It was funny, he thought, how in a moment of time you could be lifted by your belt and transferred to an entirely new life.

Now that he was home, he had lots he could show to Carol. She would like the waterfront; they could travel to the Olympic Mountains; she might like to go fishing; there must be dozens of things that were new to the area since he had left. This could be fun, this relocation. Spokane was never home. Seattle could be home again.

Of course, there was the rain and the clouds that sat oppressively gray for months at a time, but one could get used to that. He recalled the long winter grass that would crawl up the sides of pavers in their backyard and the black rash of moldy moss that would break out on the base of the garage wall. He recalled standing under the tall pine in their backyard waiting for the rain to let up so he could make a run ... *and the strange path laced with dripping ferns and spiral ended tendrils, "fingers of the forest" KT called them. The bright green jackets of closely packed trees that added mystery to their walk. She was his guide.*

The sky had all but disappeared, though he dared not look up to see. Heavy drops falling wherever they chose – as if mischievous children in the tree branches above were dropping mini water balloons at him.

You trusted that the path would get you home. Out safely; back safely. The children were on their own.

But then he had heard something other. Off the path, through the thick, chest-high overgrowth.

He told KT to stop while he pushed through the greenery in search of the noise. It sounded like a cataract breaking apart on boulders below, but the sound was oddly a kind of scream. A cry of some kind: metallic, scraping, frictive, even, and he had never heard a cataract in this part of the forest. He pushed, stumbling over rotting logs from fallen trees that the forest was rebuilding itself with.

Fall, rot, grow: the natural law of the forest.

He was newly filled with an urgency. A drive to find the source of what he heard.

He tried to push past all obstacles to observe what he was hearing. The harder he tried to reach the source of the sound, the more he worried that he could never arrive there.

His boots slid if he stepped on the fallen logs; he overextended if he stepped past them onto what he couldn't see. He stepped on boulder backs imbedded in the mossy forest floor. Despite the unstable footing, he pressed toward the sound, the cataract sound. He seemed to hear other people there. Perhaps swimming in the rain. Their voices laughed as they staggered and yelled from the water below perhaps. Then the slamming and a loud yell. The thought sent a shiver through him, and he heard less of the falling river water. He pushed at a soaked fern taller than himself; it sent alarmingly cold drops down his sleeves.

There was no opening. Nothing to see. No sound now. And with no sense of direction home, he stood for a moment in the wet. The only sound was the pop. . . pop, popping of raindrops from sky to trees to ferns and wide leaved plants and to the forest floor.

And judging only that his back represented the direction he had come, and seeing how the drooping dampness of the forest had closed in behind him, and stumbling once badly, a step that took him to the ground and soaked him, he pressed on, hoping to find KT and the path that she was holding safe for him. And she would tousle his wet hair as if to tell him, "Silly boy. There is no river over there. I don't know what you were thinking."

Carol was dressed and sitting on the bed beside him. She had combed her hand through his hair. She had a motel coffee in a small white cup wrapped with a brown plastic handle.

"I'll put this here for you."

With an uninvitingly scratchy sound, she opened the heavy drapes, leaving the sheer curtain closed. She peeked out. "It's going to be nice. A few clouds but lots of light. Get up, lunkus. I've already had a shower. Let's get something to eat."

Ch 32

Something was wrong.

They could see immediately that something had happened to the Plymouth. There was glass from the taillight on the ground. The rear bumper on the passenger side was bent away, three to four inches. The right rear fender of the wagon had also been bent. Something solid had crashed into them, had tried to go through rather than around. Luckily the car seemed still intact enough to drive.

Then it hit him. "Shit. Nice welcome to my old home city."

They spoke to the young woman at the desk, who, just coming on shift, had neither seen nor heard anything. No note had been left by the night shift. Her diligent search had been to lift one piece of paper.

"It had to be a truck," Matt offered. "There was a large truck across from us yesterday."

The girl looked at the reservation sheet. "Actually, those people had a Ford sedan, not a truck. They left early today, before I got here. That truck you saw could have belonged to anyone, I suppose." She replaced the same piece of paper she had moved twice and was giving no eye contact. The attention expressed in her voice was just above monotone.

Matt saw that this was going nowhere.

"Would you like to report some damage?"

"Some damage? Are you kidding?" Carol touched his arm; Matt settled a bit. "Yes, we would." He wanted to grab the phone but chose instead to glance meaningfully at C.

◆

The interview with the police was not very promising. They seemed more anxious to have a seat than to poke into anything but with the most mundane of questions. They left Matt and C with a heavy sense of futility as well as a report to complete.

"Did you hear what he said to me?" Matt was still fuming about being scolded by the police for thinking that they would be of any use in tracking down the culprits.

"It is what it is." She reached for her purse. "Let's walk over and get some breakfast. Thank god, we didn't have anything of value in there."

◆

Matt shoved his syrup-drenched pancakes around his plate after only a few bites.

 C told him that if he wasn't going to eat those, she would. She had already finished her two eggs and bacon. He pushed his plate across to her.

"It's not the value of the car so much as the selfish rudeness of those people. They're primitives. No, I take it back. That's an insult to the goodness of primitives."

She was in mid bite, "Of course it is. No one's arguing with you."

"Just pisses me off. "

Carol took a dripping bite of pancake. "Things work out. The car was given me in the first place, so I'm still ahead of the game." She mopped up some of the yolk with her next bite. "I won't let myself be defeated by this stupid accident."

Matt began, "Accident?"

She put her fork down and stared him away from starting the next sentence. With a resigned shake of his head, he settled in to watching traffic on the busy arterial. Cars hurried and braked, changed lanes and held up others while trying to make a left turn. The morning had turned overcast.

"Are you going to call Marianne this morning?" She made the effort.

"When we get back, if my notebook hasn't been stolen."

"Don't be a baby."

He finished his coffee and took the receipt to the register.

Carol watched over the last of her coffee and took her time, even after he had paid the bill and walked out onto the sidewalk in front of the window. He stood with his hands in his pockets, watching the busy morning traffic.

She put down her coffee, cradling it between her hands. "It'll be fine."

Ch 33

Marianne had arranged to meet them at the property, a small two-bedroom house in Ballard.

They had arrived before her and were waiting in the car.

The yellow house stood back from the sidewalk and above it by a good six feet. The wide cement porch had once been painted, seemingly in some shade of red or brick, but the paint had been left to the sun and rain over years. The canary color of the house seemed relatively recent and well maintained.

"Matt, I like it. We could plant some flowers in pots on the porch to dress it up a little, but it's a pretty house. I love the windows." Seeing something else she tapped excitedly on the car window. "Look, the door's arched. Just like my Gran's. Walking through an arch like that in Iowa brought me to some of the best experiences of my life.

Matt, still stewing over the morning's events, surveyed the house superficially. One house past the corner. He disliked how close the houses were. He had forgotten how closely their family house had been hemmed in on two sides. On one side by Marianne's. How ironic.

Marianne pulled up close behind.

Matt was out quickly to greet her. They hugged in the street while Carol closed her door and stood on the parking strip. Matt brought Marianne to Carol.

"Marianne, this is my friend Carol." The two women greeted one another, and Marianne led the way up the cement steps. "Now this house is open immediately. That's its virtue. One of them. We have another property closer to the University you can look at, but it's rented through next month." She unlocked the door and stepped inside.

Carol moved immediately to the center of the room and turned to look from every angle. Matt noticed the old steam fed radiators underneath the front windows. "We used to have radiators like this on Meridian St.", he said to Marianne.

"I remember. So did we . . . Old, but they still work well."

Carol had disappeared through the hallway and into the back rooms of the house.

"It is. Just feels unreal. Us living here together. . . Lovely. . . Sometim es impossible to believe." Matt hurried to catch up. She was standing, arms out in the midst of a wide windowed space. "This could be a reading and meditation room. Look at the yard you can see from here. It feels like its nearly inside. Like there are no walls."

The back had a small yard with two pine trees and an apple tree by the garage. Most of the bushes had been ignored, and flowers had been left to die in the rain.

It had been newly fenced all around.

"We can put in some flowers, if that would be permissible." Marianne nodded and smiled. Then feeling the impact of the room was finished, Marianne led them to complete the circle of the downstairs. "The kitchen."

Carol's excitement dimmed. She stood in the doorway and nodded. Matt looked over her shoulder. The kitchen had been let go over the years. It had the essentials but little else.

"And, passing through to the front of the house, here is the dining room." The windows looked out onto the quiet street, their cars and three houses straight across.

Marianne filled in the rest of the tour from there. "Two bedrooms and a bathroom upstairs. And a partial basement. That door was across from the sink in the kitchen . . . I don't know if it's what you were thinking, but this opened unexpectedly and . . . "

"Matt, we can't ask for more than this. Don't you think?"

"I like the house." He turned to Marianne. "So, what do we do?"

"Leave it to me. Do you have any furnishings at all?"

Matt looked at C and resisting the obvious opportunity to complain, shook his head. "No. We have no furnishings."

"Well, there are some pieces in the basement. There's a bedstead, mattress and box springs. In fact, I think there may be two. There are a couple tables, a sofa and a few chairs. Two living room chairs anyway. At least it gives you a start."

Carol hugged Marianne warmly. "We are so grateful for you helping us get situated. I can start shopping as soon as tomorrow, once I get my banking squared away. This gives us a wonderful start. Don't you think, Matt?"

"I do. I like it."

"Can we take you to lunch?" asked Carol.

"Yes. Most certainly. Just not today. Today I'm a busy gal and already late for my next appointment. But I'll be by in the next day or so, and we can sign the papers. In the meantime, enjoy getting settled in." Marianne moved to the door. "I nearly forgot. Here is the key, and here's my card if you need that for anything. I'd better get going. I need to get back to Doc soon. He's going to wonder who is the afternoon receptionist." She stepped forward to hug Matt and then Carol. "I'm so glad this worked out for both of us."

◆

The two of them stood on the faded cement porch and watched Marianne descend the stairs and get to her car. They waved as she glanced up. She drove away up the quiet street.

C squeezed Matt's side as she stood with him. They were a couple. Standing on their porch in a new city where she had met her first Seattle female friend.

Matt could feel the excitement in C's grip at his waist. He knew what she was thinking: "Some flowers here and maybe a little paint for the porch." He put his hand over her shoulders and brought her near to him. She was shuddering.

"What?"

"I can't believe this is real. That all this is coming our way."

He squeezed her to him.

"Believe."

Ch 34

Matt woke in the night. He pulled the blanket off the bed and padded to their bedroom window and, seeing nothing, shuffled across the thin carpet to the back bedroom.

He had heard a distant siren, and there was a thrumbing in the air that unsettled. Looking over the back yard he could see little, but he heard the rotor pulse of a helicopter hanging somewhere over their houses.

The labyrinth of yards and fences, of bushes, trees and stairwells gave fugitives a chance he supposed. The police sirens told the story. Apparently, someone was running. Hiding perhaps. And the search was on.

Matt wasn't afraid. He was engaged immediately, however.

This was what it was like to search. To really search.

Spokane was never like this. Seattle apparently was as dark as it was light.

The rotor pulsed more closely. It sounded nearly overhead. The single paned glass rattled in the vibration.

And then it arrived. It must be hanging above the side window. Matt crossed to see.

The beam revealed the neighbor's gray flower remnants, turned away, shielding themselves from the unearthly light. Then, with the downdraft combing the space between houses, the burning light lit the gray basement stairs that crept down to the short windowless door, padlocked and peeling. Dried leaves, awakened and animated, shuddered in the well. He saw two racoons scurry furtively to behind the trash cans beneath the wooden back stairs.

And then the light adjusted, splashing over the shingles and up into the gray eaves and back again, down over the darkest of hidden places.

And off.

What an event. The night was as busy as the daylight.

The siren had moved past but was still nearly as insistent.

The search scene dissolving, Matt descended to the main floor. He crossed to the meditation room and stood just inside the door. A single light from the garage spilled beyond the alley and backlit the yard.

This was now to be home.

Whatever person had looked out these windows a week ago had moved on, and this garden had become theirs. His and C's. And she already had plans for plantings that would make it her own.

Matt moved to the rattan chair and climbed in.

And she had already seen paint colors and curtains and bathmats and decorative cannisters in the kitchen and a vase on the dinner table. Her poem, "The Boy", lovingly framed in Spokane, was already on the mantlepiece.

It was as if she had found herself.

Why was he so blind? Why for him was there only now? Why couldn't he see what others seemed to see so easily?

He looked at his trunk, black before the charcoal window. Almost negative space. His trunk. Gift of his family. Container of all his papers and clothing and books and memories of a former life. Negative space.

Now the trunk sat before the dark window, topped by a draping of material that C had been pleased to find from a bag in the back closet. On top of the cloth, a small cobalt vase holding a clutch of artificial flowers.

Pushing himself even further into the blanket and the rattan chair, Matt settled. This was where he was to be now. Where their lives would start new.

Who had ever thought?

The night had supplanted the insistent searchlight. There was no memory of the white light in the dark window. Only the dim yellow alley light with a pine branch between it and the meditation window. The branch moving, up and down in what must be a breeze. Matt watched the alley lamp and the branch and the alley lamp and the branch.

He didn't even sigh; he slid off into sleep.

◆

He awoke tight and disoriented. The residue of a poor night's rest was upon him.

He stood, stiff and wrinkled, needing to stretch into the morning. He rewrapped the blanket and shuffled to the hallway. Turning up the thermostat, he moved into the shadowy front room whose windows would display the first light of day.

The sunlight seemed to be searching, seeking a breakthrough in the brooding overcast. The heavy cloud cover creating a blanched version of night rather than a brightness of morning.

A sudden, bright light shaft flooded a sector, shining onto some roofs, flaring against house fronts now aglow. It all but flamed, then moved along, abandoning sashes and gables, porch fronts and stairways to the early morning, dozey gray.

He looked into the sleepy morning and oddly saw his own reflection in the small pane. The shadows of the lilac's trembling leaves pocked his face as if he were masked for a Halloween scene. He looked past the blemishes.

It seemed the day would be like the night: heavy light calling up broody things, leaving hidden places around bushes and dark corridors separating the houses.

This morning was for mulling. He had forgotten that about his city.

He put his hand on the radiator. The cast iron was still cold. He thought of the water hidden away, orange and thick in its secrets. He shifted further into the swaddling of his blanket, awaiting warmth in this unfamiliar, unfurnished morning.

He moved to sit at the almost sunlit corner of the room to sort his thoughts.

He remembered the boy Lucas. Lucas had looked out with the same blemished features. Lucas had been caught like a fugitive, caught and seen. He would rather have been hiding far away.

Matt slid to a sit.

Lucas had been crouched in his own body, trapped in someone else's vision of him.

Matt remembered the feeling of looking at the boy and seeing himself. He recalled knowing what it was to hide away within himself. To keep the difference between what was seen and what he knew. Eventually he had forgotten that he had always been the bad boy and only had been pretending to be anything else. That had always been his protection. From his teachers and their judgements of his failures, from the adults ready to see him as unfit. From his father whose belt was quick to punish.

Perhaps even from himself.

From his corner Matt watched the day scud before him and felt the thoughts fly dark across his vision. The birds rode the wind on days like this, in fact they played it. Trees opened wide combing themselves luxuriously with the wind.

He sat in the joint of two burgundy walls. Watching. Wondering what would appear.

He felt lost. Waiting to see where he was. Who he was even.

Not a priest. Not a Jesuit. Not a teacher.

He rocked his head against the burgundy walls.

He was not home.

And the shadow blemishes? The shortfalls, the insufficiencies, the failures that he had kept hidden? The misgivings? Fears even?

Could he turn his face to the light, the way Lucas had?

Could he do as Larry had suggested and extend himself to himself and forgive?

Accept?

Despite?

◆

Another naked figure, blanket wrapped and squinting, shuffled into the room.

"What are you doing?" she whispered.

He laughed, recovering from his thoughts. "There's no one here. You don't have to whisper." She sat down beside him.

He spoke, "I couldn't sleep, so I came down to see what we've gotten ourselves into." He rattled his head in his best Stan Laurel.

"Matt, I'm so happy with this. We've fallen into a wonderful start. Think of it. From sleeping upstairs in a smoke polluted, rickety old house, we've arrived at this lovely home."

He let go of the last of his ruminations, "You are something else."

"Get up. The sun's already up, and we can make some breakfast and get started. She leaned over, looking his way. "I suggest covering your johnson, or I'll have to do that for you."

"I thought I had. No sense, no feeling."

He watched her walking away, stretching her blanket up behind her head like a naked fashion radical. She spun to show him.

He was up immediately.

Ch 35

At breakfast Carol had put a piece of paper on the dining table.

"I'll get the bank stuff set up today and do some household shopping. We'll have work soon and get something coming in other than the Trust. 'Til then, we're fine.

"You take care of utilities, our phone, and our key. Do you know where you might use a phone?"

"I saw a drug store on the avenue. I can walk there and use the pay phone."

"A suggestion before we start our separate errands. Let's just walk the block once. To see where we are. Where we live . . . our new home."

◆

He agreed. The block was lovely. Trees on the parking strips gave a sense of welcoming as he and C ambled from home to home as they walked the sidewalk. Some of the trees had lifted portions of the sidewalk cement with their roots, giving a hint of the neighborhood's age. Homes were of various colors. Most sat on embankments as did theirs.

"Theirs," how strange, he thought.

Most houses were quiet; likely most owners had left for work. Many were Craftsman, these houses: deep porches, second story overhang in the front, shingle siding, composition roofs. Green seemed to be the dominant color choice, but there were plenty of brown to tan to yellow to off white to Alaskan white with forest green trim. People cared for these houses.

It was easy to see where the active kids lived. Bikes and wagons were parked on porches or stood alone in the yards where they had been abandoned. Sometimes baseball gloves or a bat might be strewn on the stairs as if the athlete needed to forsake the game to enter the house.

Some houses had faces. He had seen that ever since he was a kid with a paper route. They might wink with their shades: one up, one down. They might be asleep with both shades drawn. They might be yawning or grinning or grimacing in pain. He used to enjoy throwing papers into their mouths to see if he might awaken them.

Remnants of summer gardens were common along the top of rock walls next to the sidewalk. Green wire fencing edged many of these. The remains of flourishing blooms were now gray to black with rotting. Part of the process. Bloom and decay. Beauty and death. Forever change.

The eternal oxymoron.

He would spend a little time cleaning the flower beds at their house today.

"Is it nice to be back?"

"It is. Just feels unreal. Us living here together . . . Lovely . . . Someti mes impossible to believe."

She took his arm as they walked. "Believe . . . It's you and me, kiddo."

Ch 36

Matt had quickly found work at a tavern a mile from the house. It was steady and gave him a sense of contributing. The owner had told him he would have three days of training, but Matt had been left on his own after the first night. Matt sensed the owner could not be happier than being free of the night shift.

After a few weeks, Matt was able to perform tasks unconsciously. He knew the regulars; he knew the routine. He was a quick study. New role: barkeep.

◆

One night as Matt came out of the storeroom, he sensed something had changed. He glanced up as he unloaded the supplies. A new customer, next to what they called the "shadow table" was taking off his black overcoat. He had on a black fedora and looked to either side for a place for the coat to dry. There was none. The man draped the coat over the back of a chair and sat at the dark table.

When Matt had finished his work, he noticed the new customer perusing the menu. He approached.

"Can I get you anything?"

The man pointed to the menu on the table. Matt looked over the man's shoulder and around the hat to be sure where he was pointing. "With cheese, I bet." The man nodded without turning to Matt. "Special with cheese. Can

I get you a beer?" As he nodded, the man turned away to straighten his coat across the chair next to him.

Matt finished his note to the cook and went to draw the beer.

Unusual to have new folks wander in and sit off to the back like that. The light there was awful. Usually that table filled last in the entire place.

Matt placed the beer on the table.

"Matt, I need plates," the cook shouted through the serving area.

Walking away from the dark table, Matt finished up by saying over his shoulder. "Burger should be up soon."

After sliding the stack of plates through to the cook, he turned to the bar to wipe things down and finish the restocking.

Phil waggled him over. "I'm going to be late for the game tomorrow night. Can you hold a seat for me?" Matt liked Phil.

"Sure. There'll be something for you."

And they fell into a discussion that let Phil do what he loved: show off his intricate knowledge of the team. Matt leaned into the conversation.

More new customers arrived, and Matt put his towel over his shoulder as he went to them.

Cook's bell sounded. "Order up!"

The screen door at the front slammed shut.

The night was picking up. Matt turned with the burger and glimpsed a dark figure pass by the storefront window.

He saw just enough for him to stop.

The shadow table was empty except for half the glass of beer. The coat was also gone. Matt left the meal at the bar's end.

Matt approached the table, uncertain what had just happened. Beneath the half glass of beer was piece of folded yellow paper. He opened it.

"You look good . . . Catch you later. Too loud right now." M.

The black coat, the black hat, the silent departure.

Of course.

◆

Meese stood at the tavern door without knocking, waiting for Matt to see him. He would have seemed a specter had Matt not known it was him. Matt laughed on the way to open. It was "Maltese Falcon" lighting. White light, the face shadowed by the hat, the unmoving, dark presence awaiting the moment of opportunity.

Film Noir if ever there was.

"Come in, Father." Meese crossed into the room and waited, holding onto his hat. Matt gestured to the nearest chair. "Have a seat." Meese sat, placing his hat on the table.

It was somehow very good, almost uplifting to see Meese. Matt passed on the most obvious question.

"Would you like a beer, Father?"

Meese indicated he did not . . . There was a long pause, and then he smiled.

"It was too loud. I need for us to talk."

"Sure. No problem. It's good to see you." Matt wondered what all this could be. He put his arms on the table so he could lean in closer and hear what Meese had to say.

"I wanted to know what happened." The older man had to work to be heard even in the silent room the bar had become.

Matt looked at his old neighbor. He saw for the first time that Meese had receptive as well as penetrating eyes. For the first time, Matt saw that in the filtered blue light, the man's hands seemed artificially quiet. He was stifling his usual energy.

"Father, I just wasn't cut out to be a priest."

Meese wasn't going to let it pass. "No, that's not it. Nobody is cut out to be a priest. That's the bottom line here. We go from there."

"I just meant that I had all but lost my faith, really. Saying Mass had become torturous for me. I was doing the whole thing by rote." Meese's head had begun to pulse like a metronome in acknowledgement. "And then I fell in love." . . . Matt trailed off.

They sat in silence with the sentence between them.

"I've never fallen in love." Meese's sentence was voluminous.

Matt watched the old man's face with its almost smile. He waited.

Meese began. "Why did you go? People lose their level of faith; they eventually burn through to a new level. People keep going because there is a covenant, a pledge there . . . " He ducked his head. "I'm not trying to blame; I'm trying to understand." He seemed to go somewhere and then return. "See, I have boxes of files and statistics, but they don't tell me what happened, not really. They just say: "and he stopped"; "it wasn't working"; "he walked away."

"I watched you go. And I knew I'd likely not see you anymore and that I would live at the end of that damn hallway without any hope of someone stepping through my doorway for another twenty years. There was no way in hell I was going to step through theirs. Yours, I would have . . . You, I would miss."

Matt noticed that as Meese talked he now squeezed at a dark blue rubber ball. Meese saw him watching. "My habit. Besides smoking, I mean. I apologize about the smoking by the way. It must be obnoxious.

"I hardly ever noticed."

Meese opened his hand and looked at the ball. "This is my therapy and my outlet. My game and my release. It keeps me from smoking even more. I squeeze it sometimes; I balance it on the back of my hand sometimes; I toss it against the wallpaper in the hall sometimes. I have even thrown it all the way down that damn hall and had to go search for it on the first floor... That was a bad night . . . Sorry if I ever kept you awake with the noise of it."

Matt shook his head.

"It's how I deal." The priest was becoming fidgety.

Matt wanted to ask him things. Things about his life and things about how he had managed all these years to do what he did. The priest part. He wanted that not because it would make any difference to his own choices. He just wanted to understand.

The old priest put the ball on the table, and it sat as if it were a companion pet, trained simply to be with the master. Matt folded his hands beneath his chin.

"My name is Jerry. I want you to know that. I'd like it if you'd call me that. No one does now that my dad is gone, except Bob and my mother, Flo. On my papers and on my door it says I'm Jerome, but I think of myself as Jerry. And if you can, I'd like you to think of me as Jerry. That's really who I am. It's who I've always been. Jerry.

"You know what they say," Matt began: "'to respect a person's name is to bring God to that person.'" Matt had no idea where that came from

"You're lucky. Matt Is a boy name and a man name. I've been Jerry and Jerome and even Hieronymus when the church spoke Latin. Jerry is who I am. A person's name anchors them, don't you think?"

Matt's chin lifted from his hands. 'I do. And I can call you Jerry. I'd like that. I wish I'd known before."

"Matt, now that I'm transferred over here to care for my mom, I'd like to get to know you. Jerry to Matt. Matt to Jerry. If that's OK."

"Of course. May I ask you something?" Meese just watched. "How did you . . . ?"

Meese put up his hand; Matt thought he may have overstepped. Then Meese pointed to his throat: "This, right?"

Matt sat up. "I didn't mean to be rude."

The hand went up again and Meese cleared his throat.

"When I was a kid in Montana my best friend Bobby and I were playing in the yard, doing something silly I suppose: pushing or trying to trip or trying to punch or twist away. The kind of things kids do. Well, Bobby shoved me, and I fell. Thing was, I never fell. I was the one who could usually catch him up. I was the one who could out run, out dribble, out jump, out everything. But this day, I fell. And the stupid leather punch that was in my shirt pocket, 'cause we were headed to punch up some belts in the garage, the punch ended up making a hole in my throat.

"My friend Bobby yelled out and my mother and daddy came running. Thank God.

"I do thank God . . . I see this", he put his thumb to his throat "as my second chance." He smiled. "I know I seem to be careless of that chance given my filthy habit ongoing . . . , but I'm grateful for my second chance at life. Always have been.

"I don't see this (he gestured) as something negative or something arousing anger or, even less, self pity. I see it as a reminder of how fragile I am, we are. How grateful I am for the chance.

He dipped his head. "Not everyone gets one."

He stopped, looking down at his fingers. "My habit tells me, how complicated."

He reengaged, concluding. "And that's the Jerry that only a few know. Most see only Meese.

"That's part of why I always sat alone at table. So few were willing to look beyond the surface.

"And its why I valued your brief visits to the old man across the way." He tapped rigid fingers on the table.

"Thank you for those."

He picked up the ball and began again to squeeze at it.

"Now I'm here to watch out for my mom. My friend Bobby paid for them, mom and dad, to move over years ago. Mom is still in that same apartment." Meese drifted for a moment.

"Poor Bobby. I think he hurt more than I did. I think his hurt has never gone away. Mine healed over. He has watched over my family all these years. When he graduated and got himself set up in practice, he brought my mother and daddy over to this side of the state so he could keep an eye, and he always kept me in touch with how they were.

"I see. Is she well?

"She's a smoker. She won't stop. She won't see a doctor." He started a dark laugh. "And I don't have much leverage for arguing with her . . . Since my dad's death, she's unhealthy in a lot of ways and keeps herself holed up in an apartment up on Capitol Hill. So I try to lift the blinds and open a window once a week. That doesn't sound like much, I know, but at this point it's all she lets me do." He looked into the distance.

Some days I have to sit for a very long time before she talks with me . . . She's so used to being alone." He had not really returned from the distance.

"OK." He sat up and took the ball from the table. "That's a start on Jerry Meese. Now you will owe me a starter on Matt Turner. I'll be in touch. I know how to reach you. Research, you know."

Jerry had different eyes than Meese. There was more intrigue, less judgement. More playfulness, less oppression.

◆

"There's more but I'm almost out of time. I can only go so long, and then you won't be able to hear anything, and I'll have to write, which doesn't work. So, here's the deal. I want to visit with you and have *you* do the talking. I want you tell me everything about what happened. It's happening all over, and I want to understand it. Maybe there's something we can do to help instead of losing all you good people. I need you to talk me through." His eyes were back to searching.

"Would you do that?"

Matt began, "I suppose. I don't . . . " Meese interrupted.

"I want to think that you and I had something, a brotherhood of sorts that I can rely on. I have to understand whether this whole thing" . . . He stopped. He was watching the top of the table with a narrow eyed look that Matt had seen before in their hallway.

His face began to alter. He reengaged. "You and I are alike, Matthew Thomas. We are the same; we just have chosen differently."

He picked up his hat. "I'll be in touch."

"About the study?"

"Just so we're on the level," Matt waited as Meese leaned in.

"There is no study."

Meese's face softened before Matt, and Matt saw the previously hidden outlines of a youngster he had never seen. A youngster with whom he might have played ball or walked to the river or spent the afternoon fishing. Someone he could simply be with. To him he spoke.

"I understand."

He wondered if he did.

Meese got up from the table, preparing to go back out.

"Here's what I know. Every story is different. And I call it a study so other people will listen. But these stories can't be reduced to a product. What I have learned so far is that the priestly life is just like any other calling, maybe even like falling in love: there's either life in it or death. Depends." He shifted into his overcoat.

Matt thought to ask him "on what?", but Jerry continued.

"And that's what we need to talk about. After you fill me in like I did you."

Meese fitted his hat onto his head. He turned to Matt.

There was a moment in which Meese just looked at him.

Matt nodded. "Sure, Jerry." Meese offered his hand with its pink and yellow fingers.

They shook on it.

As Meese neared the door, Matt spoke out, "I'm glad you found me." The old priest waved without turning and left the tavern.

Matt had had to check himself.

He had almost called him Father.

Ch 37

Carol had made arrangements at The Boathouse for lunch. She had heard how enthusiastically people talked about eating there. And she wanted to treat Marianne, to thank her.

It seemed somehow predictable that she would arrive first. Matt had waved to her over the sound of the vacuum as she left the house. He had given her a thumbs up. She would have kissed him, but he was involved with his chores and needed a shower.

◆

Carol had rehearsed her facts in the mirror as she got ready for the outing. Neighbor, best friend of KT as kids, kids were almost raised by Tritons, Matt and Marianne had been in a show together at some point. She had gone East to school and married there. That didn't last all that long, and Marianne was back helping her father, Bob, the dentist. Doc, he was called.

What Matt didn't know KT had. She and Marianne had been best pals all through school. Matt joined them because he would have been left out otherwise. Marianne called him Matty. Partly, as an endearment, partly to intimidate him. As a kid, he never knew quite which, according to KT. Neither had she. Marianne liked it that way.

Marianne could be very loyal. She could be kind and generous. Carol had already seen that to be true.

Marianne could be mean. The dark sculpted brows could direct destructive energy down on people. KT had felt bad about saying this, but she thought Carol should know. Then KT had laughed. "I remember taking her by the ears and kissing her forcibly on the forehead. — Her ears stick out. I had sometimes made fun of them. — She didn't know what to do when I grabbed her by her ears. And we both started laughing. She was never mean to me again. I never made fun of her ears again. It was our bargain."

Carol was just finishing her review of KT's call when Marianne appeared at the hostess station. She was such a beautiful woman in her Kelly green suit, matching shoes and purse. Her white blouse was immaculate. Her smile as she approached, wide and easy.

Carol adjusted her sweater and tried to stand.

"No, no, no. Have a seat." Marianne put out a hand which Carol took as they sat. They unfolded their napkins as the server came with water.

"A Chardonnay, please. Mont St. Michelle if you have it."

Carol passed. "I'm fine with just water and tea with my meal."

Marianne sipped at her water and leaned forward as she put it down. "So, tell me about you. I know all about Matty."

Carol began from a dead stop. "A thumbnail for you.

"I was named Carol because I was born just before Christmas, and that was maybe the only sweet thing my momma and daddy did for me.

I'm from Texas. My daddy walked out of our lives when I was in grade school, and I went off to live with my gran and help out with things. I have a sister.

I write. I teach. I haven't published much, but I will eventually. Takes time. I work as a hostess to make ends meet.

I met Matt doing theater and writing up a teacher profile on him.

We came this way to be near the water, which I've never been and for Matt to be in his home town. And we love living on 26th. Thank you so much!"

Carol felt gushy, but she wasn't done. "And I hope you and I can become friends since I so appreciate your kindness in helping us get set up, and I'd like to get to know you better and return the kindness as I can."

The waiter put Marianne's wine on the table, and she immediately lifted it. "I'd like a Cobb salad." She looked at Carol. "If you haven't tried it, their Cobb is wonderful." Carol felt a pressure to be ready, but she was glad not to have to work through the menu. Salad it was.

"A shrimp salad for me."

"You'll love it. . ." Marianne adjusted forward. "I'd like us to be friends also. And just so you know, I'm glad to help you two get settled. KT told me about Matty's struggles, and I just want to help.

"I'm going to start by getting to work on Doc to get you into something long term or permanent on your house. Doc has too many properties. He doesn't even know what he has. I do. I deal with them. We can let go of some to good buyers.

"We'll see what we can wrangle." She smiled beautifully.

Marianne began a travelogue of Seattle. Carol discovered soon enough that she needn't remark, just nod occasionally as she thought about her face and how to show interest.

In the midst of the monologue, and for the first time, Carol remembered about Marianne's ears. She wished she hadn't.

When their meals arrived, and Marianne ordered a wine with her meal, Carol found herself mesmerized at the difference between Marianne sleekly coifed and classily outfitted and Marianne with two wines and with ears just waiting to pop free of the elegant sandy hair and flap both women into a Disney cartoon.

What had happened?

Carol was able to regain her presence by ticking through her salad until she realized how the tiny shrimp were curled like little ears. Little pink ears. And she needed to eat enough to make everything seem normal. She concentrated on the lettuce and chasing a set of small cherry tomatoes as Marianne finished her narration.

What was this?

She decided it was something to put aside. It was a defense of some kind. A shield. Marianne's "wrangle" had tripped Carol into a step away, a place of watching someone at work perhaps. Something KT had overlooked or forgotten.

"Do you come here often?" Carol cut into the dwindling narrative line. "Are there always so many boats docked?" Both women looked. "Do they all get used?", Carol mused. The silence had settled in. "So, do people actually use these boats to get around or just to ride on the water for a while?"

"I have no idea." Marianne glanced out at the water and then sipped. "I just think they are picturesque. But I don't think I know anyone who owns one. I probably do, but I can't think of who."

"How was your salad?" Carol asked as Marianne lay her napkin across the top of her plate.

"Very good. And yours?" Marianne began with a mirror and lipstick. "You were smart to order the shrimp. Here we are in the seafood capital of the Northwest. Order seafood. Smart." She put her makeup into her small green purse.

"Carol, I've enjoyed being with you. I would like to do this again when I don't have to run. I apologize for being so rushed. But we gave each other a beginning. I'd like us to continue." The ears disappeared, and a beautiful woman smiled back at her.

"Give my love to Matty. I'll connect with you soon for a lunch date on the Hill where I can take more time."

Carol stood. Marianne embraced her warmly. "Welcome, my friend. Call me. You have my number."

With that Carol watched Marianne scoop her purse from the table. It wasn't until Marianne was nearly to the door that Carol observed the generous payment she had left for both lunches.

Making a quick turn to smile goodbye, Marianne waved and was out through the doors before Carol could formulate a sentence.

Carol finished her tea trying to sort her feelings in the aftertaste as she watched gulls play the wind and land acrobatically, replacing one another jealously on the pier post in the marina.

Ch 38

November, 1974

Within a month their lives had changed and moved into new rhythms.

They had contracted with Doc and Marianne to rent long term and had signed a year's lease. Carol and Marianne had even talked about an option to buy, but, though inclined, Doc had not yet committed. He would soon.

Carol loved the house.

She had planted as she had hoped. With some of Matt's heavy lifting, she had planted in front of the backyard fence with a few azaleas. Neglected daisies were trimmed back and would bloom next season along the side fence, along with cosmos. On the tree side of the back she had trimmed a large lilac bush, and nearer the house, shaped the two lavender bushes. In her mind the back was no longer a yard. It was a garden.

A rhododendron bush now fronted the dining room window and would provide a dark red flower when it bloomed. She tended to each planting with motherly attention, but the rhodie was her favorite. The bush of expectation.

"I've heard," C told him as they were putting the rhodie into the earth, "that the Scots look on the rhodie as a useless bush since nothing grows beneath them. All the more for you and me." She sat on the edge of the porch, watching. Her straw sunhat threw a shadow across her face and chest.

He had finally gotten the ball of the plant around to the point where it settled into the hole he had dug. He twisted to make it sit down in the hole. Then he set to filling and packing beneath the plant, throwing dirt at odd angles and trying to tamp with his shovel. Tomorrow he would feel this in his back.

Matt had already stripped and repainted the front porch. A half dozen pots now lined the front perimeter, each with its own colorful geranium.

C had a job as a hostess at Black Angus in the afternoon and early evening. She was teaching two sections of Creative Writing at North Seattle Community College. She had been hired early enough to be included in the Winter Catalogue. She was proudly "official."

Matt had struck out at Seattle U and at the University of Washington. He had a nibble from Western Washington University in Bellingham, but he would have had to pass on that anyway. He was plenty busy with his part time job as well as taking care of the house. He was no longer sure he wanted to walk into a classroom.

He would find something.

He was able to walk everywhere else he needed to go. The tavern was about a mile from home. He would walk there and most times get dropped back home after closing. He worked only six hours a shift. Usual was four days a week. Business was usually modest to slow. So it was easy to punch the clock. A dry place out of the rain with a TV behind the bar. He spent most of the shift pouring, wiping down, washing up, leaning and listening to the music and sometimes to a customer or two. It paid the bills. For now that was enough. He didn't have to preach or pray. He was able to converse and call it good.

◆

With November came the rains. Every single day rain. All shapes and sizes rain. Rain in drizzle, rain in mist, rain in downpour, in showers, in partial showers, intermittent, steady, or light, or heavy rain, in deluge, in flooding, in monsoons. Gutters overflowing rain, storm drain backup rain, auto spraying puddled rain, city bus hissing rain. Gray clouds gave way to overcast, giving way to partial clearing which, when coupled with onshore flow, made for a heavy raining darkness and, for the duration, called for rain gear and boots.

Matt would still walk. He would walk to the avenue to shop according to the list C had left him. To work, to the library to renew or return, to the coffee shop, to the deli he would walk. He could navigate the neighborhood efficiently enough to do most everything on foot.

This time of year, walkers often looked like hooded monks trudging through the slog. Umbrellas rarely worked. This weather needed determination, conviction, personal dedication. And a wide brimmed hat with a draw string.

This kind of walking could set a person to singing show tunes or to pondering or to musing or observing. Matt did all of these on occasion.

On this overcast day, he had amused himself by thinking about his journeying. The christening, the launching, the dedicated voyage he had begun years before. People had politely applauded at his send off. They would not want to do it themselves, but more power to someone who did. Best wishes for the new beginning.

That suddenly had altered. It was silent when he had transferred to the smaller boat with Carol. No one in fact was there to see them off, but they had embarked with hopeful hearts to sail west.

And then the surprise highway attack from the crazyman. They had been lucky he had not sunk them altogether.

Matt still had not got to the bottom of all that. But it seemed over. In Carol's mind it was over. He needed to let it go.

And then there were the pirates who had crashed into their car had ended his joyous entry into Seattle. They might as well have thrown boulders to sink him altogether. They had started his descent, left him to work through the exposure he was facing. His fantasy had burst. Seattle was never going to be an Eden. But was it going to be home? What was it he was looking for when he said that word? Was there a way of melding the Matt who loved her and the Matt hidden, huddled beneath the surface?

He had not spoken of his fear, but that didn't lessen it.

He might as well have been left on a raft. Whittled down to the most meager of crafts, he was, he felt, in some essential way, by himself, trying to make his way.

Though, granted, she was at the prow, hopeful. He knew that he needed his own ability to see.

His walking kept him active, grounded, animated. At home "chores" as Carol called them, bent him over, made him weary. He tried to ignore the drudgery of the dusting, the mopping, the doing of dishes, the mowing, the making of the bed, the scouring of the shower, the washing, drying and folding of their clothes. The menial jobs from the seminary had groomed a strong work ethic for tasks such as these. In fact, with the radio on and a duster in hand and perhaps even an apron, he had discovered it could be great, even elegant fun when he had the entire stage to himself to sweep and turn and finally to take a deep bow.

He kept that to himself, however. Made him feel frivolous.

◆

On this day, he had stayed in to put a final polish on the kitchen. They had special guests coming. Larry and KT were coming by for dinner and to be with them in their new home. Matt had already begun preparing the soup, and Carol had left for the store to purchase bread and flowers and a bottle or two of wine.

Matt checked the glasses to rid them of any smudges from handling. He put a final polish on the plates and wiped the silver one last time. The utensils weren't the best, but they were clean.

Matt expected that Larry would pull him aside and inquire about his status. Matt had been in correspondence with the Provincial since he had written the formal letter requesting to be returned to the laity. Things were in the works. He was not responsible for the timing. Who knew when the Church would respond, but that was not really a deep concern. He knew who he was, and it was not a priest.

◆

Carol returned with the cut flowers for the table. She was damp from the walk across the back yard from the garage. That was something they would change if they could redesign anything, but the house had been built at the turn of the century, and garages were on alleys, not tucked into the living space of the home.

"Are we all set?" She kissed him.

"If we have bread and wine."

"On the drainboard."

He kissed her. "Lovely day, wouldn't you say?"

C was looking out the dining room window. "This weather can get to you if you pay attention. How many days has it poured?"

"Most of the month. This is the month of rain, when monks scurry and trudge."

"What?"

"Something I heard."

"Whatever. It's not the most uplifting."

"Agreed." He put down the dish towel. "What do you say I build a fire later?"

They'd had the dry wood from the garage piled next to the fireplace for aesthetic purposes almost since they had moved in.

"Do it. I'm glad I bought three bottles of wine. We can swing the sofa around when we want to sit at the fire. That'll be nice way to finish the evening, don't you think?"

"You know, I never thought I'd be a chef, a maître d and room designer, but here I am." He became W.C. Fields in the blink of an eye, the white towel over his arm: "How did you get so lucky, my little Chickadee?"

She gave him an odd look. She then kissed him and disappeared to hang up her coat.

The towel still perched over his forearm, Matt pulled the cork out of a bottle of red to let it breathe.

He shouted so she could hear how good his rendering of the comedian was: "It ain't what they call you; it's what you answer to."

Ch 39

Matt was fussing with the end of the meal when Carol came into the kitchen.

"Will you start the fire now? I'll take care of all this."

Larry and KT were seated separately. KT was on the sofa and Larry in the half round easy chair. Another chair was open for Matt, and Carol could sit on the couch.

"Wine for anybody?"

"No, but I reserve the right to change my mind." KT swirled her quarter glass and took a sip. "Little bro, you two have put together quite a home in such a short time. This is lovely. How lucky for you that Doc and Marianne had it available."

Matt snapped some of the kindling into smaller segments. "Exactly. We couldn't have been more fortunate. Carol designed a garden and planted all through the back. Did you see that?"

KT had; Larry had not.

"It'll be beautiful through the spring and summer if all goes as planned. The back room on this floor is for meditation or contemplation, whichever one happens, I guess." Matt sipped his wine before adding, "If sitting in a wicker chair, looking out onto beauty is praying."

"Why wouldn't it be?" asked Larry.

There was a moment's pause.

Larry, sensing something, changed the direction of things: "What's it been like to be back in Seattle?"

Matt finished twisting the paper for under the stack of wood pieces, "Good. I've enjoyed being back. When I was in Spokane, I could have been in Billings or in Wichita, or in Pittsburgh. I lived in a building, not in a community. Here, I'm living alongside a group of people working in the community, trying to do the same things we are. Or, that's the feel. We're neighbors, trying to make a go of it, as they say. I like that." He had finished setting the fire and had pushed back along the floor to lean against the sofa rather than use the chair. KT rubbed his head once, and all watched the fire.

"Who's up for coffee?" Carol had come to the arch between the living and dining rooms.

"I am," said Larry.

"So there are two of us." Carol disappeared through the archway.

Larry watched her go. "She's wonderful, Matt. You're a lucky man." KT sipped at her wine.

"I know. I've never had this kind of connection with another person. She's a dream and a . . "

"A dream and a . . . ? Go on. Ears are itching. Ears are itching." She had turned the corner into the last part of the conversation.

"A dream and an eavesdropper."

Carol brought Larry his coffee and crossed to sit in the single chair left open.

"You two can see what I have to put up with," she tried her coffee.

Larry rested his coffee on his lap. "So, it sounds like Matt is comfortable here. This part of the state is new to you, Carol. How do you like it.?"

"I love it. I'm teaching, and I have an evening job, and I love the neighborhood, and I don't know how we could be happier. Spokane is in the rearview mirror." She turned to Matt. "Matt, wouldn't you say that overall this has been a good move for us?"

He answered Larry. "I'm *not* teaching, but you know, I don't think I'm ready to be back in the classroom right now. If it happens, it'll happen, but right now I think I'm doing well to get my feet wet with things that others learn when they're in their twenties. Things our training ignored. Life skill types of things. I'm way behind."

"What do you mean?", asked Larry.

"If I needed my room painted, I asked, and it got done. If I needed to fly to Omaha, I didn't have to save for the ticket. If I needed to drive to Ritzville, I climbed into some car or other – there was always one available – a car that someone else had serviced. I didn't have to make many decisions at all.

"I need to make a million more decisions about how to live my life and how to get things done. What to fix for dinner, what style phone do we want, what's the best use of my time, how can I get all my errands done without a car? I never had to deal with any of that before."

Larry spoke up. "Because of the small community I live in, I have much more latitude. I have to make decisions about where we live and how to shop and stay on budget for the house. My life is more normal than yours was."

Matt toasted him. "'Abnormal' was more the word for mine. I'm now needing to learn how to . . . how to work with responsibilities for my own life.

"My biggest change is interpersonal. I'm needing to learn how to be open rather than just disappearing into the communal TV room. Or better yet, I don't do what I used to and just close my door like all the others in the hallway and then take out a book.

"Now I have to work to be open to conversation. I could hide away from that before. Thank god for C's patience with me. She's seeing me through."

Carol slid her foot encouragingly under Matt's butt.

KT put her hand on Matt's shoulder. "It's a major lifestyle change for you. Besides, we're always learning. All of us." Then she glanced Larry's direction. "With the exception of Larry, of course."

Larry toasted her, smiling.

They had talked at some length after that. Matt offering more wine, Larry told about his new assignment in Seattle doing similar retreat work to what he had done in Portland. KT told of how she wasn't doing anything special and then proceeded to list a half dozen things she was doing regularly to assist people. Though it was never said, there was something about Larry's new placement that had seemed to change her situation in Portland. Something she may still be working through.

Carol told about her class and the students who were enthused with some of the projects she was giving them. Both Larry and KT seemed very interested in what projects she had for the students and for herself. She told them about something Matt had never heard.

"I'm considering working up a play on what it means to come home. Don't have a lot of particulars yet, but somehow the project seems to be calling. It's a lot of what our lives have been involved with in the last year. . . And will be for a while."

"May always be," said Larry. "Great project. I want to know where that goes. I have lots of folks for whom that would be a strong, meaningful image."

KT yawned in spite of herself. Carol finished the last bit of her wine. "Well, we've outlasted the fire. That must be a good sign. KT, let me show you up to your very own room. Matt already took your bag up." As Carol took KT to the stairs, Matt started collecting the coffee cups and wine glasses. He waved a wine glass at Larry, "C'mon."

As they headed to the kitchen, Matt turned to Larry, "I'm glad you're going to be here in Seattle. Maybe I can help with some of what you're doing. I don't have much time, but I have a little. Could be a nice connection for you and me. Let me know if I can help."

"I will. There could be something there. I'll check with my team and see." He put his glass into the washer. Matt sensed an odd distance. Something new. A sense that his offer was never going anywhere.

"Just so you know, you are one lucky guy. You two seem great together. You don't need me to tell you this, but I wanted you to know what I think."

"Good to know, Larry. Thanks."

"God, you're right. You do have a lot to learn." Larry pulled out all the silver Matt had put into the washer. "You never put the silver in all clumped together. Didn't anybody ever teach you?"

◆

Matt gave a final wave to Larry's car as it pulled away from the curb. He came in and began closing down the blinds; he turned off the far lamp. In the residual light, he sat to watch the embers of the fire.

C had come up behind, and she rested her hands on his shoulders.

"KT is happy to be staying over. We had a nice chat; I like her." She crossed down to sit with Matt. She was silent for a while. She rubbed her hand along Matt's leg. "Do you ever miss church and all?"

"Not really."

"Not any of it?"

"You know, we had all the elements of church right here tonight minus the vestments, and I didn't have to preach." She looked at him quizzically. He added, "A meal, our community, and sharing. Natural church. Church without the stained glass."

She snuggled into him. "I'm glad we have our home. " He helped her lie across his lap, and he stroked her arm.

They sat like this for some time, silently. "Fires take time to die down, don't they", she mused.

"Everything does. Wants a chance to rekindle. Will burn every last cinder. Even when it seems out, it's still burning . . . Another first, you know: a fire in our fireplace."

"And your sister staying over. And folks in for a meal. It was nice to meet Larry."

They watched the fire begin to smolder.

"I couldn't be happier, Matt."

He rubbed her arm.

They watched, each thinking about what it meant to be in their new home.

◆

Upstairs, they climbed into cold sheets. The chill drew a vocalized shudder and a scurry to snuggle.

"Do you think they've slept together?" she mused after some moments.

"I hadn't really thought about it." He took a moment. He felt odd that he had not told her already. "I guess I would say, 'likely'. Not recently though."

"I think they've been lovers." She was silent a long while. "I admire how they're living now, then."

Something prompted him. "Would you do that?"

"If I were her? . . . I think I would always love, no matter what. I think my body would cherish its memories, and my spirit would always have a wound. But I would love. As long as I had my life." She grew quiet.

"I think that's what love is."

He pulled her even closer to him, spooning her. As if she was his very self, he held on.

◆

He had returned along the dusty road. He had watched his sandals land and lift repeatedly.

No one had recognized him on the streets even though this had been his home for so many years. The years and all his adventures must have changed him, or people grew away from the expectation of seeing him. Everything changes.

Expectations must as well.

246

The veil of mist began subtly at the base of the path and insinuated itself and then built, winding with every turn. It was now everywhere. Beyond it was only a suggestion that memory might fill; eye could not see.

And memory was frail. What was beyond the path, he only thought he knew. As the path climbed, he grew more chilled, and so he shifted and pulled to tighten his clothing. He wrapped a scarf over his head and across his mouth and nose. No one would know him now if they had seen him in the mist.

The path left him standing before the castle which was enormous seeming to his eye. Thick growth had attached itself to every crevice. In the dark, the castle loomed. The deep green brooded in the night glistening leaves. The window cuts showed no evidence of the castle he sought: no light, no laughter, no clatter of dishes or scraping of furniture moved. No rustle of human passage. No call or whinny of activity from the courtyard. The secrets of leaves only. It was a secret he did not know, seemingly could never know. The leaves would not disclose the hidden door he knew was there. Only upon working his arm through the branches and pushing with all his body and with his fingers prying as far as possible into the workings of the growth could he know. He soaked himself with the dampness of the leaves as he reached arduoulsy into them. Numbing his reach and deadening his grasp, he touched the door but with no hope of opening it.

They, if there was a "they," were locked in. He, if that was him, was locked out.

A cadaverous fear rose.

He was gone. Missing. On the way to being forgotten. His castle had forgotten to keep room for him. His former home now hid behind a welter of winding leaves.

A shock of laughter burst from somewhere behind the dark vines. There was life here. In some dark space made light where people had gathered around a table perhaps. With favorite stories perhaps.

The laughter left him more aware of his darkness and the mist in which he stood alone.

Disconnected.

All other travelers were home. He would never catch up to them. To himself. He felt as if he would never be intact. Home. Nothing belonged to him that had been his. Nothing. Who he had been. What he had had. Nothing.

The struggle to get home, the joy at the prospect evaporated. Not only had the residence forgotten, it seemed that he had moved into a new place where the hand that would knock, the voice that would call out, the name that would be called into the night had all vaporized into the damp fog.

Oblivion. Imminent oblivion. It must be what the dead experience if the dead experience.

Cadaverous fear.

Ch 40

Carol stood before the meditation room window. Her flannel "guest in the house" nightgown and lined slippers were not quite enough to keep her warm, so she retrieved the afghan she kept on the chair in the study.

Looking out the meditation window into the dark, she kept all the lights off save for the backdoor light that spilled over the pavers leading to the gate. To look at the garden she and Matt had planted was to look into the future. Her hope would be the sprouting, the blossoming, the bloom, the release of beauty all season long. She needed to hold that in the darkness, in the rain, and on the edge of winter.

Beauty leads on.

She sat in the rattan chair and pondered the shadows of her yard.

She remembered that before her father had left, she had received, one Christmas, a bike, a used Schwinn with white wall tires. She had sneaked out of bed and come downstairs, past her parents' room and through the door to the basement. She had been able to turn on the light and had sat in her pj's contemplating the burnished blue against the bright chrome handlebars of the Schwinn. It had a new seat and a basket, and her mother had picked up two cut plastic streamers, each of which fit into the black rubber handle grips. The horse of her dreams had become a bike to take her wherever she could pedal. She could now go to the library, past the old City Hall, over to Stephenville City Park, or past Tarleton State, and, if she was feeling strong, out to the high school and back. This bike, resting against the dirty cement basement wall, was her ride to freedom. A new door had opened in her life.

She remembered the feeling of anticipation, of expectation, of potential, and like the streamers, of freedom. She would wear her hair loose sometimes just for that reason when she rode. She would stand on her pedals and coast, streamers flying.

She could go anywhere in the town. She could do runs to the store for something forgotten; she could return her books on time instead of waiting on her mother; she could ride to City Park and swing or just lie on the grass if she wanted. Her yellow, dusty yard had become expansive. Her daily plans had too. She was growing up. Moving beyond borders.

And this backyard garden, small as it was, would take her away from any confines. Would let her stand at the window on a rainy day and sip her tea, watching the flowers bob their heads and drink in the rain. She had a window of hope.

She no longer needed to watch from behind anything. No longer needed to hide.

She was standing on her pedals. Her hand freed her hair from the afghan. Hope was in the air.

She was moving ahead in her life. She and Matt together had planted. She and Matt together could enjoy the tiny yard and all the widening expanse it gave to their thoughts. Always widening. She loved that.

She might save for a fountain in the yard. That would fit in perfectly.

Had she felt free to, as a girl, she would have sat all night on that basement stair. But she had needed to creep back to bed.

But now, Carol nodded into sleep, and only in the first light did she hear movement on the stairs and rise, her afghan still around her, and go to the kitchen to start the day.

Ch 41

KT had her coffee and was at the dining table when Matt came downstairs. "Carol's at the store, sleepy head. Good morning."

He had gone straight to the kitchen and was pouring his own cup of coffee.

"Did you sleep OK?" he asked. "We've never had anyone in that bed before."

"Slept wonderfully. Cold outside, comfy inside. A nice meal in the belly and a few glasses of wine. How could you have directed it any better?"

"Glad you were our first guest. Something right about that."

"Same here."

"What would you like to do today?"

"I have a few Seattle things to shop for, but I can do that even after I leave here. I don't have to waste our visit time. It's only a couple hours to home. I'd just like to avoid rush hour in Portland."

He crossed to look out the rhodie window, coffee in hand. "Looks like anything could happen. Could pour, could just brood. Who knows?"

"Much like Portland. Makes monks of us all." He turned and looked at her. He let it go.

Matt held his coffee close. "Want to walk? We could walk around the lake or on the waterfront. We have an extra jacket if you need."

"I'm always ready for weather. I have clothes in the trunk of the car. We might want to see if Carol has plans. But in general, I vote for the lake."

◆

Green Lake was always busy. Walkers, joggers, bikers, talkers, story tellers, listeners, laughers, meditators, grinders, frowners, gawkers, showoffs, dog walkers. Dancers with music in their ears, runners in training, trout fishermen on their way to a break in the reeds, roller skaters, people pushing a pace in secret races with someone and then with another. People dressed in sweats, people in shorts and singlets, people bundled in jackets zipped, people in tees and workout pants. People with new exercise togs; folks in clothes from the hall closet.

A carousel of journeyers. A microcosm of travelers. A world in motion. Everyone on the move.

◆

The threesome started by the wading pool on the north side. This time of year, it was dry; but during the summer, mothers and children dipped and submerged, laughed and spluttered here. And at the hub of it all, the spraying fountain. The airborne water would just skyward, then fall into a spray, dousing the ecstatic youngsters, knee deep and waiting to scream in delight. The tumult of screams and young joy centered there. In the summer, the excitement could have told a blind man where to take off his shoes to cool his feet.

Carol mused for a moment. "I imagine that in summer this is as glorious as life itself with the sun and silver spray. And the children. And right next to the lake they will swim in when they are bigger. Like life itself. Keeps stretchin' out. Getting bigger."

KT had spent many a summer day there. "Exactly . . . " She took some time. "Today it reminds me of my clients. The water is turned off. They're dry. They know there should be something more than what they're experiencing."

Matt peered. The entire pool was silent and gray. He saw the old blemishes, the black tar repairs snaking at odd angles along the cracks in the gray cement. Some of them would have to be redone before water filled it once again.

He remembered being at this place as a kid. Hanging at the edge, reluctant to mix into the melee. His mother had patiently sat at the edge, her feet in the pool, urging him to join his sister in the freedom of the spray.

He remembered the discomfort he had felt and the later scene he had created when they took him for swimming lessons at the lake. He had cried and stood frozen, up to his suit on the cement stairs while the others had already begun to swing their arms in a vague swimming motion just like the instructor.

His father had yanked him from the steps, and his mother had sat him on the blanket with his towel.

Matt had nothing to say.

They moved to the path that circled the lake.

Carol and KT kept a pace with Matt listening in.

"Your play interests me, Carol. What are you thinking about? I mean 'home' is a broad topic."

"Maybe how it keeps in, and it keeps out. It holds what belongs; it bars what doesn't. It contains and rejects. Mine isn't yours. So, it's almost like each person." She walked some. "So, I want to look at what it is in essence as well as in metaphor."

"What do you mean?" KT leaned in to hear Carol's answer as two bike riders passed dangerously close.

"We have lots of meanings for home. Home is the place where a person can be and is expected to be themselves. No need to perform for anyone. No judgement. Mine wasn't like that, but I think it should've been."

"Most of our homes were probably not perfect. I know ours wasn't." KT glanced at Matt, checking for agreement.

She spoke to C. "When you grew up, did your mom and dad support you and give you your sense of confidence in yourself? You're a very confident person."

"In a backhanded way . . . And thank you . . . What I mean is I suppose they gave me a sense of confidence because they did very little to give me confidence, and so I was left on my own to find my own way."

KT, nearest the bike lane, looked back for upcoming bikers before she spoke: "So, in your play, what would be some of the marks of home or coming home?"

"Part of me thinks of it as a place. A place of freedom. A place where one lives in the truth of both gift and deficit. No hiding. Light, harsh light: no imposters, no shadow. It's a place of truth: both good and bad. I'm a frump; I'm a princess. Zits and curlers; mascara and prom dress. All of it.

"Honesty. I agree with you. No pretense, no fakery."

"That's the exterior place we call home." Carol stopped, waiting for Matt who had fallen off pace. "But the real home is inside us."

As he neared, the women began walking immediately.

"Really, the word seems a metaphor for being human. We are who we are, and we need to find a way to live with ourselves." They walked a bit. "And then also with the others who are there with us . . . and that can be painful sometimes."

KT waited a moment and then posed the question as they walked. "So, is it even a place, a destination?"

Carol kicked a larger stone off the cinder path. "Recently, I'm thinking home, as aspiration, is a state of becoming. Movement, being rather than residence." She walked some.

"Our journey. The growing into ourselves. Avoiding nothing."

KT was with her. "And arriving?"

"Maybe. Maybe for a while. But maybe always on the move. Not settling in or getting there. More like growing. The constancy of the change. I like that. The constancy of the change. If I say it enough, I remember it."

Carol moved into a silence while the other two walked with her.

KT had a thought ready after they had been passed by the joggers who had been creeping up on them. "When I come home, I relax into being at home. Being whole. For me, it's a place where I'm most honestly and fully myself. No pressure to be anything else."

Carol chewed on that briefly. "Maybe the word is even a synonym for the essence of our life itself. There's a beauty in that truth, if so. Being. Our home is us being truly us. Us, becoming our honest best."

KT added excitedly, "So, coming home is being who we are without excuse or reservation."

"That's good." She turned to look at KT. "This has been a help." Carol started to laugh at the insight.

"What?" KT asked.

"So now I just need to shape that into a play. Should be no problem." They both laughed.

"At least you have a focus to look at. That's a great start."

They continued to weave among the walkers and runners and riders, and their conversation became more topical to the lake and its denizens. Matt had his history of fishing the lake and taking swim lessons here and being afflicted with "Green Lake itch" as a child. This narration seemed to make him more comfortable.

They had circled the lake and were back to where KT had parked.

Matt jumped in: "If we cut through here, we can get a coffee. Anyone interested?"

The dark, entangled castle from his dream kept haunting Matt.

Cadaverous fear.

He had been anxious to turn the conversation to something lighter. Thank goodness that had worked.

He ordered a coffee while the two women preferred tea.

C pushed the creamer to KT. "With Larry up here now, will you be able to help out with the family retreats anymore?"

"I don't know where that's going to go. That's fine. I know that Larry wants me to do that, but I have to see what that looks like. I have lots of Portland commitments. Things get complicated. So, we'll see."

"I like that. The 'we'll see'. Someday I want to come visit you at your house, if that's not too forward."

"Not at all. Love to have you. We'll keep connected I suspect."

Matt had fallen quiet, measuring out the cream with his coffee spoon. His hand was unexpectedly trembling. He spilled onto the table top and looked up.

He smiled: "That'll be good."

Ch 42

KT turned away from the dining room window. "I had better hit the road. It looks ominous, like a month of rain is ready to level us. Wish me luck that I can get out of town before it cuts loose."

They waved good bye to KT from the porch. The air was changing. Carol walked the line of planters, pulling any weeds she found. Matt went inside.

As if he was drawn, he walked to the meditation room and sat in the wicker chair overlooking the back yard. A wicked headache felt like it had punctured his forehead. It had settled in his eye.

He heard Carol come in and shut the front door.

"I'm going to write for a while, so I'll be in the study." And she was gone. Her door closed.

◆

Sissy,

Sorry that it has been a while since I wrote. Today I have a sense of family in my heart, and it feels like time to catch you up on our lives in the Pacific Northwest.

Of course, I hope also that you are well, still loving your work and finding the Bay area exciting. Let me know if any of that is not true. Promise?

I am well. I love Seattle, and my work is showing some promise. You know me well enough to know that my being a writer is always about teetering off this idea to leap to that one, to catch my balance before jumping to the midstream boulder while the river courses by. I'm always about to get good and soaked if I misstep.

My writing is a challenge these days. We're up to so much. Moving in, welcoming friends, trying to find incomes that support our home and our lives together. All these things distract if I'm not careful.

But they also prompt.

They remind me of the searches that I'm in the midst of: the search to anchor myself in a community, to be useful within that community as a teacher, to learn to become a good partner to Matt who sometimes struggles with the newness of his life. I know that must sound odd, and I'll try to explain at some point, or I will have recognized that it was a phase and drop it out of my concerns altogether.

I think we have discovered a foundation in one another that's going to allow us to be happy here. Our house is nice; in fact, we couldn't ask for better, given our meager finances. We have friends here. I've met a few teachers who I would like to invite into my life. Matt's life is more restricted than that, but that's temporary. He'll find something soon that lets him expand his talents whether it's for directing or teaching again or working with social programs or whatever. He just needs time. He's way too talented to be undiscovered for long.

We can thrive here. And we have even been able to make this place our own by planting and decorating because the owners are friends of Matt's from his childhood and have done everything they could to help us feel at home.

That's what's true. We feel at home.

The concept is on my mind these days, and I will write more about it when I write again. For now, I'm feeling it. At some later point I'll try to talk about it. I know you look forward to that. "O", I can hear you saying, "the joy of having a sibling who writes about ideas for a living."

My joy is having you as my one and only link to our wind blown past, to the faded house and the brown back yard in Stephenville, to my earliest years, to our shared clothes, our talks whispered in the dark of our little pink bedroom, to the secrets we kept and the things we knew before mom had any idea. And the games we played together, needing nothing but a single Barbie and a cardboard box for her house. Remember?

I love having you as my sis. Be well. Know that I'm thriving two states north of you. But thought and love and concern ignore those boundaries. Hope to see you in our home one of these days.

PS. (You will love Matt. I do.)

Carol.

She took the small bud vase from the top of the desk. She lifted it to the light. She thought she would give that to Matt and tell him he was her flower, her most lovely possession.

◆

In the meditation room, Matt sat in the rattan chair. He tried with his eyes open. He tried with his eyes closed.

Matt had never felt like he was feeling. Every breath seemed to struggle to go deep without any of the satisfaction, his entire chest lifting and emptying, his chin lifting to allow his chest room, his entire face seeming to open to intake as much air as possible. As if every facet of his face was grasping after breath. It was as if he was experiencing a lift off, and yet a gravitational drag as he was trying to fly out of his body. He felt pushed down and pulled up and helplessly out of breath. He felt a deeply breathless panic.

His castle dream was melting any resolve. Home. The dream reconstituted itself as he sat before the wide window. He was at the castle entry, but as close as he was, he was excluded. What should be his dwelling, his home, seemed as distant as the fact that the yard was hers, the plantings were hers. He resented none of that. He loved the joy it brought her, the brightness his exertions at planting had brought to her cheek.

But his eye was dark. His cheek cool. The city, the neighborhood even that which he had known as home was not really home any longer. This house was not; the garden was not. He had not returned to a place of nurturance. The dark dream was very clear about that. He was not home; he was banished somehow and forgotten.

Laughter was for those inside with the light.

The feeling was clear: he had returned but he was not home. He had felt the image before: a discarded piece of gray plastic wrapping — tossed up weightlessly and blown away. Tossed. Blown away. Gone up into a night or, like this very minute, up into a thunderhead darkness that loomed, pressing spirits down before the release of a hard slanting rainfall.

And then the blockage released; the plug gave way. He wept without any recourse. He wept helplessly in the wicker in front of the window that looked out onto her peaceful garden.

Unseen, a gull cried somewhere nearby.

The dark sky was Matt's only witness.

Ch 43

By the time Carol came out of her study, Matt had packed a small bag and left the house. She found his note propped on the dining room table.

C,

I love you.

I need to go away for a bit. I am not right, and I want to be. I want to be fully there for you. You deserve every bit of my best self.

Give me some time to put this all together. I will be back, if you'll have me.

It's you I love.

Matt.

Carol folded the note in half and then in half again. She pushed it from her to the center of the table. She could feel herself preparing to respond, but she had no idea how it would be. Outside their window the leaves of the dark green rhodie repeatedly ducked in the punishment from the heavy rain. She watched it and rose to go to the kitchen.

It wasn't until the water began to boil in the teapot and she had taken her favorite cup from the cupboard to the countertop that she felt the quaking take over.

"God damn you!" Feral, she could not have growled with more intense anger.

She looked at the bud vase sitting innocently on the countertop. It took her breath.

She grabbed for her cup and viciously threw it, smashing it against the far wall of the kitchen.

"God damn you, Matt Turner!

She could go no farther; crumpling, she slid down the face of the lower cupboard doors and shook. As if thrown or knocked to the cold kitchen floor, she began to weep in hot, angry sobs.

Ch 44

Work had been slow.

Or he had been slow.

He wasn't really there. He found himself wiping tables he had cleaned earlier, then adjusting the condiments with unneeded precision. Had he been a smoker, he would have stood outside in the front door alcove or in the dark recess behind the building, having his smoke and watching the rain destroy the sheen on the puddles. But he was not a smoker. And he had nowhere else to be. He was still damp from the walk to work. He would have to play this out.

◆

Finally: Closing time. His energy rose as he began his routine. At last customers headed out. At last Chuck, the cook, finished his kitchen clean up.

"Need a lift?" Chuck had slid onto one of the stools.

"I'm fine. The rain's stopped. I'll finish up here and walk. I feel like I need the exercise; the night was so slow. Be good to stretch the legs."

"I know what you mean." Chuck got off the stool. "Tomorrow, then." And he was out the door.

Matt locked it and shut the place down.

◆

In the silence the shadows deepened. As Matt pulled the till from the register, he glanced toward the windows and a sense of movement. Someone who had missed last call, no doubt. It happens.

The front door rattled twice, impatiently tried. The figure put both hands up trying to see into the room. Finally, aware that he was locked out, he turned toward the street, apparently surveying his choices. His wide brimmed leather hat hung over his upturned collar.

Matt moved to the door. He had forgotten. He pulled the blind. He turned off the neon. That was an error he would not make again soon.

◆

In the back room he tallied the day's receipts and the cash drawer and spun the safe's lock to end his day of work. But unlike other days, he did not leave and begin the mile walk home.

He sat in the broken leather chair in the corner of the backroom. And fearing that he might be discovered, he turned out the light and settled in as well as he could.

When you don't belong where you are, the darkness is full of threats.

◆

She would have found his note by now. She had not called. She would not show up.

Throughout the shift part of him had been waiting for her to appear at the door, beaten up by the rain that had pummeled her on her angry walk here or her angry walk from the parking lot in the back. Or maybe she would not be angry. Just hurt. The daisy coronet rose to his mind.

What had he done?

Here he was. No longer a leader, a teacher. He was now a wiper, a sweeper, a tapster. A hider.

He tried to sleep, but in the backroom of the tavern, he heard sounds he had never heard with the lights on. It may have been that there were mice. It may have been the building breathing or settling: it was whatever goes on anyway, but in the light is never heard. He stayed awake listening. And wondering.

What had he done wrong? He had followed his heart, hadn't he? He was with a woman who loved him. The woman who had saved him from his former life. He only knew that where she saw joy, he saw panic. Where Larry and KT saw promise, he saw fear. What was he missing? Why was he so blind? Or was it why was he so afraid?

The room grew chill with the hours. He wasn't sure this plan was going to work. He wanted to be next to C, to be warm against her body, to be free of the demons that kept at him whenever he got close to sleep.

◆

He woke with a start in the morning. The sound of the newspaper pushed through the mail slot and slapping onto the floor woke him.

He had passed the night. Never had night been so long and so unsettling. But he had passed the night.

◆

For a week he slept sitting in the backroom of the tavern. He had taken extra closing shifts. He had let the cook know each evening that he had a ride coming by. The cook no longer even asked about giving him a ride home. On any off days Matt booked a motel room and took a shower and watched bad TV and dozed. On the days he was working, he was back to his old routine.

Matt would be out early in the morning, locking up behind him. He had stuffed his bag onto the back of the top shelf. No one else in the place could reach up there.

He sometimes had caught the bus to the U District; sometimes he had wandered downtown. He had walked from the U District up, past his old high school and past St. Mark's and onto Capitol Hill.

He was never sure what he was looking for on these day trips. He just knew that he didn't have a place to go, nowhere to be. He walked along, knowing the places as part of his history and knowing that the places no longer knew him. He was another person walking the streets, headed somewhere. He felt as he looked: lost.

He had chosen to embrace the combustion that had shaken him so, to find out what it was made from and to dismantle the source piece by piece if he was able. If nothing else, he would no longer be split apart.

He had heard from Meese, in a letter delivered to the tavern. He had not answered. Now was not the time.

◆

It happened toward the end of his shift on a Thursday that he turned to serve the new person beyond the register. It was usual to hope that anyone who came in this late would be gone quickly so closing would not be delayed. He wiped the bar on his way, and moving past the register, saw that it was Marianne. He looked away and back.

"Just water, Matt."

He drew her a water glass and wiped the bar by habit as he put it in front of her.

"Here. This is for you. Doc got it a couple days ago. The open envelope was for his note. The sealed one inside is yours."

Matt put the envelope in his back pocket as he continued to wipe at the bar. Marianne watched him with intent curiosity.

"Matt, where are you staying? C called KT, and KT let me know you two were split. Where are you staying? KT is very worried about you."

"Nights, I've been here."

"Matt, I'm going to stay in my car outside till after you close. Come with me after you lock up. Get the hell out of here."

"I'm OK here."

"You're fucking kidding yourself. You're not OK here. This is your job, not your home. My car is the white sedan right in front."

"Where would we go?"

"I have a place for you to stay. You need a base, Matt. Not a . . . whatever. Are you sleeping, what, in the backroom?" She could tell that she had hit it. "Whatever is happening you need to treat yourself better than spending half your time in a tavern backroom. Respect yourself."

The two dart players finished their beers and put jackets on. "G'nite, Matt."

"Night, you two." He crossed from behind the bar to pick up the glasses. Only Phil at the end of the bar and Marianne were left. Matt started his routine by collecting dirty ashtrays, dumping them, and cleaning the filth from the glass. He then put up all the chairs and went into the women's bathroom. No one had used it all night, so he simply looked and went back out. The men's room required a sweep out and a sink cleaning. He replaced the paper in there. As he emerged from the men's, Phil was nearly at the door.

"G'nite, Matt."

"Phil."

"Can I help?" Marianne asked.

"It'll be quicker if I do it all. I have a system."

"Am I OK or in the way?"

"You're OK."

Ch 45

They didn't talk much. He had asked where they were headed; she had told him to relax and come with her.

Once they began to drive, his mind eliminated destinations.

She had come up Capitol Hill

She pulled over at Harvard St.

"This apartment is used only for emergencies. Dad lives in Mukilteo, and I live in Edmonds. If we get caught really late at the office, we come here. It's only two blocks away. But no one uses it this time of year. So it's sitting empty . . ." She had turned off the engine, and they sat in the darkness. "Why have you been trying to sleep in a tavern and walking the streets during the day, hiding like a convict?"

He said nothing.

"Am I wrong?"

He shook his head.

"You need to be somewhere." She gathered her purse and opened the car door. "Here it is. Follow me."

◆

They got to the third floor. The hall had a red carpet down the middle. He could see only four doors on this side of the third floor. The walls were plaster painted a light green. Each of the doors was polished dark hardwood.

"We're on the corner. It's quiet. Only one person adjoins, and she's a deaf, gray haired lady with a cat. She's nearly a figment of everyone's imagination she's seen so rarely."

Marianne opened the door into a lovely apartment with hard wood floors, coved plaster walls and windows on both sides of the corner. The bedroom was to one side, and the kitchen was to the other. The front room was nicely furnished.

"I can't stay here."

"I'm not asking you." She took his hand and placed the keys in them. "The office pays the rent for this as part of doing business in a busy part of a busy city.

"Two blocks from here is shopping, Fred Meyer, a bike shop, a café, a realty office, two, maybe three fast food places depending. A Baskin Robbins. What more could you want in a loaner?"

He had wandered over to look out the window and down to the street below. She continued, "It's pretty quiet. Two blocks over is where the action is.

"By the by, if you're willing to put in the mileage, there are at last four bars within an easy walk of here. I would think that if your hours are flexible, you might be able to land a job on the hill.

"There might even be something in our office. We're in need of an office staff person at the moment. Don't know if you might be interested in that. If you are, drop by and give your name to "Harps", Peggy Harper. Tell her I recommended that you come by. A word of warning, you may have to work for her, and she can be a tough bird. Think on that.

"There are nice people to have lunch with in that office, so I've heard." She smiled.

He had wandered into the kitchen and was looking over the round oak table in the corner as if he was considering to buy.

"If nothing else works out, you are on the bus line, and forty-five to sixty minutes will get you to where you're working now.

"Marianne, I don't think . . . " She interrupted.

"I didn't ask. Matt, understand something. People love you. They understand that you need some time. They don't think that you should be punished, let alone be punishing yourself.

"You're the only one who sees a mark on your forehead.

"So put your bag in the bedroom, put the keys on the dresser, and relax. This is yours, no problem."

He just looked at her.

She took his hand. She kissed it and looked him in the eye. "Let it be."

And then she crossed to the door. "And now I'm on my way." She turned back and winked with a warm smile. Welcome to your new domicile." She swept both arms in a grand gesture.

"Are you driving home now?"

"Yes, I am. There's a reason this didn't happen last night, my friend. I had work today; I have tomorrow, I mean today, off. I'm a planner; saves a lot of suffering."

He crossed to her and opened his arms. "Thank you."

She inserted herself and hugged him. She looked at him, a long count. "Don't lose the keys. I don't know if there is a second set." She moved toward the door. "I'll see you from time to time. Sleep well."

And she was gone.

He watched out the window as occasional late night traffic passed below. He saw her reach where she had parked. She did not look up, but opening her door, she held up her hand and waved.

Ch 46

As he sat on the couch, he opened the envelope she had given him. Inside was a meek, single sheet of lined paper too narrow for the wide envelope and folded multiple times to become even smaller. The letter seemed to want to disappear.

Son,

I am writing to both you and your sister. I am sending this to Dr. Triton at his business since I am not sure where my children are. My fault.

I'm coming to the West Coast soon, and I'd like to see you.

I have to admit, that sentence makes me shaky. You may not want to see me. But I need to push through, or things will never change for me. I need to make some amends.

You can help me.

I'll be asking you to forgive me for all I did to you as you were growing up. I was not a real father to you, and I need you to forgive me. I am so sorry.

I understand if you don't want to see me. But that is a risk I need to take. I'm trying to be better. To grow up.

If you can leave word with Dr. Triton, I'll come to you or not, the way you wish. I don't deserve no more than that. I deserve less. I really deserve nothing at all from you. You probably have little desire to see me. But you see, I am trying to get rid of the person I used to be when I was with the family. Like a snake does with its skin.

Even that's wrong. I don't want to be a snake anymore.

There are so many things I regret. Most of them involve you and your sister. Mostly you.

I'm so sorry.

It was unsigned.

Matt folded the note and returned it to the envelope.

◆

Matt felt suddenly weak and lightheaded. He needed something to eat.

There was nothing in the refrigerator, and the cupboards had only a small selection of canned soup and canned vegetables and boxes of cereal. There was certainly nothing that was going to erase his hunger.

He turned out the kitchen light.

He sat on the couch in the near dark. A single streetlight shone outside. He remembered the sound of the bottle hitting the radiator and the window, the ugly tire marks on the parking strip. Matt remembered the hidings he had received, red stripes that hurt for four days and the cold eye his father gave when he pulled the belt from his pants. The two of them had never been close. He remembered how his father stood at the ready when it was time for a whipping.

Matt knew he was trapped. He had to respond.

Now he was being asked to make room for this monster. He was being asked to look at things differently.

He was not going to answer right away. He was going to take his time. After all, he had his own troubles at the moment, and this just compounded things.

He didn't need this.

He spun the note onto the coffee table and put his feet up to sit in the dark.

Thoughts morphed into almost sleep and then back again as he sat in the dark. Things forgotten became things remembered. How he maneuvered always to be last into the family car. How his father had watched him in the rearview mirror. He saw the eyes.

◆

It was going to take some time.

It didn't need to be settled right away. After all, it had taken years for the letter to be written.

He frowned at the envelope on the coffee table as if it were the man himself.

Passing through the front room, he turned off the front hall light and entered the bedroom. A double bed, a dresser, a small closet with a topcoat and some rain boots. An umbrella leaned against the inside wall. The bathroom was in black and white tile with a pedestal sink. It had a shower.

He turned on the lamp at the bedside table and turned off the overhead. He felt odd, like he was an intruder and should sleep on top of the bedspread, but he turned down the bed and after undressing, slid into the clean sheets.

He drifted. The note had knocked him off the vague course he had. He didn't remember his father to have the kind of face that could speak the words of the note.

His father had rarely spoken to him. He had glared and given head nods and finger wags. He had bared his teeth and made ugly exasperated sounds.

They had never talked.

Matt couldn't even picture the face that owned the words of this note. He had no memory malleable enough to imagine it.

His father had been stone.

He remembered anger. The eye. He remembered his own resolve that needed to be found for him to survive beyond the monstrous beatings.

Did people change from primal to civil?

Could his father have made such a change? And why should Matt bring him back into his life?

He settled into a steady breath. Where would all this take him? Where would he wash ashore this time?

The night was full of sound he had never heard. The passing traffic. Somewhere a shout in the street. Loud conversation as a bar emptied. The slam of a car door. Another.

It seemed as he was afloat watching the night clouds shape and reshape his world. He was not afraid. He was alert. Alone. Alive. Headed into ever more darkness. Probably in a slow spin. He couldn't tell.

Derelict? Was that it?

The morning light woke him. He was disoriented but soon recalled where he was and what had happened. He lay in the bed with a sense that the chair in the backroom of the tavern had never given.

It led him to sit on the edge of the bed. This had brought him to prayer so often. Today it took him to his breath. Was he at the start of something? Or the end?

Was there even a difference?

He could see the warm colors of the morning in the far room.

But there was another feeling. He was encased. He sat on the edge of two worlds. He could be alive, his arms free, his legs, his heart, his breath, his soul. Or he could sit. In membrane. Unborn.

He could feel the need for a choice, like a tidal rise, finding its time.

There was no more hiding, no more running away. The issue was in his feet. He needed to choose.

He stepped into the living room. And he stood in a ray of filtered morning light. As he looked down it seemed as though a spotlight had found him in the prison yard.

He stood in the middle trying to catch up to himself.

Breathing.

At the moment it was all he had.

Ch 47

Finally, a day just to catch her breath.

She stood at her window looking out at the Sound.

Nothing more to do than observe and be.

She retreated to her couch.

Marianne loved her home. She had kept her eye open a long time watching for it. Brick. Two story. Newer. Hillside Edmonds with a view of the Sound and the ferries crossing. On a summer afternoon it was nearly hypnotizing to watch from, with the sunsheen on the water, the ferries working toward or from Kingston, an unfolding of clouds hanging in a drift across the wide sky.

She loved watching. Everything was constantly altering. The intensity and angle of the sun, the coursing of traffic onto or off of the ferry, the breeze in the few remaining pines, the tankers and container ships, the passenger ships heading north in the AM and returning in the PM or the few with longer trips – north on a Monday; south a week later. She watched for patterns and sometimes found them. She kept tide charts even though she could not see the rise and fall. She kept a seasonal ferry schedule even though she knew it by heart. It gave great satisfaction to have a sense of order in the midst of such seemingly random change.

Had she really put her mind to it, she could have told the time of year and time of day by observing the sun, the temperature and five minutes of the movement outside her window. She was good at it.

She was good at figuring.

That was why it was so relaxing, after a glass of wine in the evening, to watch the day come to its apparent conclusion. Though well she knew that shipping never slept; tides never stopped breathing; moons waxed and waned with regularity.

Then, over coffee in the morning, to watch the day stretch into becoming itself, moving in every direction.

She loved her house.

She loved having a day off, which was rare. It meant, this time of year, that she could start a fire in the main floor fireplace in the morning and putter throughout the house keeping the dust and cobwebs at bay. After vacuuming and perhaps doing a few of the windows on the basement level, she could sit on the creaking leather sofa with a book or with the radio on low.

She worked hard, not just because she liked to satisfy so many of the needs of her personality, she worked hard because it felt so good not to. In this house, it felt wonderful. In this way she looked on her life with appreciation.

If she turned on the tv, at some point, nearly always, she became bored or even melancholy. Pretend people pretending at life.

A book called one to imagine, to observe detail, to rise in judgment or wince in disappointment. Often books stayed in her imagination through the day. As if the people in the story were the people in her life.

A screen more usually just called one to have eyes open. During reruns, she rarely remembered whether she had seen a show already or not.

Her work was so analytical; her relaxation was in being a genial observer.

At least that was how it had been. Two years ago when she had bought the house.

But she had worn down in the weather and with the divorce. Her view during the last winter had grown darker, grayer, less vibrant. More wine, less window.

Something had happened this year. When she had gone cross state to see her childhood friend Matt at his ordination. She realized she missed him. She had thought about it on the way home. She had thought about it after dropping her father in Mukilteo. She had thought about it over wine the evening of her return. Thoughts of Matt had travelled into work with her the next day. She found herself pulling out her yearbooks. Despite being two birth years apart, he was only a year behind in school and was in plays with her. She remembered standing with him at the final applause for their *Our Town*. She had euphorically slipped her hand into his; he had squeezed and briefly hooked her arm toward his side.

After, she had stood at the makeup room door, waiting for him, watching him put cold cream on his face as he chattered, using half a box of tissues to scrape it off. He was no longer the little neighbor boy. His chest was strong, no longer white, flat, and flexible. He filled out his running shorts. She needed to move from the doorway, but she could feel the heat in her face.

Her last year in school Matty, KT and she and her family had spent much of the summer at the family lake house. She had seen how quickly he had learned to water ski behind their boat. She had hiked with him, and they had cowboy camped over two nights. She had let him see her in the morning after only the briefest of finger combs through her hair.

On the second night, lying head to head in their bags near their fire, he had touched her on her head in their almost sleep.

She had plans. He was making plans. They would part after that summer.

She had held his hand on her hair and rubbed the back of it before rolling toward the last of the fire.

The memory still lived in the rhythm of her heartbeat as she gazed onto the bright winter water and remembered.

She was still in the memory when the phone rang.

Ch 48

He had found coffee and with it a semblance of life, but that feeling was short lived.

It was cold in the apartment, and he felt silly putting on a coat for inside. He felt strange looking for the heat. Trying to find a spare blanket to wrap up with.

Everything reminded him that he was out of place.

He could hear traffic and the day awakening around him. That seemed to deepen his sense of being out of rhythm. Out of place.

The coffee mug was not his. The furnishings, the simple hangings on the walls, the windows, the views. He was in a place he had never been. Left to his own devices.

Marooned.

All the generous friendship in the world was not changing that.

He needed to get out. Needed to move.

To?

Perhaps he would discover something that would help him feel less alone. Less "marooned." Was that the word? He had never used that word in any sentence. He had not thought it forever. Only pirates and seafarers and adventurers of old were marooned. The boys in *Lord of the Flies* were marooned. Odysseus. Robinson Crusoe was marooned.

He remembered being young and, while playing on the beach, finding the hull of forsaken boat on the seashore at White Rock. It had lain there a long while from the looks of it. A gaping hole was torn in the side of the wreck. The hull had dug its way into the beach, almost as if it belonged. But everything gave the lie to that. It did not belong. It was derelict and abandoned. It had belonged at sea.

Huge, orangebacked King crabs clawed awkwardly in the dark shallows within the wreck. Cumbersomely climbing and spitting in bubbles below their bulbous eyes. Creatures of the sea.

He recalled standing for what seemed a very long time, mesmerized by the breakage.

This is what could happen. And he would never get home.

The wreckage. The collision of life and death. And the creatures that crawl through things.

The sorting for meaning. We must carry those images with us forever not because we know what they mean but because we haven't placed them into meaning yet, and they still tease us into wondering.

And why was his mind on a beach and his body in a strange three-story building in a neighborhood he had never known?

Where was he in all this?

The collision of images jolted him. It was time. He needed to move.

He dressed, and, with a deep sigh, determined to purchase a loaf of bread and some eggs, he exited into the still dark hall. As he locked the door, he heard a cough from behind the next door down.

He was not alone on this island. He had forgotten the report about his neighbor.

He heard another cough and then a spasm of wet coughing. It made his chest tight to hear. How could she have time to catch her breath with such spasms? The image was painful to contemplate. The coughs slowed but continued as he made his way to the hall stairs and down. Interesting to him that he had heard nothing when in the corner apartment. Insulated.

It increased his feeling of being disjointed.

◆

He descended the stairs.

On a small table in the lobby of the apartment building stood a decorative fountain he hadn't noticed. He must have been distracted by all the bustle of moving in, he thought. The modest fountain was flanked by miniature but leggy greenery that hid the table. A small card fronted the fountain. "Vida." Whoever she was. A woman's touch. He would never think of such a thing.

He saw now the small upper bowl overflowed into the larger middle bowl and that bowl overflowed into the larger bowl at the base. And then the pump moved the water through the cycle again and again, giving a feeling of vibrancy, perhaps expansion or purpose, a reminder of nature, perhaps of life itself. He didn't know.

Why did people do this kind of decorating? Why were a wild plant and water feature placed within the wood and carpet lobby of an apartment building?

He spent a moment trying to sense the change the fountain made.

The change was in the air.

It transformed the hallway into a lobby, a place to be, not just to pass through, he supposed. He pointedly ignored that part of him that wanted to track the power cord under the carpet and exceeding that, beneath the black duct tape to the plug near the super's door. He just tried to feel the fountain. It transformed the moment. He stood observing.

It distracted. That must be it.

One bowl bubbling would probably do the same thing, he thought.

◆

Marianne was right. Two blocks over was where the action was. He walked for six or seven blocks in the chill of the morning sun just to see the variety of businesses on Broadway. And the foot traffic and the parking places already taken. He saw Doc's office and looked in the window. No one he knew. A half dozen folks with magazines and a bird like woman behind the desk intently considering something in front of her. She had the phone on her shoulder. She was awkwardly asquint as she bared her teeth and struggled with the typewriter. May be Harps . . .

Perhaps another time.

As he turned, he became aware of just how many bundled up people were on the move this time of day. He was taken aback. So many people were out. He had come to this place with a sense of being marooned, and he had discovered so many people were busily on the move. Briskly, with purpose. Belonging.

Oddly it reinforced his sense of isolation. He was not like them. They knew something he did not. They likely were something he was not.

◆

A café was two doors down from Doc's. He went in, all thoughts of buying groceries and cooking giving way simply to eating. He had not really eaten in some days.

He chose a booth to sit in rather than at the counter. He wanted the option to write down some of his thoughts from the night or about his waking time. Whatever came to the surface. He had taken a small pad from the nightstand for that purpose, should it arise.

He had felt his mind searching.

He didn't even have to pause over the menu. He ordered as the server brought the water. "Two blueberry hotcakes with two eggs over medium and two pieces of bacon, extra crispy. A hot coffee, with cream please."

Strange, he thought, how food grounds us. Calms and focuses us. Eating alone gives one time to consider, to observe one's surroundings without being ostracized as a gawker. It gives time for mulling and for considering. For chewing on things.

This would be a good place to catch his breath. So much had happened. His alienation in the back room. His being transported to a modern, cavernously beautiful corner apartment by a friend. His immersion into the thoughts that his untethered time brought.

What word came to mind?

Awash? Afloat? Navigating? Journeying? He felt badly that Carol was alone. Remorseful?

But he was incomplete.

They had been together for so much of this trip. What had happened, really?

Lost?

◆

This café would be a good place to write about some things at length. Perhaps something definite would make its way to the surface. He was tired of living in this world of questions. This must be what it was like for Carol. He had never really been a writer. But how interesting.

At the booth nearly across and only a few yards away, a young couple was finishing their meal and giving the last scraps to their curly headed toddler. He was not getting enough, however, and began to crawl across the table towards his father's plate. Neither parent acted to discipline him. They simply kept up their conversation. The youngster lifted a remnant piece of toast and jam. Without even looking, the mother took the toast back to the plate. The boy had left a blotch of raspberry jam on his cheek as he eyed the remaining scrambled eggs on the mother's plate.

Matt watched somewhat in amazement. It was their peacefulness, their naturalness that amazed him. Their hands attended to the boy; their faces attended to each other and to the conversation. Now the father, now the mother fed the boy as they exchanged their thoughts over the last of the breakfast.

She gathered him to her lap.

Matt's family had taught obedience in greater proportion than this kind of love. For his family: this behavior is for here; that for there. His family had loved him; he knew his mother had at least, but because they had loved him in their way, they wanted him to know how to sit. "Sit up straight." (He could hear the voice. He did not look toward the glare. He knew that eye.)

How to fit in with manners: "Elbows off."

How to ask rather than reach. The slap: "Born in a boarding house?".

To wait while "adults finished talking." Even when they talked forever.

His musing drew him to look out the front window. Every person from every family, had learned to grow beyond their upbringing. He would need to lean in instead of turn away. His father was back with him, obviously.

Just what he didn't need.

◆

His food arrived. He managed the arrangement of everything but did not let go of the musing. He poured the maple syrup from every possible direction. As if the pancakes were his thoughts. He was coming at things from every angle but had not the pleasure yet of a satisfying bite. He lifted the eggs with his fork, and placing them on top of the stack, cut into the eggs to run into the crevices of the cakes. He nibbled at the edge of a bacon piece, letting his cakes absorb all he had poured into them.

His seminary training had been similar to his upbringing. This is what is expected. We work now; we pray now; we walk now; we sleep for this number of hours. We have recreation with these assigned brothers this week. We go to this priest for permission and that priest for advice. We take our major studies now, philosophy now, theology now. We bond by similar behavior.

Sometimes, but rarely, by heart.

There had been no slap, no punishing glare. Things had been more subtle than that. It was the rigidity that was linking the memories.

Finding the connection.

And he was here, unmoored. Marooned. With no direction home. He smiled.

He looked up from his meal. The family was preparing to go. While the mother helped the youngster into his coat, the father reached across the table and in one movement wiped the boy's cheek clean. It was as if there had never been such a mark on the child's face.

◆

The moment came without Matt's seeking. He watched, mesmerized, as three worlds fused.

This child was Lucas, the boy with the burns. The child was Meese. The child was Matt himself.

And Matt was the father as well as the child.

Matt was stunned. He wanted not to think about it; he wanted to let it manifest itself.

The purity of infant skin, the naturalness of an easy wipe. The cleansing, the wiping away. The return to what was really true, not what had been taken as true, made to be true.

Forgiveness of some sort. Return to innocence and to its essential guileless and thoroughly enabling embrace.

Pieces jostled.

And there was no ignoring the release, the opening of long closed caverns, the invitation to step freely into the sun of a cold winter's day.

He no longer breathed the same.

He pulled the notepaper in front of him and wrote across the top: "The markings of life experience on the face of innocence. . . Love sees beyond blemish . . .

He had not eaten a bite.

"Even in the mirror," . . . as he wrote the words, he looked at them as if they had been penned by another's hand. He felt them seep into his understanding.

◆

The luminous image of the youngster with the burns was as clear to Matt as if the boy had never stepped into the night years before. As if the boy had stood in the vestibule until each of them had understood what they saw in the other. Until Matt had known why he was so bonded to the blemished boy. And what the memory of the boy had been trying to reveal.

Until he was shown, in one moment, every portion of that.

The shadowy image of Meese leaning forward across the table, so close that Matt had seen him as never before, in his youth instead of his age: "We are the same, you and I." Beneath the jaundicing, the nicotine mask, was a young face, speaking. Was young Jerry Meese.

Was himself.

◆

He watched the young family exit, and he pulled his coffee to his lips as he considered his thoughts.

He was being asked to trust himself. To sail a course of his own devising, instinctively bringing himself home. To trust that he could be loved even if he found himself without a compass or "crawling in the middle of a table".

To trust that she could love him. (He knew she did.) But that he could love her. Ah! That he could match up to what others had learned years earlier and better than he. That he could trust himself and his own real choices and his ability to be what he wanted with all his heart.

He had been an actor taking on expectations, roles, all these years. That was what needed to change.

O, there it was!

He was stunned. He put the pencil down and looked away, laughing at the news.

That was what she had been talking about when she said, "Socrates." She hadn't been talking about his asking questions at all.

She had been talking about knowing himself.

It went deeper than he had thought.

Carol had known it already. Somehow she had known something from the start.

Now it seemed to be his turn.

His own feelings had been of inadequacy.

Inadequacy. Yes, that was it. Arising from his behavior which had been so in need of correction that he no longer trusted himself or allowed himself to stand in the light he needed for growth. Instead, pretending at every turn, he had become or continued to be the schoolboy hiding pee-soaked towels in the hamper. The watchful schoolboy who tried to keep hidden even from himself this secret: he did not measure up.

And so, he had pretended there was no wine dark stain, no birthmark, no scarring, no welts needing explanation. And to others there seemed to be none. He seemed to seem whole.

Meanwhile, over years, in the mind of his mind, he knew otherwise. Knew his fractures, the hideous bad mark he was cursed to carry.

And so, within the roles he had hoped to inhabit, somewhere cowering in a cavern, was a little boy fearing to be found, fearing to be discovered, fearing the light all others enjoyed freely as self.

Hidden and alertly watchful, attentive to every sound that may threaten, he had sat.

And here, in this plain unremarkable café, he observed the truth about the years of being hidden.

He now saw the boy that had been and still was himself, and his body began to mourn and cheer all at once. He smiled through what recognition had brought. Instead of confusion this eruption of awareness brought a different feel: relief from the burden of pretense. He no longer needed to mistrust or even hide himself. That game could be over.

He could, right now, no matter any bad mark, wipe it clean of stain, and more – allow it to be gone.

He might become . . . whole was it?

He looked to the street. To the crossers and walkers and shoppers and people bundled against the cold and squinting into the light. People busy about their lives. He wanted to leave now, into the light they all seemed to be enjoying.

He stood and tossed his napkin over the uneaten meal.

Whatever.

He had things to do.

Ch 49

Carol just had to get out of the house. So, in the morning she had taken the Plymouth north on the freeway to the first community whose name she recognized: Edmonds.

She followed the exit to the ferry, judging that it would lead her to the water. That was what she needed. She needed cleansing. Movement. To be washed. To be alive with motion and purpose the way the salt water always was.

She parked part way to the ferry dock and walked down the remaining arterial and then past the restaurants fronting the shore. She passed a boat storage and came to a small park near what seemed the end of the road.

A boy and his father were flying a kite. The boy would run while the father gently cradled the kite in his elevated hands, so it could be free to fly away at the boy's pull. The wind was perhaps too strong for kite flying since the boy's efforts caused repeated crashes and rescues and resets and starts.

It made Carol think of her father and how she missed belonging to him even though she had spent her whole life running from anything he had ever held onto.

It made Carol wish for her father to be connected to her even by the narrowest of strings.

It made Carol push her chin into the wind and watch as long as her misting eyes allowed.

The boy ran by one of the tables set out for picnickers. All of them were empty.

Only one new arrival walked into the wind along the raised shorewalk in the distance. And from the looks of things, he might not be there for long. The cold wind was enough to yank repeatedly at his wide brimmed, leather hat. She watched him tug at his coat for warmth as he looked out at the Sound.

And though the day was cold and darkening, the boy's mother and smaller brother were watching the youngster's forays into the wind, ready to cheer him on, to lift the kite with their enthusiasm if possible.

Next to the mother, obediently perched, sat the family's black lab. He too had come to be part of, though for the moment he was called to sit. His eyes never left the boy. His red tongue lolling, the dog panted in the chill air and watched more intently even than those at the table. At first beckon, he would run with the boy. At first beckon.

Carol knew that expectant look. She had seen Random so many times watch for his cue and leap into a wanton run into the wind of the Texas plain. It was usually a ball he chased, certainly not a kite. How many solid red rubber balls had had wide divots torn from them by Random's enthusiasm. She had thrown ball after ball: terrible, drool laden, torn-to-pieces rubber balls, so that she could see the circular sweep of his tail as he chased the ball in its bounces. So that she could see his smiling face as he trotted happily back for another throw in the game he loved.

How could all this converge here, so far away from Texas? So far away from her past pushed down and replaced by a present in which she now felt stranded.

Part of who we have become.

She found herself smiling and misty all at the same time. Life was sweeping before her everywhere she looked. In every runner, slow ambler, ferry watcher, windblown dog walker or winter smiler she saw. Her life was being told her in small, and her feelings were being evoked so that her face danced with uncertainty as to what to feel.

She was alone. This was not what she anticipated on this journey. She had had enough of that already. But she would be patient. She was done with the tunnel of anger. She had caught her breath and stood up in her kitchen. She had picked up the pieces of the smashed tea cup. She had placed the bud vase on the windowsill to show in the sunlight. She had become quiet and had begun to breathe evenly. That seemed for the moment to be what she was being asked. Patience. Long suffering. Allowance for the universe to take her where she needed to go. This was the hope beyond pain.

She sat on an empty picnic table, and without anyone with whom to share, she watched. She remembered. She cheered. And she told herself that the cold wind was blowing tears up in her eyes.

Dark clouds were coming in. The family on some cue, stood and moved or wound the string and cradled the kite and without instruction left.

She petted the dog as it passed her.

The visitors' car backed noisily out of the gravel parking area.

◆

She had better get home before the clouds opened with weather that looked like it could be punishing.

Ch 50

Matt entered the apartment from the dark hallway. Nothing had changed. It was still alien. The air was exactly the same air as when he left. Stagnant. Stopped. A bell jar.

Where should he begin? What would be the change? How could he return to the little yellow house and be content that he was home?

Matt opened the apartment door and entered from the dark hallway. He hung his jacket in the hall closet.

The room was as he had left it. Cold and foreign. Nothing had changed itself. He was going to have to do that.

That kept him standing there for a moment contemplating where to begin. He could not tell what to do with what he had learned.

He crossed the room to the couch and fell into the corner of it to sort his thoughts.

After a moment he leaned over the notepad on the coffee table and began:

C,

I am so sorry for these last days. Please forgive me. I have sorted through things and am feeling ready to come home. If you will have me. Please understand that I would never have done anything to hurt you. I am sorry for any pain my absence has caused you. I just needed to work through some things.

We can talk. I am ready for that. More than anything else, know that I love you. I love you. I love you.

Please phone if that's good. (He got up and crossed the room to see the number.) 759 2616.

I love you.

Matt.

He left it on the table.

He picked it up.

He folded the note in half and then in half again and put it into his back pocket.

He could not just stay here forever.

◆

When he had left the café, he immediately had felt the cold sun pushing him farther into his jacket. A dark sky had begun to drop a heavy snow onto the avenue. He had hurried back to the apartment. For?

The letter from his father still sat staring as if it had eyes to see. To look at him. To glare.

Carol would be getting home soon to the empty house that had lain open to the chill all day since no one was at home.

KT was at such a distance in her warm woodburning little house.

And Larry was off somewhere. Who knew?

Change was up to him.

◆

The snow, supplanting the cold brightness of the day, had begun to darken all and thicken in its fall.

A seagull screeched once, wheeling somewhere over the building. It drew a smile to Matt's face. Had he not been here, he never would have heard such a sound. Things align. And he knew that sound was meant for him. He had heard it before. He remembered.

Matt sat on the edge of the sofa and watched across the room the thick flakes waft or plummet, kite or tumble in strange mixtures each at its own speed and direction. Filling the gray sky, descending in wide swirls, colliding silently with the window. Alighting on the long tree fingers he could see. Beginning to cap the telephone pole and its gray transformer.

◆

Matt heard what seemed to be someone at the door. There was no knock. Only some unusual shuffling sounds that in this quiet corner of the building drew attention. He went to the door and listened.

As he watched, the knob turned. Since Matt had thrown the lock, the door was not going to open, nonetheless the trying of the door alerted him. He stood still behind the door, uncertain whether it might be Doc or Marianne or someone else from the office who was stranded on this awful snow darkening afternoon. Someone who had been told to rely on the apartment as a refuge.

Matt began to think in terms of welcome and opened the locked door.

There stood a small gray woman in her worn, print housecoat, who, as he opened the door suppressed a wet cough into her hand beneath an apparently painful squint.

"May I help you?" Matt asked, noticing the plate she had in her other hand.

Tending to her free hand, she smiled. "I wanted to bring you something since you're new here. Think of it as a traveler's gift." With that she put the plate into his hand and passed through into the center of the apartment, leaving Matt to shut the door and to try to assess what was happening.

"Thanks for the gift. How did you know someone was in here?"

She spun dramatically, hardly letting go of her assay of the apartment. "The walls have ears, as they say."

Matt was uncertain just who might have said that, but letting it go, he moved to take the plate to the kitchen. He saw for the first time that the dish contained the remains of a casserole of some sort, perhaps fish . . . and some cheese . . . and noodles that looked stiff and dry.

She interrupted his growing alarm.

"Been years since I've been in here." He turned to see her making what was almost a dance rotation, arms extended. He couldn't tell if she was responding to some interior score or simply enjoying the width of the room. Likely he would never know, but he enjoyed watching her. There was something fresh surfacing. Her face relaxed during the single turn she made so carefully. It was, in a slowed motion, as if she were a young woman, fresh, dancing in the cleansing breeze of a summer afternoon. As if she had spun herself, for just a moment, back in time.

She had not always been so worn.

He was beginning to see her.

She dropped her arms and smoothing the front of her housecoat, crossed to closely observe "The Beached Skiff", the only painting on the interior wall.

He put the half-eaten casserole on the counter but found it difficult to turn away from it.

"I hear them when they come, but I don't like to interrupt Bob, and the daughter is not one to mess with." She moved from the picture to the corner of the couch at the far side of the room. "I recall one time when I did, and she was not pleasant, shall we say. It was clear I was not welcome . . . I was for Bob, but not for the girl."

"Bob?"

"The Doc." She nodded as if Matt had said it. "Bob."

"Doc Triton?"

"The same. She sat on the arm of the couch. "Bob is how I know him. He and our son Jerry grew up the best of friends. Bob has been very, very good to us. He found us our place. We've lived here for years. Way before Albert passed.

He knew the story he had been told. He was sensing even more. Deciding he would let this revelation unreel without remark, Matt began by asking, "so how did you know I was not Bob over here?"

"Bob plays his horn. Always plays before he goes to bed for the night. He and Jerry used to both play. School band in Missoula. Jerry doesn't play anymore, but Bob does." She wiped at her face with a sleeve. She began to get off the couch arm and wander to the corner where the windows joined.

She turned and looked at him, sizing him up. "I knew you weren't Bob."

She watched the snow now as she spoke.

"And I knew you weren't the girl because I heard the two of you, and then I heard someone leave and saw her getting into her car down there. I'm in the apartment next." She was making sure he knew her story by pointing each direction as the story unfolded.

"Anyway . . . I haven't seen the snow from the corner here, and I wanted to see it. I have a side window that looks at the one street, but I keep the blinds down, and besides, the street's not much to look at."

He wasn't sure what to say, and so he just waited.

"Blinds been closed since Albert passed. Nothing much to see most days. If there is, I can peek out the side of the blinds from time to time. Anyway. This snow is special, and I wanted to see the grandness of it all. She swept with a crimped and somehow painful gesture that dropped unceremoniously. "Reminds me of home."

She looked at him as if he might have something to say. But when he only smiled and looked toward the window, she watched him in the silence.

Finally, she spoke. "I imagined you were hungry."

He began readying something to answer when she moved abruptly toward the door. Once there, she turned, and without speaking, took a last look as if she might have to paint his portrait or give a police report on the state of the room. She had kind but tired eyes which he sensed had seen a great deal of life. She had Jerry's eyes.

"Here long?"

"Just for a bit," he replied.

She flipped her hand past her ear. "Well, you can bring the dish back when you're finished. I'm always there . . . Flo." She extended her hand. He remembered it was the hand that had stifled the cough.

Matt waved. "Thank you, Flo. I'll have that dish back to you tomorrow. Thanks for your thoughtfulness."

Scarcely seeming to listen, she had moved back to the picture. "Thought you might be hungry."

He waited for her to finish her rumination.

She did. She moved to the door, idly turning over the key set lying on the hall table. Opening the door for herself, she turned to Matt. "Hope I'm not too noisy over there. I try not to be. I know the folks that live in this building like quiet. So I try . . . Anyway." She raised her hand and nodded to conclude.

She left as she had come, with a virulent wet cough into her right hand and a scarcely disguised wipe on the side of her housecoat.

As she moved into the shadow of the hallway, Matt went to the door and closed it before crossing to the sink to wash his hands. He left the food on the counter.

Flo. He had seen her now.

Jerry's Flo.

Ch 51

Matt had listened to the coughing woman reenter her apartment.
He let himself collapse into the sofa.

It was getting darker. And colder. And there he saw his father's note still sitting untouched. He breathed out, stretching his neck.

He pushed his head into the cushions and soon after found himself drifting much like the snow, his thoughts floating at all angles.

◆

He still had not eaten.

He got up and began moving toward the kitchen, stopping at the far living room windows. He could see now that the snow was serious. Already the streets were whitened, and the cars were turning ghostly. Tracks etched in the streets were beginning to disappear. And all the sky was heavy with gray. He couldn't tell, but he may be trying to see into the heavens through the thickness of enough snow to transform an entire city.

If he were with Carol, they would be in front of the fire. It would be their first snow together in their home.

He needed to stop thinking like that if he was going to be patient enough to truly find his way.

Going to the cupboards he pulled down a box of Cheerios. These would do. He sat on the sofa. Snow was really coming down now. Box still in hand, he went to the window and could see that the walks were covered and the parking strips had disappeared. It was a world one needed to remember, transitioning. The house across the way had build-up over all its flared porch roof. The cars on the street were now covered. It was getting deep.

There was a knock at the door.

He delayed, wondering who it might be who knew where he was. Had the coughing woman returned to the hallway? He had not heard her door. But then he had not heard her the last time.

Could Carol have found the apartment and come to take him home?

Or had Doc given the address to Matt's father, his repentant former neighbor? Matt was not ready for that confrontation.

Matt hesitated and listened to the silence. He would need to be prepared.

In the center of the room, he stood in what he momentarily saw was almost comic paralysis.

He needed to be done with hiding.

He opened the door.

"May I come in?" Marianne had a bag of groceries on her hip. The cold had reddened her nose and put water in the corners of her eyes.

"Of course. Come in, come in. Here, let me take that." He took the bag to the coffee table as Marianne closed the door and stood just inside, wrapping her coat to her ribs for warmth.

"Come, have a seat." She sat on the sofa, still holding the coat and herself tightly. "I need a favor I think."

He sat on the edge of the coffee table.

"I wasn't supposed to be in today, as you know. But the office called for something they couldn't unravel, and here I am. And now this snow. I started to drive off the hill, but I only got a block or so and realized this is too dangerous without chains." She shifted.

"You have to go all the way to Edmonds in this? The freeway has to be as awful as the surface streets are. I wouldn't try it without chains."

"The thing is, I don't have chains. I looked in the trunk. I thought I had bought some with the car, but I don't know what became of them."

"A service station might have your size."

"That's what I'm hoping, but I'm not brave enough to drive to a station to buy a set. I was thinking that if I asked you . . . "

"I can do that. There should be four or five stations around. Somebody must have your size chain."

"If you would do that. I can't tell you . . . I would cook us some spaghetti. I bought the makings from Fred Meyer. That way you have a nice dinner, and I get a way home."

"No. Sure. Be glad to help. Let me get my coat." He took the groceries off the coffee table. Coming back into the room, "I'll get my coat."

She was still shivering as she dug the car keys out of her coat pocket. "It's the little Toyota. White."

"I remember."

"O, right. Sorry. This snow has me a little sideways."

"OK. I'll check out the chain thing, and you'll be all set."

He went to the door.

She called out. "Don't go too fast. You won't be able to keep hold of it."

"Not to worry. I'll be back in no time."

He closed the door and skipped down the stairs and into the lobby. He closed his coat as tightly as he could and stepped carefully down the front steps. The snow was almost like in the movies where the hero is fighting against the elements to make his way home. The snow was not as soft and pleasant as it had seemed from the third story. It stung and pricked at his face. He hurried, even losing his footing as he tried to turn the corner on the sidewalk.

Her Toyota was just ahead. Of all the parked cars, hers had the least snow on it. She must have had it under cover or brushed the snow off before she started out.

He got the same story at each station. Only a few stations carried cable chains, and he was too late anyway. Most places had sold out hours ago when the first snow had hit the hill.

He turned onto E Aloha street to give it one last try. He thought he remembered a station off that street. As soon as he started onto the street, he realized his error. He had turned onto one of the hills which later in the evening would be blocked to traffic. He was headed down a grand slide that was only going to end at the blinking red light at the intersection below. He tried shifting to a lower gear. He pumped at the brakes. He squeezed the brakes softly. He slowly pulled back on the parking brake.

Everything happened slowly: the twist her car began to take, the headlights coming from the left along the arterial, his entry into the arterial, the lurch and unsettling shove of the impact, the slide, the stop in the snow still coming down.

His door had broken open and left him to tumble across the ice. He watched as it happened. He was more surprised than hurt. He tried to recover immediately so as to dispel the apparent seriousness of the collision. He was rattled but seemingly unhurt.

His hip perhaps.

There was minor bumper, headlight, and fender damage to the arterial car. Marianne's car had a dented left rear, and the trunk no longer sat flush. The arterial driver was concerned that Matt may have been hurt. Matt raised both arms and twisted in the snowfall showing he was not broken. The driver seemed satisfied though concerned. Both drivers were anxious to get out of the cold, and both cars seemed drivable. They exchanged insurance information, and each car left the scene after a final reassurance that Matt was going to be alright.

Something was off, but . . .

He wasn't sure how to tell Marianne about her car. But he would think of something.

◆

The apartment was bright and warm. Music from a portable transistor radio was coming from the kitchen. The room smelled wonderful. Two places were set on the coffee table, only one of them had a wine glass. The opened bottle was at the corner of the table.

Matt hung up his coat and poured a wine for himself. He walked into the kitchen and smelled the full aroma of the spaghetti. Only then did he realize how hungry he was.

He saw that his father's letter was now on the oaken kitchen table. So were the pen and the notepaper Matt had used.

Crossing back into the front room, he heard the curtain in the shower.

"Marianne?"

"Be out in a sec. Finally, I'm getting warm."

"Smells great in here."

"Did you get the chains?"

It was going to be much easier this way to tell her what had happened to her car.

"I didn't. I searched all the stations I could find, and no one had any left. And I ended up getting dinged by a guy on 10th."

"Are you OK?" He thought he saw her briefly peer out of the bedroom doorway.

"I'm fine. No one was hurt. Both cars had pretty minor damage." He took a sip of his wine and looked toward the window. "It's just treacherous out there."

"I'm glad it was you and not me. No. I mean, I wouldn't have known what to do."

"Not a major thing. We both were wanting to get out of the snow."

◆

He moved to the window to watch the continuing onslaught of the snowfall.

Flakes swirled furiously as if hurled by some unseen hand, and he saw, in the reflection, himself watching, and he saw the warm wood of the apartment and the darkness of the open bedroom door.

And he remembered a night when they had been young teens, the night at the train tracks.

He thought of it at this moment perhaps because he had never known where to put the experience.

So many things he didn't know where to put.

◆

They had climbed the rocks at Richmond Beach while the families started a bonfire below. She had dared him to stand still while the train passed, after he had put the nickels onto the rail. She had challenged him. They were not supposed to be up there, but she knew not to tell. He would be in for another whipping if word got out. She knew that.

They half leaned, half lay over the yellow white boulders at the top of the hill next to the tracks. He was excited to be on an adventure with her.

He had heard the train first and had stood. She had just rolled over, laid out langorously: "show me," she seemed to say.

He kept the coins in his hand. He might have balanced while walking on the rail, but she had seen that before.

The train was nearing.

The sections of the train would speed past him, he knew that: car after car after car. Most would be dark and filthy. A cold, fatal bludgeon to anyone stupid enough to think they could hitch a ride like in the movies. Door open; door closed; door open; open, open, open, open. Inscrutable into the night. He remembered imagining it all. He knew what he would see.

The train horn shocked him to a start as the engine made the turn before the beach boulders.

Quickly he put the coins on the track. Then he stepped slightly back onto the shoulder of sharp rocks.

He waved.

The train blared a deafening warning as the dark, one eyed engine bore down on him. He stepped another step and felt the sudden impact of wind knocking him nearly off balance: the immense hurtle of the train, the single hard beam of white light, the height of it all, the muscular, metallic onset of noise and clamber and power and fierce passage. He felt the train yank at him, tear at his clothing, as he set his feet in the metallic breath of the screaming monster. The noise! He could not turn his back. The train still yanked at his clothes as if it would leave him naked and exposed.

What was this?

He had seen trains before. At some distance. But this was not what he had seen! He was freezing now, clenched and shivering in the whirling pull, the swirling suction of the menacing steel. Holding. Barely holding.

And she was there, with him. She had wrapped him to herself from behind, turned him, and pulled him away. He had gone with her, but then he had tried to watch even while she held. He felt her body struggling to hold him even as he watched the train. She was warm. She could not be closer as she held. And even with the threat of savagery so close that they might be yanked into death with one misstep, he felt his groin start to stiffen against her.

She had felt it, too.

What was this?

He pulled away. That was not it. He needed to see the passage.

Matt didn't fear dying. He stepped toward the train.

She grabbed to regain him. He, and now she, were being blown and sucked, battered and nearly tumbled, pushed and pulled seemingly from the face of the earth. Part of him bent, as if to kneel; part of him braced trying to find balance. She held tightly trying to be an anchor for him.

His arms momentarily kited, and his white shirt unfurled, shuddering like feathers.

In the maelstrom of noise and blown dust she was with him. Holding. They moved reactively, nearly as one. He no longer knew which way to go.

As if in victory, he screamed out raggedly, but he heard no sound. He was being devoured by the punishment of this air. Left as a shell by the train noise. At each moment he felt like he might fly up crazily, like a plastic bag in an alley. He might adhere to the cold, hard metal, or just as likely, fill with this energy and, like a makeshift parachute, drift for a terribly violent moment and fall back to the planet somewhere down the track.

The thought had mesmerized him, left him – set feet against sharp stones—watching, magnetized by energies he had never known before.

What he thought he knew, he hadn't.

And then it was gone.

And Marianne had fallen to a sit and was as stunned as he, caught in the same magnetic pull.

What had happened?

An intimacy of some kind. A holding on. The tenuous but bonding struggle of two bodies within the menacing dark. Had that been all?

She had felt him changing in her arms. He had felt her trembling.

◆

She had seemed as frightened by the moment as he. He saw her crawl to a kneel, realize something and fix her glasses.

And she saw him: his twisted hair, his new white shirt pulled and hanging out.

She had studied him for a moment before blinking. Before scurrying off. He had watched her go. It rattled him. He recalled being rattled. More than by the train.

He had been left alone.

◆

And now here he was, alone again, watching.

◆

What had actually happened that evening at the train tracks? He had never put words to it.

◆

Outside the apartment the snow billowed and swirled, tumbling like the thin remains of small ghostly shadows falling from a dark grey murderous sky. Some flakes floated; some plummeted; some dallied, almost rising as he watched; some seemed to slide forever along. Some collided with the glass and slid into mourning down the pane toward the white sill.

◆

Marianne came out of the bedroom still drying at her hair. She had put on a pair of flannel pajama pants he had seen in one of the drawers, and she was wearing one of his white tee shirts. Beneath the shirt she was loose.

"I'm glad you're not hurt, Matty. Thank you so much for even trying to find chains for me." She disappeared into the bedroom again.

"I'm having a glass of your wine. Is that OK?"

"Yes. That's yours. I have mine in here. I'll be out in a minute."

He was out of balance a bit. He could feel that. He was not certain what he was to do to make things normal. He wanted that more than anything. To have things be normal.

"Can I dish up the pasta?"

"Sure. There's some Parmesan in the fridge. I got it for us."

"Perfect meal for this evening."

"I'm glad . . . Almost done in here."

◆

The meal was easy. The spaghetti was a distracting adventure in itself, and the wine seemed to put them each at ease. Marianne asked him if he had been to his childhood house, and that started a run of nostalgia stories that both revived and embellished the youth that both of them had had together. Secrets became stories, became jokes, became their bond. He loved her "offended face" when he told her of being able to see into her room from his. He had let her stew before telling her that he could only see her from the ears up. She slapped at him. He held his "wounded" arm. That was enough. She slapped again, and they both laughed easily. The stories left him relaxed into the sofa and her sitting cross legged, facing him. They had found a smiling peace.

She told him of moving off to college at Northwestern, which he remembered, and how she had met her future husband there. She shared how they had selected Minneapolis as where they would settle and where he would be able to build his career. She poured another drink, and Matt felt the evening becoming more serious as she confided that the marriage had failed with her husband's need to travel and work long hours when home. They had parted less than amicably. Her husband never did understand why she couldn't be happy with all that the money provided. So, she became the bad guy and filed the papers and eventually got enough from that relationship to get back to the Northwest and begin again. Actually, Doc had helped her until all the papers were final. That had taken a while.

She suspected the only reason it happened when it did was that her ex had met somebody. Asshole.

Matt told the brief story of his failure to thrive as a priest. He stopped short of telling fully how C had opened his eyes to what life could be. He spoke of needing to leave the house due to his need to find some time to think things through.

◆

"Did you hear from your father?" she asked.

He smiled.

"I figured that was what was in the envelope that came to Doc."

"I did." Matt sipped at his wine.

"Was that good?"

"I don't know." He twisted on the cushion so as to face her. "He wants to see me and KT." He took a moment. "I'm not real excited to do that."

"I understand. I remember him pretty clearly."

"You know, everyone deserves a second chance, but he made things pretty ugly for us."

"For you especially."

"Anyway." Matt shifted on the couch. "I'll think about it. It's not like he's staying up the block, and I need to have decided by tomorrow."

"I know." She put her hand on his leg and rubbed in a small circle. "You'll do the right thing."

"I'll try." He felt hollow.

"You'll do more than that. Give yourself credit. You're a better person than you know."

She offered her glass in a toast. He followed on cue.

"To an improved future for us both."

They had finished the wine.

Matt got up from the couch. He started to walk but discovered that his leg was stiff. His back as well. It took him a few steps to find his pace without limping.

"You're sure you're alright?"

"Yeah. Just a little stiff from the collision." He finished his cross and looked out at the snow. It had not relented and was whipping around the streetlamps and slashing down at one severe angle only to come the next second from the opposite side. No cars passed through the intersection. The home across from the apartment was dark and piled high with snow at every possible landing. The scene was lovely even though tumultuous.

"It's really quite beautiful, all this upheaval. Such a change." He stood watching as he spoke.

"What do you see, Matt?"

Matt laughed; he spread his arms and put his hands onto the windows as if it could draw him closer. "Beginnings and endings."

"I'll get the lights," Marianne started across the room.

He watched the snowfall. There was something more. Something that hadn't yet come to words. Something hanging in the gray-white air.

The bewildering train experience and now this.

It seemed that this "something" was waiting for recognition before revealing its name.

Things were like this storm, he thought. The descent of millions of small moments affecting what you have seen so that it could become, almost miraculously, what you had never seen.

Perhaps that was it.

Expectation blinds us. We only awaken when we are baffled or surprised enough to wonder. And watch carefully.

◆

The room light went off. Marianne came to behind Matt to watch.

They stood quietly for some moments.

Marianne spoke, "It's lovely. . . I've always loved the snow."

◆

They stood quietly for some moments. Waiting. Listening.

"You're right, Matty. What I see from here is quite beautiful." She put her arm around him and put her hand onto his stomach. She rested her chin on his shoulder. "Quite beautiful."

Matt saw the muted reflection of the two of them in the window. He felt her body settle in closely behind him. She kissed his neck.

Matt placed his hand on hers. She began to lift at his shirt. He turned.

Facing her, he saw the eyes he had seen at the tavern in Spokane before she had kissed him goodbye. Present. Frank.

He spent the moment looking and discovered that he saw the adventuring young woman who had fallen down stunned after holding him, saving him, from the train.

 She kissed him now, on his lips.

He looked away. "I have to go." He did not move.

She moved her hands to his face. "No, you don't. You're fine. . ." She watched him. "You have nowhere to go, Matt." She was peaceful.

He closed his eyes, but he knew what she looked like. He was frozen. He looked at her eyes. She was present. Mild eyed.

She kissed him again, her face staying close to his. He could feel her warmth radiating. She took his face in her hands.

"Stay."

He had never heard such meaning in any word. He felt, it seemed, the width of all the world, the weight of all decisions, of all promises, of all guilt, of all betrayal, of all desire, of all fear, of all his life.

"I have to go." It was all he had to offer.

"You don't. You choose to go . . . What is it? . . . Matt, I . . . " she stopped and looked at him as he had never seen her look. She was a naked he had never seen in anyone before.

Her eyes began to flood. She turned away to hide it.

He moved to her and held her from behind. He wanted to keep her from the pain.

She stayed rigid, breathing. And then she leaned into his body. He closed his eyes and stood with her, close. It was he who was breathing now.

They stood in their clutch in the half- light while outside and all around, down every street, and over every house, down past every streetlight, some dark celestial something, passing slowly overhead, was, with only the slightest of sounds, discarding against every window what looked like the ghosts of millions of small white birds.

◆

He kissed her, on the top of her head, once.

She took his hand and slid it onto her stomach and up to her breast. She held him there.

She was so warm, so expectant. He could feel her heart as he held her. He had thought of such a moment as this. But not such as this.

There was nothing he could think to say. Things were past saying.

He stepped away. He crossed the room to get his jacket.

"Marianne." She stayed turned away, her shoulder sloping with the hold she kept on herself. "I can't. I would turn into . . . " He lost himself in the sentence before it formed . . . "If I stay, I'll lose you . . . I don't want that."

She turned and smiled briefly, not so naked as before. "You and I have . . . " She had to stop. There was a moment. And then she walked away to the window.

◆

The last he saw, she was still holding herself and was, it seemed, watching the tumult wrap around the lamplight.

He closed the door.

◆

As she looked, she saw the heavy flakes sailing and falling like pieces of a torn, intimate diary, casting brief shadows across the window and across her face, frozen in its forlorn gaze.

The silent snow had covered her white car, had erased the sidewalks, hidden the streets and left her watching.

The world she loved to watch was disappearing.

It was going to demand a new beginning.

She didn't know whether she was up to it.

The snow had changed everything.

◆

As he reached the sidewalk, he did not look up. He pushed into the snow with shallow breath and a kind of blind impulse. He had never felt such a weltering onslaught. He could not stand and feel. He walked. He could do nothing but push through the flurry.

He did not wave to her. He squinted and struck out down the abandoned, muted street.

Ch 52

Busses run infrequently at night.

He tucked himself into a storefront across from the café. Though he was out of the storm, he felt the buffeting. The wind and his nerves made him shiver.

The storm had transformed everything he looked at. It had blown snow into the semblance of frowns above the apartment windows at the corner. Spear point triangles of snow had been pushed methodically into every doorway he passed on Broadway. Brickwork wore scruffy white fuzz beards. In the street, the snow had built into a scar tissue where tires of passing cars had packed the flakes. The world was wild and darkly alive. He stood uncertain whether he was excited or afraid. He just knew he was chattering beneath his coat.

He had made a choice that he had never wanted to make. He had changed an entire history in one moment. He was still trying to recover from that severance that had pushed him out into the rampage of the night. He sought the only comfort he knew as certain: the collar of his coat.

The bus was nearly empty, and the garish light did nothing to help him calm. He watched the homes, the cars, the bending tree branches absorb the weight and silence of the snow as he moved in a chattering passage on the snow-chained bus.

The snow and its muting were no different at the next stop, or the next. He got off on 65th and began the walk to 26th. He pushed ahead, rattled but intent, into the cold. Worst case, he would drop by the bar and see about his job or go to his motel. Worst case.

Carol may still be ready to kill him.

A strange, limping, rhythmic mantra rose as he crunched his way through the mounded snow. He heard his boots squeak unevenly. He felt like a wounded tar, a pegleg even, making his way uncertainly on land. He was not used to moving in such discomfort.

He watched his good boot kick through and destroy the silent, pristine curvatures of the snow. His path was not about beauty or loveliness. His path was about directness and redemption and a trust that every footfall would take him forward instead of down on his butt. He had been there already. He was done with that.

For the moment his odyssey stopped. It was time to catch his breath. In the wind he set himself with an uncertain stagger.

He had arrived.

He stood beneath the old streetlight at the corner two blocks from Carol's house. In the black night the white snow pelted him. The dark houses kept stern watch from their elevated banks. He stood as if in a great but broken hall with all expectation focused down on him. There was no one else out in the night, in the storm.

This silent, nocturnal hall was his: he could lay claim to himself here or disappear into the shadows. Own it or leave it. Come home or make do. For a moment he felt the chill of his own smallness in the cavernous night.

Who was he anyway? What was he doing here?

What? Those questions were done. Those questions had frozen him too long.

He had not come so far just to stand timid and impassive in a snowy downpour.

He had come here by choice. He would finally slay his old self, the hider, the fearful watcher in the night. And in slaying him, he would slay the many roles he may have taken. The roles of false suitors, pretenders. He grew steely.

They must be gone, those roles. Eliminated. Slain.

He would have no more of it. He was here to claim victory, not to give that watcher new life.

He now, in the light, in the wind, and in the black of a swirling night, was leaving himself free to stand in this wide hall of his return. He was about to come home.

It was time to put his plan together.

As soon as he thought that, he laughed into the pelting snow. There was no plan. He was simply going home. They would talk. He would prove, no matter what it took, that he was himself. And he was hers.

If she would have him.

◆

She wished in looking out the dining room window at the cold and the vertical explosions of blown snow that she was not alone with only a sputtering candle. That she was not alone in this room or in her bed or in her home. She wished her heart would quiet and would dull the pain she was feeling. She wished that she might at least pick up a pen and write.

She slid the candle to the center of the table.

Sitting in near darkness with her elbows on the table and wrapped in a blanket from the bed, she sipped at her tea in the quiet of the house. She felt her body begin to weep, not from her sadness or her pain, for she had already held both of those in her hands. She wept from her inability to do anything more than love him. The change was up to him. She would see what she would see.

The lesson she had learned long ago was needing to be faced again.

She would search for the strength to do that.

◆

There was a clatter at the door.

She opened cautiously.

Matt, fallen and snow-covered, was lying on his back.

She could not help herself; she stepped out and reached for him. She helped him up. And even in the swirling snow they stood.

Letting go of all thought in the cold air, she helped him inside.

Once inside, she stepped back. Looking at the snow inside his glasses and inside the neck of his coat and all down the front of his pants brought on her own quizzical disbelief. She stepped away and tugged her robe more tightly around her. She shook her head.

He saw her response even while cleaning his glasses. He undid his coat and flapped the snow out of his collar.

Remembering that she wanted to listen, she asked him, "What were you doing out there?"

"I fell coming up the walkway. Face plant. And then I fell once I got onto the porch, and I crashed into the screen door. It was like a comedy routine."

She turned partly away.

His story was a mixture of earnestness and comedic disbelief. "I walked all the way from the bus with no problem and then fell twice coming up from the sidewalk." Then realizing that he had not entirely addressed her question, "I came to chat if you're OK doing that."

Her voice was steady. She didn't look at him but put out her hand. "Give me your coat and hat. I'll put them in the bathtub."

When she returned, he was still standing in his stocking feet, just to the side of the tile rectangle inside the front door.

◆

She stood at the end of the couch. "I don't have a fire for you." Both of them were silent. "I was using the blanket to stay warm."

"I wasn't expecting anything. I came to give you a letter I wrote, and to talk with you. I mostly came first to apologize for needing to be away and then to ask you to forgive me."

She had become busy. She had turned on the other lights in the room and had retrieved the blanket from the dining room floor where she had dropped it.

"Come, sit," she gestured toward the couch. He moved toward it. "Can I get you some tea?"

"That would be good."

"You can sit with this over you. I'll get the tea and something warm from upstairs. I'll be right back."

He put the blanket on the sofa and went to the fireplace to start a fire. He was just finished lighting the crumpled paper when she returned with his tea.

"Thank you. That'll be nice."

Facing the fire and placing more small pieces of kindling, he said, "The letter I wrote you is in my back pocket. You can read it while I get this going."

Carol put his tea on the hearth and took the letter from his back pocket. She sat on one end of the sofa. Matt tended the fire as she read. She was quiet a long while.

"Thank you for writing this. I trust we'll have some time to talk about it all. Not now, but at some time. There's a lot here to talk about."

She put her hands into her lap and watched them as if they held the clarity she wished her words to carry.

She found a way to begin. "Before I got better, I thought of all kinds of things that I needed to say to you the next time I saw you. And before that I thought of all kinds of things I needed to do for myself to protect me from being hurt like this again.

"Matt, I was so . . ." she looked away, "so angry with you." Her tears began.

"You hurt me. That was all I felt. You hurt me, and I didn't know why. The man I had let touch me had hurt me instead.

"I always thought . . . " She stopped. "I always thought you loved me . . . As much as I loved you.

"It was probably my mistake. But I thought that we were special. Not like my mom and my dad. Not like your mom and your dad. Not like anyone I had ever met before . . . Not just . . . not just a fling, a dangerous, forbidden something . . . In my mind we were lovers, Matt. As careful with each other as with ourselves. At home whether in front of a fire or over ice cream or in bed. Lovers."

She was looking off. He, looking down.

"I loved you, Matt. I don't say that to just anyone. In fact, past Sissy, I never say that.

"It occurred to me that I have protected myself and secretly readied myself for you coming into my life ever since I was little and was sent away." She looked at him directly.

"Matt, I . . . " She walked to the mantle and picked up a journal lying there. She took a moment. " With you I found my truest laughter; I uncovered my smile . . . I unboxed my shrunken hope to fly free . . . My life changed. I put cut flowers on the small table in my room. I stood on my bedroom porch and opened my face to the sun and tilted back my head to feel it all. Every bit of it." She closed the journal.

"Every bit, Matt."

She looked straight ahead, away from him.

"Sometimes I nearly wept with how happy I was with you." She turned to face him. "I loved you."

She shifted. She caught her breath, preparing. "I still do . . . But once a person has surrendered, betrayal is doubly difficult to absorb. Once a person has left themselves unguarded . . ."

"I just have to think what to do with all this . . . " She looked over at him a long while. "Can I ever laugh with you again? Can I let myself be seen unguarded? Can I allow myself to think that you love me? Do I dare trust?"

She let the words finish.

"I just have to think what to do with all that." She was looking into the carpet.

She looked up at him. "As you need me to understand you, I need you to understand me."

She started to break apart.

Matt wasn't certain whether it was a sadness or pain or . . .

"Matthew Thomas Turner" . . . she stopped, unable to go on. He was uncertain whether she was addressing him or reading his headstone.

Her face was working to find a resting place.

"I do love you. And I'll search for what to do with that. But I need to step back so I'm sure you're with me."

He shifted. She pulled her breath with a struggle.

She looked directly at him: "I'm hurt. I can't change that yet . . . So I'm not going to make sense here . . . I need you gone so I can heal . . . And at the same time, I need you here to heal." She was reaching down for the next sentence. "I need you to listen, Matt, but I need you to ignore almost everything I said." There fell a silence. "I'm almost afraid to talk."

She found it: "I need time to see us without seeing pain."

Carol came to him. He stood. She kissed him on his cheek.

319

And then she turned away.

He understood.

He went to get his wraps. Returning, he kissed his fingers and touched her cheek. She was turned toward the fire and weeping.

At the door he looked where she looked: at their fire. "Please. I hope you can forgive me."

She didn't turn, but he continued, "I do love you."

She heard the slamming of the screen door. She was alone again. She listened for what was next.

It was silent.

She stepped toward the mantle to return the journal. She picked up her framed poem. She read to the small, nearly prose stanza: " I have seen you . . . and you have made me smile."

◆

The snow was still falling. His arrival footprints were covered already. He stood at the top of the steps trying to catch his breath and find his way. The swirl of the snow no longer elevated the neighborhood into fantasy. He angled his face into the flakes.

He was moving from being warmed in front of her fire to being chilled with the insistence of the sudden, icy wind.

He looked up. The snow seemed to lead to an infinite darkness of pieces aswirl –like his own world.

Oddly all that left him immobile.

It took him several moments to settle back into his body and ignore the blizzard.

He began to move down to the sidewalk. He stepped unsteadily, like a youngster, using the rail for support until he reached the lower steps where he moved with careful uncertainty. It wasn't just the snow this time. His body was weak with the trauma of what had just happened.

He walked while waiting to reenter his body fully.

At the sidewalk, he needed to return left toward the bus or to walk the other direction, perhaps toward the tavern and the possibilities that might still exist there.

He would go to the right.

He began his walk painfully in the snow.

He would try again. He had hurt her, and she needed time. He would try again. Being with her was what he wanted.

He was certain.

His life would not go far if he was without her. That was not what he wanted to be.

A set of headlights slowly turned at the upcoming corner.

He made the turn himself and watched as the taillights continued down the snowy street.

Matt would take this side street to the tavern. All streets lead somewhere, if you know where you want to be. He would ask for his job. He had always done well by them. He would . . .

He felt a tug at his coat.

Turning, he saw her in open, unclasped rainboots, her crimson velour robe beneath her raincoat. She was clutching at a purple scarf wrapped around her throat and head.

He began, "What are you. . . ?" She put her hand to her mouth.

It wasn't the time for words.

She took his arm and turned him so they would continue along into the deeply fallen snow. He limping, she shuffling in her open, awkward boots.

They walked around the remainder of the block. Matt had placed his arm around her, and it took them a while to find a gait that was sympathetic. He with his ailing hip; she with her slippery boots. They began to laugh at one point their pace was so uncoordinated. She bolted in a comedic, lurching run toward the streetlight at the back of the block.

He heard her laugh loudly as she undid her scarf and dragged it behind like a wild, flying banner. She ran backwards; she turned again, laughing all the while.

She bent over, winded, and then rose to taunt him for being slow. And then she ran further ahead, past the back corner, onward, toward the corner where they lived.

Matt watched her, amazed. He pushed forward, his bad hip making him awkward.

When he arrived at their corner, she had already stopped. Her purple scarf draped on her shoulder, her raincoat lolling open over her robe, Carol looked up; Matt moved to her.

She watched him from the slightest of angles, protectively. He took her face in his hands.

She smiled and fully gave him her face.

They kissed. Still holding him, Carol took one small step back, enough to see him. "Can you stay with me?"

"Always," Matt responded.

"I'm freezing. I'm going in." She had begun to shiver, and her lips were dark in the awful light. She started her intent walk the one door toward their house.

"Come soon." Not needing to look, she called it over her shoulder.

"I'll be right in." He watched her make her awkward way to their stairs and, holding to the rail, up to the porch and in.

Matt stood for a moment before walking into the street. It only seemed right to walk where he had never walked before. It only seemed right to see things new and not by habit.

It was time.

◆

The reach of the cathedral sky seemed infinite. The descent of the now silver-white snow still falling seemed silently, magically restorative, clarifying. This was its own luminous moment in the shadow of night.

These were the moments when God sometimes came out of hiding.

Matt wanted to pay attention.

Besides, he had always prayed better in the dark.

◆

His thoughts took him to his childhood. Oddly, the opposite of now. The quiet of a summer evening on their lawns, with various neighbor folks out on their porches. The kids at play between, around and behind while the adults lounge or read or talk about the day.

And then a burst of screeching laughter. A shout protesting. One or other child racing to home base. "Home Free!" Another, breaking for the base! The frustrated keeper of the base turning, too late to catch them.

A lull while the keeper, invisibly tethered to the base, makes a search.

Tension hanging while hiders wait, watching around edges of things.

Some children hang back, frozen; some peek timidly from corners, some from behind a shrub or down beneath a front rockery. Waiting to make their run.

Enough! The keeper had had enough.

The call gets made. Game over. "Ollie, Ollie, Oxen Free". Come home all!

He remembered the freedom of playing the game. The giddy freedom of pushing against the shadowed shingles of a house or along the bumper of a parked car or behind a too narrow Hawthorne tree. Hoping against hope he would not be spied. The judgement of whether or not to dash. Running without noise! The tag of the base. The leap. And the swagger and such a laugh in victory!

Innocence is for memory. Never to return but never fully to depart either. And the moment was flooding him with memory.

He stood alone just watching. Waiting to hear. Alive.

It came to him.

Jesus and Odysseus had both been children at play. Both perhaps had hurried to dusty home bases in some ancient version of Hide and Seek. Both had laughed at the victory. Both had grown through awkward moments and trials. Both had come to their ideas, their gifts, their dearest convictions. Both had become men.

Matt scooped snow from the fender of a car and turned it into a ball.

Both stories were the same. The displacement, the watching, the delay, the embrace of the journey, the challenges and ultimate acceptance of a truth. There was in fact only one story. Only one. Only one, and he was standing in the midst of it in an abandoned street on such a cold and transformational evening of snow.

And he was not Father; he was Matt.

He waited. It came quickly.

Meese was Jerry with the receptive eyes; Flo was graceful beyond words to tell; Dr. Triton was Bobby, the most faithful of friends; and . . . Marianne.

Alone at the window.

He stood listening to the silence. In the movement of the unpredictable, animated white air, the moment continued.

So words and silence and moments of waiting were also elements of the sacred.

Beauty leads. Carol was right. Beauty leads us to see what custom and story, expectation and language has hidden from our eye.

He tossed the ball and caught it. Tossed the ball and caught it.

Beauty leads; watching leads; listening leads. Compassion for hidden human suffering, that also leads. It was coming to him.

Eyes always have more to see. His eyes did certainly.

So, this was it.

Return was not the end. Return was the beginning.

He stood still with his thoughts until they were done. Until they were his to keep.

◆

The neighborhood was no longer weighed down with a draping of ominous and blinding snowfall. It was being sprinkled with a vibrant display of near glitter

The quiet houses stood as silent witness to his homecoming as he moved through the glisten in his slow walk.

He was happy, slightly limping down the middle of the street, beyond the snowbound cars. He was happy beneath the dark sky. He was happy watching their house come into full view beyond the tree.

He would love it if he could stay in this moment forever. "This is it!" He caught his breath.

◆

Candlelight now appeared in their single dining room window. The warm eye gleaming. Welcome for the traveler.

He could see it all right before him. The little yellow house was theirs. Was them.

For the first time in a very long time, he was really home.

She would have him.

◆

Closing the cover on the matchbook, Carol watched from the dining room window as he stood in the street looking to the house. He then turned, seemingly trying to place himself in the world of snow. He seemed to be memorizing his surroundings as if he would need to recall the moment as special.

She liked that. She relaxed in her chair.

Who knew? He might be seeing the world for the first time. Feeling it that way. He was such a romantic. That was not all bad.

She watched him. Perhaps maternally, as one watches first steps or sits astounded having seen a notoriously awkward teen execute a lyrical, or intricate dance. She saw him, alive and feeling, slowly turning in the middle of a snow bound city street.

A grown man. In some way beginning.

Beauty leads. It does.

She loved him.

She watched quietly as he brushed the blown snow from his pants. He cut sideways and nearly fell between the cars before plodding carefully toward the stairs.

She placed her hands in her lap and watched as Matt, all elbows and with the all the uncertainty of a youngster, picked his way up the slippery stairs.

Once he was in, she would move the small candle to the mantle next to her poem so they might sit in the gloaming of their fire and still have light to talk.

Or perhaps just sit.

Or perhaps . . . Who knew?

The future was a mystery. And that was fine.

Now was their time.

◆

"That which we are, we are," she found herself quoting aloud.

"We'll be fine.

"We've made it around the corner."

The main thing: he was home.

That was a start.

◆

She rose from the table, and retrieving her journal from the mantlepiece, she returned.

Opening the small book, she began to write.

Acknowledgements:

Thank you to all who from the beginning of this multiyear process have helped in a variety of ways to bring Ollie, Ollie, Oxen Free to its conclusion.

Alan Watt brought me into his writing and rewriting classes and kept sharpening my understanding of story telling. I recommended LA Writer's Lab to anyone asking and to many who didn't. Colleen Craig with her editor's eye and generous encouragement led me through some of the darkest of times and helped sharpen my eye. J Terry McLaughlin made time to read revision after revision after revision and maintained a fresh take each time and with a hand on my shoulder told me what he saw; Shannon Sullivan took much of the early, underdeveloped story and encouraged me to build on it; Jim Hushagen encouraged my early efforts, (what more can we ask?). Barbara Walker asked for clarity and helped me find as much as I have. Margaret Garrison called me to do more. David Wilkinson with whom exploration sparked my imagination. Monica Bergers who supported me and encouraged me throughout the challenge of rewriting.

To Nancy, my wife, who has loved me and lived through another creative process with me.

Thank you so much, each and all.

Questions for group discussion of
Ollie, Ollie, Oxen Free

What connection might the title have with the story being told?

Does the title reflect upon all the characters or only some? Does a theme arise from this?

Does the story show change for each of the main characters? Why would you say that?

What might the future hold for Matt and Carol in their relationship given what you know of them?

What connections does the story exhibit with *The Odyssey*?

What purpose might that serve?

What did Carol observe about Matt, the Odyssey teacher, that he was not ready to recognize?

Does *Ollie* still connect to the epic story at its completion? How so?

What do we see in Carol's story that differentiates it from Matt's?

What might be some adjectives appropriate to Carol? Where do those attributes appear?

What seems to be the function of the "Meese" character in the story?

What are some of the lessons or themes that this story brings to mind?

Does the story hold universal lessons, or is it unique to one person's experience?

Why would you, if you would, recommend this story to someone else?